for Ray Repp

Roxie & Fred

a novel

Richard Alther

REGENT PRESS
Berkeley, California

[paperback]
ISBN 13: 978-1-58790-382-3
ISBN 10: 1-58790-382-2

[e-book]
ISBN 13: 978-1-58790-383-0
ISBN 10: 1-58790-383-0

Library of Congress Catalog Number: 2017933613

Manufactured in the U.S.A.
REGENT PRESS
Berkeley, California
www.regentpress.net

Roxie
&Fred

For John Robbins.

Thank you so much
for supporting my story
with your wonderful words.

Wishing you all best.

Richard Alther

9/17

"We've had Colette's aging courtesan Lea and her young lover Cheri; the unlikely pairing of the movie couple Harold (age 20) and Maud (age 79); and most recently, the 39-year-old President of France, Emmanuel Macron, and his 24-years-older wife Brigitte. So the timing seems perfect for *Roxie & Fred*, Richard Alther's novel of friendship and sex between and 88-year-old woman (in excellent shape!) and a 40-years-her-junior man (who requires a diet and some exercise to keep up). Readers will enjoy the warm-hearted celebration of this zesty old woman savoring the hell out of her final years."
— JUDITH VIORST, BESTSELLING AUTHOR OF *I'M TOO YOUNG TO BE SEVENTY*

"Brilliantly written! I really enjoyed this book, I couldn't put it down, a wonderful love story with so much depth. I felt inspired and very young when I finished it. What a delight."
— NICOLA GRIFFIN, INTERNATIONALLY ACCLAIMED MATURE MODEL

"I devoured every word of Roxie & Fred. I read this book reading five pages forward, two back, chewing, chewing. Richard Alther is so brave, and open, revealing, and strong, wise and irreverent. And I could go on and on with not one word sufficing."
— DEVARSHI STEVEN HARTMAN, AUTHOR, FOUNDER PRANOTTHAN YOGA SCHOOL

"This exploration of the role of art in modern society leaves us with a vision of possibilities yet to be discovered in our own lives. ROXIE & FRED is an engaging, thoughtful, truly exhilarating novel. It raises questions about what it means to be alive."
— WILLIAM JOHN KENNEDY, CORNELL UNIVERSITY, PROFESSOR OF COMPARATIVE LITERATURE

"BRAVO! to Richard Alther. I am not a very sentimental guy, but he brought tears to my eyes. All of it written in prose that approaches poetry. I am sure I missed much and will re-read it, but I must say I loved it."
— JIM SELSOR, WEST POINT, RETIRED ARMY COLONEL

"A fascinating page-turner that gives you an entirely new way of thinking about aging, health and romance. If you take care of yourself, maybe you have a lot more to look forward to than you've thought!"
— JOHN ROBBINS, AUTHOR OF *HEALTHY AT 100* AND PRESIDENT OF THE FOOD REVOLUTION NETWORK

"Keep at it, Richard. You can bloody well write, and with great facility."
— DORIS LESSING, WINNER OF THE NOBEL PRIZE FOR LITERATURE

"When this astonishing novel wasn't cheering me up with its sweet and melancholy saga of late-life love, it was breaking my heart — and I was grateful for both. What a pleasure to spend time with these two fascinatingly complex souls--both of them—like all of this wonderful novel--brimming with life. I don't often get choked up reading fiction, but Alther sure got me with this one, even reading it for a second time. Lovely. "
— RICHARD STEVENSON, AUTHOR OF THE AWARD-WINNING DON STRACHEY MYSTERIES

Sell your cleverness and buy bewilderment.
— *Rumi*

Watch, and walk away.
— *Arthur Diekman*

Chapter 1

ROXIE

HER MEN AND CHILDREN ARE BUT MEMORIES. Bliss to be alone. She reaches for the weeds, one by one, as if addressing them singly here in her vast garden excludes her, releases her even if fleetingly from any thoughts whatsoever, frees her from being boxed within the cloister of her past. Wishful thinking! The men, marvelous to miserable, no longer hanging upon her and she on them, now loom damnably outsize in her weary head.

So here she squats in her lush vegetable garden instead of over some lover in bed. I'm more than enough company for myself, she thinks, shifting to the next row of salad greens threatened by crabgrass.

Enough chard for an army. Ludicrous. She wonders if there's an enticement she could rig up for rabbits or deer to share in the bounty.

Oh the reckless, fantastic sex with Harold unearthing that buried treasure in her body. Mostly it was the sheer thrill of him masquerading as her "beau," an endearment likely still in fashion among his family and hers, the Boston Brahmins whom she eventually fled. Golly they had them all fooled, off to the dance indeed!

9

Even though her knees are cushioned with thick squares of foam, she wonders when they—the knees not the foam—will collapse. The soil is wonderfully moist from recent, gentle rains, and so the weeds slip right out. She takes her time; what has she got if not time? Gripping the stem and pulling not yanking, the weed and she become one in purpose, like the pistols of a flower aligned with the beak of a hummingbird, seemingly disparate but all of a piece.

On the other hand she can see the hummingbird bedeviled in its frenzied pursuit. Also with this ant here struggling like Sisyphus, its cargo thrice its size.

Listen to yourself, she chuckles, crawling on to tender asparagus spears being strangled by vile witchgrass. Harold, light years ago! As if the juices are still flowing. Companionship could be sweet, she supposes. What, corralled with others my age in a "home"? Facing day in, day out, those with rigor mortis of the mind let alone the flesh?

Beautiful loam packs her nails. This transports her into the tawny arms of Amos, part man, primarily animal, stealthy as a leopard terrifying the white invaders of his Rhodesian veld he was ambushing with Molotov cocktails. She, too, was caked in filth, lubricated with sweat under the fiery sun, romanced by those heavenly violet jacaranda blooms, becoming his mate, bearing his baby, how could she not? They were fused, not as a couple but inseparable from his soil, his people, their edible roots, poisonous plants, their prey more the cocksure Dutch than the camouflaged crocodiles.

Back to my pretty snow-peas!

No less taxing were the years, the decades, of children hanging on her, pleading with her to play, to intervene, to wipe hot tears of anguish while she stood there as Gulliver towering among the Lilliputians, an oasis of calm. Invisible she was, be it Head Start or the orphanages or day care centers, soothing battered women, doing what she did best.

Africa. Teaching women to compost. To garden. To leave the children to her care so they could grow food and compensate for the men, eager rebels, slaughtering themselves in the bush.

Abruptly she stands, to relieve her back, her knees, mostly the accretion of incessant memories stacked like stone upon stone, layer upon layer, year after year, until she's straddled with a monument. Africa...the children...her own.

She wipes hands on her smock, pausing and inhaling the perfume of pines as if she needs further affirmation of being gloriously swallowed by these woods.

Ordinarily she hikes the hills, mountainsides if not the peaks. "Power walks," she gathers it's called, her tromping over meadows of mustard and grass. But these days the vegetables demand and get the attention of her twisting torso, duplicating her yoga positions. Arched above intruders of her asparagus bed she becomes a giant Praying Mantis. Indoors that's her Downward Facing Dog.

Next she's hunching over the low incubator window box of seedlings. "Bless your hearts," she croons to the tiny tomatoes as if one could believe that tome of yesteryear, "The Secret Life of Plants." They flourish with Mozart, wither with rock. She chuckles at her silliness, knowing she could purchase established plants at the farmers' market and pluck ripe fruit in a matter of weeks. I like it my way, she tells herself, thinning the miniscule seedlings of lettuces, spinach, squash and the rest. Stretch the journey out like one's life since it's all fleeting as a snowflake.

She works quickly now, tending the infant plants. She tries to shut herself up, to thwart her reaching for Manny. She has kept him alive—his voice, his ironic smile—as if lovingly caged like a parrot assigned an exclusive part of her brain. Now how many mature peppers will she need? But puckish Manny, the best of her men, interferes as is his wont, really hers. Although long gone he remains, as before, a slab of composure upon which she rests.

"Oh, Manny," she remembers saying early on. "I can feel like a parasite, sucking on my big host until I'm bloated and momentarily sated. What's in it for you?"

Of course he would smirk and narrow his eyes, always before speaking. "Suck away, darling. Be my guest."

He alone of his family was not gassed. His legacy was to seek joy wherever it might lurk. This infused her and a legion of others with warning to never complain.

Thank god we didn't marry, she thinks. Thank god we had no kids. Together.

"Start a new school," he would scold. "You've double the energy and know-how of those assholes."

"It's all about the children for me, Manny dearest. You know that."

"I know you. You get things going."

"Hiring, firing, managing the money? Please."

"You draw talent to you like a queen bee."

"I try to be indifferent. I want to be a medium."

She is turning the compost, adding the shriveled

beets and carrots from winter storage more resembling petrified relics from an archeological dig. Leave Manny be. Yet beyond the badinage he is woven into the very fibers of her heart, silent and unseen, overseeing her each and every breath.

Time for tea.

Stepping inside she chooses chamomile from her bunches of dried herbs hanging from the cabin's lowest kitchen beam. The skylight she had built transforms the various plants to dazzling, gently twisting mobiles, even on days that are gray. She sets the kettle to boil and scoops the chamomile into the tea caddy. "About time for some peonies in here," she addresses the butcher-block and lesser surfaces of dull and battered wood. The browning lilacs have had their star turn but the peonies are budding up. She selects her favorite mug, ungainly and thick, likely from a beginner at the crafts collective — those young folks were so earnest, and carries it outdoors, perching on the broad tree stump.

The birdfeeder is momentarily at peace. No hyperactive squirrels. No shrill mockingbirds. Lovely.

She gazes at the rippling surface of her pond. Never a dull moment for that weathervane. She contemplates the vast bulk of water nestled so solidly in its basin, all of that anchored in bedrock, the surface play a trifle by comparison. Her breathing is slow and steady after the effort of yard work. She stares at the mountain ridge peeking through the break of maples. No more bank account, just cash in the box. Gas, provisions, so simple. Plenty of big bills for taxes and medical — what medical? — tucked away in some envelope, someplace. She trades rhubarb and strawberries with Hank to tend the car. No more magazines and newspapers keeping her informed of all she'd rather be unaware. She knows she is losing her grip but isn't that the point? Barely take in the pleasures and pains of the past, give them a nod now and then, let them ossify if they must in the mausoleum of my memory bank. Dwell instead on her seedlings, cloches for the cabbage, the endlessly re-read classics to feed the whole of her.

So she has a son who is over fifty by now, part brown, part white, part black, who knows? She has left him like all the children from here to Kathmandu and back, and good for them, good for her, all of us on our own, she thinks. He was but two years old, releasing them both from knowledge, connection, history. Of course she wonders about him every now and then but sets it aloft, a puff of milkweed in the wind. Take root, or not. How blessed she has been, and remains, to leap over one hurdle after another into the next abyss, somehow a branch materializing onto which she can temporarily cling.

No she is not free of herself, she presumes the ultimate goal. But at least she can receive and dismiss thoughts in equal rhythm set to a metronome she has tried to make of her mind.

"Sammy! What are you doing here?" she exclaims, startled from her reverie. He is the most brazen of her chipmunks, impatient for his treat. She collects herself and gets the stash of peanuts. Once settled on her porch rocker she begins shelling. Sammy scampers through the hole in the screen door she made for him as she continues chatting and he reluctantly proceeds across the floor like an intruder on tiptoes. "Shame on me," she says, "for my gender bias. Maybe you're Samantha, the leader of the pack."

The chipmunk bounds onto her lap and, nostrils a-twitter, jerkily pokes left, right, center. She holds the peanut with a steady hand and—zip—it disappears into the creature's cheek. She keeps shelling as Sammy's beady eyes dart every-which-way. A half-dozen nuts shoved in there and off he goes as a few other chipmunks skitter to and fro on her patch of wild grass and dandelions. Once she's got a handful shelled, she opens the door and tosses them, shaking the odd skins and bits off her smock and onto the ground.

She thinks about taking her book to the hammock strung between the shagbark hickories but decides to leave it on her nightstand. Meditation for now; maybe a little nap. Soon she is lulled by the creek of the chain twisting around rugged bark until the hammock is at rest. Welcome back, Manny dear. Oh how he could reflect her from the multi-faceted prism of his Falstaffian self. She was headstrong, as he could be as owner of his architectural firm. Lion to lamb, he could pirouette from one stance to another, a performer of many parts, while she held herself hostage to ongoing anxiety. He would laugh at her impatience, frustration, anger. He countered how even in college she found refuge as a volunteer counseling abused women, pregnant teens. What was her travail compared to theirs? Answering the city hotline she clutched the phone as she took in the man's belligerent bellowing, the woman's hysterical sobbing, somehow turning herself steady as a brain surgeon extracting the phone number, the address. She forgot herself, her uptight, disdainful parents, her world she fiercely attempted to drown with her studies, but not quite. Was her outreach a semblance of magnanimity or simply her parachute? And then she got married to Harold, ideally her next escape hatch. "Well, it was before any feminism took hold for you to lean on, my dear, my perky pet," Manny could carry on with the swagger of a tenured don.

She looks point-blank at darning needles attempting to copulate on the bar of the hammock. As if her own mindless, besotted fornicating with Harold could offer another step up the ladder and away. She smiles at her folly, the deep-seated smile of forgiveness she has so long granted herself. Their daughter Abigail, abandoned by her mother at age twelve, hasn't wanted to see her or speak to her for years—most of Abby's lifetime. Funny how she called her Abby to piss off Harold's mother who insisted on the name from her son's blue stocking lineage which reeked of choke collars, ascots, crinolines and girdles. Abigail, the woman reverted to, last she'd heard.

The darning needles are replaced by gnats, swallows, the odd butterfly. So much for the nap.

She hoists herself up from the hammock to retrieve her sketch pad and pencils from the kitchen, slamming the screen door, setting the roustabout chipmunks for cover. Back outdoors she nestles into a bed of volunteer Veronica, the elegant ground cover that spreads like crabgrass. She is poised pondside, mountaintops prevailing over the scene like seated royalty. But it's the solitary maple that beckons, distinguished in its singularity.

At the foot of the mountain vista the maple is regal in its way. She picks a pencil at random and starts moving it across the paper without taking her eyes off the tree itself, a discordant symphony of clashing components competing for her attention. You will each get your due, she tells the trunk, the tiniest of still-sprouting leaves, the tangle of branches and even the corpulent, exposed gnarls of root, as if they too, like sons of the lord, must exert their claim in the line of succession.

The longer she sketches the less she's the conductor, more the instruments of the million possible combination of notes. The leaves rustle like synchronized swimmers, each with instant gyrations but coordinated overall. Her hand is dancing like a dervish while she herself is tagging along for the ride. Henry Moore pops into her head, perhaps because of the backdrop of massive rounded mountaintops. All those sculptures of men on horseback brandishing swords, she scoffs. Moore's momentous shapes were womanly if not maternal. Tits and ass and billowing flanks as if erupting from the earth, not overwhelming but welded to it. Monumental still. Huge like a man. I like that, she snickers to herself. Shaped like men should be. Sprawled on the ground, embracing it, lying still.

"Where am I?" she mutters to herself. Sammy and his/her cohorts are scouting about for second helpings. She heaves a sigh. Guess I'm inspired from the few times in the drawing group. She looks at her effort, puzzled, about to right it on her lap. But no, this is what happened. The thick trunk is suggested, nothing overly realistic, at the top of the page, as if it was given birth from the nearby actual tree but upside-down in its rendering. The myriad leaves flutter at the bottom of the piece, while branches and twigs twist and roam at random, happily mired in the middle, unable to make up their minds. Is this where I'm at, totally topsy-turvy in the world? An upside-down tree! I'll be no more an artist than I was a mother. At least with art it's never too late.

She sets down her materials and sits in the Lotus position, forearms collapsed on her thighs. The Buddha was a she, rounded and squat like a Henry Moore? Never mind. Only the breathing matters. She attempts to isolate everything in the moment, like pulling one weed at a time, like washing a dish, acknowledging and honoring it, whether leftover Royal Doulton from Harold's family jewels or seconds from the collective's kiln. Carefully drying each one. Then stacking, taking pleasure with every step so she could be suspended as from a plumb line when motionless. If all of her life could be so lived, might she arrive at a point where questions are still necessary but not the answers? When she reflects on the havoc of the past—so much drama—it makes life at a standstill all the richer by contrast. I can look at the rushing brook feeding this pond, she thinks, watchful like I am right now rather than having to ride the rapids...

Sammy pounces atop her lap, sniffs and swivels upright like the periscope of a submarine and then sinks out of sight.

The thoughts come and go, like Sammy, her breath ever slower.

I could die, she thinks, and not notice! In some ways she's already dead, capable as she can often get at such thorough release. It makes sense to have a dress rehearsal for death, she continues to ponder. The show goes on and then it ends. No big deal. The cabin is near-empty. So much given away. Friends, the flea market, do with it what you will. The tattered tapestry hand-woven by the women refugees whom she taught and loved in Nepal—the crude strings of beads from the mothers in Zimbabwe—still then Harold's Rhodesia, sorry, Harold, but they were almost free—whom she taught to raise vegetables instead of their babies while she did that...no, these few cherished things she still keeps but doesn't own. They're immaterial, like she regards her various scars, not in a physical sense but as the roadmap of her soul.

She's still in a trance, her gaze held by the woods and beyond. Yes I loved them all. Manny's may be the dominant thread stitching me together, but it took more than his. I loved the ones I was with, and they are with me still. I am not a monk in a carrel, this sylvan idyll notwithstanding.

She glances at the skin of her forearms. Aged but supple and smooth like fine oiled hide. What about these arms? she considers. Could they ever wrap again around a man? Could these legs encircle and seize a lover, this center still cushion, pulse, lower and lift, move to the musk of the moment? If I can squat for an hour thinning seedlings...

She beams at the beauty of the trees surrounding her, the quivering skin of the pond, the throbbing of so many living things while they reign. Which includes her, like it or not.

"These spots!" and here she erupts in a laugh at her mottled hands and arms, legs not hidden by her smock scratched by brambles, violet with veins. The spots are simply more keepsakes. How many sunrises and sunsets has her body been painted upon? Spots, scars, all of it snapshots in an overflowing album.

But there's always room for more, one new thought forever angling with another.

Suddenly she recalls a pronouncement from

Harold's ninety-nine-year-old grandmother, socialite more born to carouse with her hems at that age cut just to the top of her knees. "Honey, the legs are the last things to go."

That one she cannot rebut, even here in the pristine outback.

Chapter 2

FRED

EVEN TO HIM, FRED SEEMS THE UNLIKELIEST master of his craft of watercolor, his six-foot-four hulk craned over the paper, poised he figures he must appear like a circus elephant en pointe. With a dash of dark umber, he's startled by his apparent decision to infuse a broad puddle of pale cream with its opposite. Will the umber now dominate or the muted ivory dilute the whole patch into a dull fog? Let the pigments figure it out, he's off to swirls of crimson taking shape ever so gradually as the paper inevitably dries.

He halts, regaining his breath which has been on hold.

His fixation with June's welfare threatens to spring forth like a coiled snake.

How could I leave the woman I have loved for work I love even more?

Fred is trying to paint but there she is, forever in his head, months now on his own. Even when they were together, rapture for his work seemed like cheating on her. That June is so agreeable, endlessly deferential, diminishes him all the more for having chosen her. Whatever will I accomplish that could sanction the dissolution of a marriage, the upheaval of a family? Fred assails himself, his hands and paints fortunately occupied otherwise. He can see from hindsight already: I married my care-giving, saintly mother. The hell with being an artist. How am I to take my measure as a man?

He sloshes his brush into the rinse water, then into the clear. He pauses, ordinarily a good thing to avoid overworking, but instead is racked with remorse. Life without a woman? He can't imagine. A sweet young thing? He shakes his head. Another artist with much in common? Could they withdraw from their cubicles of creativity for a relationship to flower?

He knows this much: he must harness some force—maybe not another woman, or person—to blast his butt off home base. I need to discover my capacity for obsession, he is thinking, toiling away again at his present work. A scuba diver daring to a deeper level every time. Confront one's utter insignificance on overcrowded but safe dry land and become submerged with an irreducible self.

He needn't be Prometheus. Why should he insist on being a solo act if a mentor could lead the way? Fine, if he could figure out the goal. But back to his starting point: a female would be, has been, a distraction, a balm, a folding of his wings that are longing to take flight.

Shut up and address the work! Push the umber to the edge, Fred. Let it harden, let it stain as outline of desiccated petal, all the more deadened in contrast to the broad sweep of the flower slightly turning brown but with the pinks of its former glory still intact.

And shut off these thoughts, too. They're deflecting

a mischievous idea in his depths...a bloody carmine coursing across the whole...indelible from which there'd be no retreat.

June. Wonderful June. Blushing and sweet, uncompromised in her prettiness as these peonies. At this he tightens his grip on a slender sable with surgical skill and delves into the maze of the interlacing petals, some asserting themselves, others submitting to shadow. This precision is backtracking from the prior daredevil rush of colors as he chooses from three brushes clamped between the fingers of his painting hand plus one in his teeth, selected for whatever reason, he hasn't a clue. He's slipped into his habit of steely control, what he's done all these years of exhibiting his salable, accessible, evanescent landscapes and still lifes for which he's become well known and amply rewarded, eight galleries coast to coast.

Insipid, he now regards these paintings. Moving on. Beyond her, too.

The paper is drying. Soon it's the challenge of restraint, to call a truce in the battle, as if he and the paints have been jousting for the entertainment of others. If he doesn't screw this up it's because he's now more witness than manipulator to the washes hemorrhaging into whatever dry blotters they can find. It strains his resolve to remain neutral as the fittest, most intense hues survive, a brawl as brutal as a cockfight if you're that subtle rose madder struggling to avoid annihilation.

He sighs.

June is all-forgiving, even of his decision to switch from feeding the galleries his steady stream of paintings, handsomely framed and matted, to this, his current maelstrom of watercolors nine of out ten of which land in the reject pile. June is even encouraging him. Forever she's been the rock from which he casts off, and returns. Until now.

"Oh, Fred," she smiled when he first tossed out the possibility of dumping his enviable status as an artist who actually sold all he produced. "Look, honey, this is not nearly the leap like when you left the ad agency to paint fulltime. The kids have always earned their spending money and now they're practically launched. Well, Nell almost has a grip."

June is graying at the temples, her mid-forties to his nearing fifty, but she refuses to fuss with her hair. Why should she? Blessed like a brunette Miss America with mahogany brown eyes, plus a grin that precluded her having to say a word, she exudes a confidence at her core, a readiness to lend a helping hand, wherever, however. She herself is as right with the world as a newborn, oblivious of any wrongs.

"Maybe I can teach," he said. "Some extra income."

"We can sell this place, Fred. The kids are gone."

"It's always about me, June. This is your chance to...spend more time on your jewelry-making. Forget about money, live off our savings."

She reached up and fondled his messy tumbles of red hair. "We can think about it. You're a painter, always been. The graphic artist years. It was torture. You found those discarded canvases or ones for two bucks at a garage sale, and painted over them all weekend, nights." And here June's smile dropped, the gravity of his proposition settling in. Normally she is a woman of few words, letting him and others talk in circles, whether she keeps her opinions to herself or whether, in fact, she holds none which became more apparent to him as the years unfurled. Affable June could infuriate him, Fred forced to carve out his stances without benefit of options she might suggest or, better yet, opposing views to hone his own. But at this moment of his throwing out for them—the careful, conscientious mid-life suburbanites—the notion of altering his career from the comfort of success to an untested platform—abstract art, god forbid—was radical indeed. Her casting her brown eyes aside, her head imperceptibly tilting, these signals were all she need convey. Hers was the reaction of a soft sea creature suddenly, painfully poked. And with that came a flash of disgust with her, his predictable, unchallenging foil for more than half their lives. And what kind of partnership is that?

Fred is stirred into action, having been slumped like the rounded bulk of a Buddha over the block of his finest Arches French cold-pressed watercolor paper. The peonies. They'll be here and gone, just like this painting, a keeper or no. And on to the next. Enough with the thinking. Total absence of thought is the whole purpose of painting for him. Not the prior stroke nor the one to come, but this one dash now, that's it and all there is. Painting is the only time he can shut down the hectoring machinery of forward motion or past regret. Suspended, he becomes as now taking stock of his watercolor, in the no-man's-land of balancing composition and color. Never too much of one or the other. An even match between spareness and articulation. The reject pile overflows with vacuous, ill-defined washes appealing as dishwater. Plus his more typical

overreaches of irrevocable darks, muddy and bleak as
New England in March.

He makes brilliant one of the peonies in full bloom,
at first with a blunt-edged plush sable. Next, before he
realizes it, he is depicting the fallen, dried petals, not to
be forgotten in the scheme of this lifecycle. He is working feverishly, his last chance to reach a climax on this
foray. He chuckles, thinking of his boy-cub manhan-
dling of poor June's clit, the clit unbeknownst to her as
well at that point, his following the tips from *Playboy*
on how to bring her off, how to forestall his selfish,
obtuse pleasure, how to take the lead. Well, he is darn
agile with these brushes. Should be by now. But with
peonies, still? Nature? How will I ever leap beyond
external sources of inspiration? he assaults himself. To
let it all erupt from within?

What's wrong with nature, his thoughts spin on
with his strokes. Why not as much a statement, point of
view, proclamation as a Dali? So often an angry or arro-
gant this-is-what-I-think-and-feel take-it-or-leave-it
plastering of cacophonous splotches across a contemporary canvas. Even a symphonic, heavenly blend of
Frankenthaler's embracing a stretch of twenty feet,
Fred tries to convince himself, matters not one whit.
The process is the payoff. Okay, so I'm a slow learner,
he muses, dabbing a tissue to blot up some heavy
ochre murk. So I started with red barns, blue skies, age
twelve. One of his first little oils on cardboard-backed
canvas from the stationery shop bled with oranges,
reds, screaming yellows he'd never before attempted.
"Fred's Italian sunset," his German dad praised it
until much later he realized this crack was more of his
father's Wop-Dago-Kike-Yid-Spic habit of speech.

Fred forces himself to take a break even though the passion of watercolor is the rollercoaster ride, unlike the cerebral necessity of oils. That, ideally, lies ahead: the capacity to coequally think and not think in the stroke-by-stroke application of this more momentous, earthshaking medium. Who cares about limpid water-colors? Feminine pastime, the stuff of ladies' leagues. Charles Demuth, one of his heroes, sublime composer of delicacy with verve, was a flaming homosexual. Who gives a damn? Do I, still? Apparently, if this is the conversation while I'm tending my posies. *Shit.* He interrupts a critical negative shape, the outline of prom-inent petals defined by the gray-blue background, not the flower itself. The positive and negative, they're the yin and yang of spectacular watercolor. Fluids coming to hold their shape. The mind of the viewer's, his above all, uncertain of what to make of the work typically follows the urge to label the thing, to create a picture. But no, frustrate that! Seduce the eye first of course but entice the guts to let go, taste an emotion, grieve a loved one, rekindle a memory, conjure the unknown. Isn't this the idea of art? Enough with words and pic-tures. Poetry is the point.

He jabs a stiff brush into the moist cake of Prussian blue. More to do.

June again floods his brain. Hasn't she always, even before he was thinking about a separation and leaving her in the lurch? In many ways he'd left her from day one, first flirting in the cafeteria of his highfalutin col-lege, she of the kitchen staff...it was all he could do to keep from flunking out, him the Valedictorian of an all-American high school thrust into a sea of multi-lin-gual preppies and debutantes? June's wholesome smile was a permission slip to his groin. She was a withdrawal to a safety zone after the parade of his schoolboy loves. Priscilla, blue-eyed and blond, eyelashes lowered, turning bright pink as he slid his sweating, meaty paw to her petite hand at the movies, sixth grade. But she acquiesced. And so did the sassy, viper-tongued girls he progressed to in high school. Or rather, he, big red oaf, submitted to them. Dumbstruck, he was thrilled to be whiplashed by the cheekiest, brainiest girls in class. He loved to be the butt of their teasing, found it sexy, exhilarating, the polar opposite the lasses were to his mother Rose. Rose was the pliable role model for his ultimate selection of June. Irish Catholic Rose was the pin cushion for his dad Al, a blustering, pig-headed German-American. How Al winked upon the hoopla of that junior high hayride where Fred was ecstatically entangled with Angela, followed by her whimpering at his roaming hand on her tits which Fred took as approval and then her crying in pain. His enormous thigh was crushing her leg.

At this fiasco his reputation as a potential boyfriend swelled, of all things, despite his total humiliation at this tale broadcast from school to town. The looser girls in high school toyed with him, ridiculed his white skin, freckles, dimples and bulk, all the while his under-standing, bottom line, they wanted to get laid…by Big Fred, heaviest tackle on the team, but truly because he was shy, he was safe, "Ferdie," gentle like Ferdinand the Bull, and a Nerd and a Brain, top in the class and safe for that, too. So when Pam's parent's were out of town and she said "Screw the movies" and they drove to her empty ranch house and undressed, she taking charge, laughing, her with open mouth and wet lips, him praying he didn't explode over her belly before he got inside given those grave warnings from *Playboy*, his first time getting this far, turned out it was true for her, too. She and he got it halfway in prompting a soaking bloody mess, Pam leaping up, horrified, screaming, him scrambling for his clothes. This, too, got to be the talk of the school and the town. His father Al was unable to conceal his gloating. "Now listen to your mother. It's way too soon, son," he babbled as convincingly as a wobbling drunk to a highway patrolman. "Gotta turn those grades into earning you five figures someday," he added, about which he was dead serious.

Chrissy, Val and Mary Lou followed in succession to the end of his senior year, going all the way but hardly distracting him from the SATs, the choice of full scholarships, desperate to prove himself for real. So burly and strong he once broke a kid's leg completing a tackle. Physical gifts he took for granted. But he lived with the marshmallow inside, others seeing the stony mask. Even into manhood there's this kid cowering under a marvelous disguise. No more than a costume as if it's forever Halloween.

The paper is dry. Fred re-wets the splay of a flower in too-heightened definition. If this is a floral piece so be it, but it's the meandering arc of its short life, not a celebration at its pinnacle, the usual way. He is fighting to break that mold. Yes, it's beautiful but he wishes it was ugly, more of the bouquet's dull and dying bits.

Some seismic streak seizes him. He picks up his largest, fattest sable, drenches it in clear water and wipes out half the painting. Next he grabs a dry brush to soak up some of this excess. It's like he's smashed fine porcelain with a sledgehammer, the splintering of his elegant effort into jagged shards but these mostly erased.

He's removed obsequious, pandering detail. Less is more! For decades he put in every twig as if he was stalled in beginner mode. He is not a beginner. This is not for sale. Think Rothko. Two slabs, often not even two different hues. Just variations of burgundy. Bruises light and dark. Two stacked squares. How simple, how serene, a mandala upon which to lose your mind. How confrontational and bold, a bull's eye, stop sign, harbinger of death. Rothko for Fred is all this and more. Maybe, someday, he too could shoot for such. And shooting not arriving will be the goal. Will he have the guts? Will he leave her for real, his foundation and nest, the mother of their children now nineteen and twenty-one, them understandably unformed but *him* at forty eight? She's a boulder, you're a pebble long since ground down. And *peonies*.

His present enterprise has trundled along to the syncopation of his prattle. Not a disaster, more joyride in truth. He stands and hoists the block up at an angle. Peonies. It's my statement. It's both a blur and dramatic heaves of color. It's powerful. It's anti-war, a plea from anguished humanity, a far cry from facile rendering. It's my "Guernica," he silently declares, but as ravaged, boisterous flowers. My peonies a la Picasso.

Chapter 3

ROXIE, EARLIER

"**R**os, I can't believe your mother lets you wear slacks to school," said her best friend Kay as they were fanning through movie magazines in Roxie's bedroom.

"She doesn't. I do it anyway," replied Roxie evenly. It wasn't much of a challenge to outwit her mother who rushed from one church ladies' function to another. "I bring them neatly folded to school with my books and change in the girl's room. I told my teacher my mother said it was okay, that I get so cold." Kay was paying more attention to the glamour magazines than listening to Roxie, who had lost interest in movie stars. Roxie was scanning the news section of her father's paper — war and strife all over, subjects that galvanized her father but things her mother ignored.

"I'm the only one who calls you Ros," said Kay looking up. "Rosamund is ridiculous, worse than my Kathleen. You need a nickname that's fun. Ros is better. How about Rosie?"

"You know Mother loves to pronounce it — Ros-a-mund — like a court lady in some Shakespeare play. She was a great-grandmother of my father's. He's got the blood line that Mother's always going on about. Like the highboy in their bedroom from the Revolutionary War! Who cares? Not my father."

The girls at fifteen were well along in social studies, world geography and history, but Roxie was riveted by the newspaper pictures of war-ravaged families, the wailing, lost children especially. They didn't talk about that in her private school.

Roxie's mother had been a nurse from a tidy but much simpler section of the city. Her father was a Harvard-educated physician who earned lots of money as a cardiologist and surgeon for the Charles Street crowd. Roxie came to understand he loved his job but didn't need to work. Their four-story town-house on Commonwealth Avenue was filled with Oriental carpets and English antiques, lined with shelf upon shelf of fancy porcelain, and shuttered from the outside by floor-to-ceiling crewelwork curtains. It was given to her parents by his parents when they married. If her mother bid on one more gilded clock at a charity auction, her father said, she'd "have to give away one that was already overcrowding a mantelpiece."

It was fun to visit with friends in her bedroom, especially to thwart her mother who urged her to play canasta or whist on the gaming table in the library. The panels there were near pitch-black. She was terrified of sitting on and collapsing the Colonial daybed with its spindly legs. But here with Kay, a chum from early childhood, from "a proper family" approved by her mother, she was becoming bored. All Kay wanted to chat about now, besides the hairstyles and dresses of movie stars, was boys. Roxie liked boys well enough, in theory, but they were even more boring than the girls. All boys talked about were guns, Gary Cooper, and sports.

It was Roxie's father who delighted her. She was happy to be an only child, his sole attraction.

"Why did you become a doctor instead of a banker like your dad?" she once asked.

"Bankers, at least the ones in my family, sit in committee meetings and lunch at the clubs. They just pay lip service to the customers. Except for the few really loaded ones." He was only in his forties but had beautiful coils of gray hair twisting around his ears, thick and wavy on top. She thought he was very handsome. He smoked a pipe so she got to inhale the aroma, sweet as licorice.

"What's lip service?" She was sitting on the floor of his study, the curtains pulled back to create a flood of light.

"It means going through the motions with people but not really caring."

"But you do. That's why you're a doctor."

He smiled and drew on his pipe. "I like helping people. I believe if you're privileged you have an obligation to assist the needy. But that's just part of it. Healing folks who are really down, even close to dying—I don't know. It's just the way I've felt since I was a boy."

"Dad." She hesitated, fingering a fringe of the Oriental's edge. "I feel that way. But I'm a girl."

"I know you do, Rosamund. I keep the stack of newspapers for you. You're not too young to understand your own privilege and all the trouble in the world."

Roxie clambered up and tapped her father' knee, to let him get back to work, to not be a pest. She left the study enfolding the next stack of papers. She paused at the big door hoping he might say something and let her linger. "Thanks, Dad," she uttered softly and slipped back to her room. Roxie realized, in a way both unsettling and inspiring, that her father seemed to enjoy time with her more than he did with his wife.

"I know!" cried Kay, interrupting the quiet time they'd been separately sharing, as if they'd been two kids on a scavenger hunt who made it back to home base. "You can be called Roxie. Sexier than Rosie. Almost like you were a starlet."

"My mother would blow a fuse."

"She won't have to know. Just in school. Just with friends. We're teenagers, Ros—no, *Roxie*. Forget the recitals, stupid piano and ballet. We'll be going to dances and teas. You have to introduce yourself to the boy. Seriously, if I can be Kay instead of Kathleen..."

"Okay, okay." She grinned and halted her pal but she liked the idea. And not just to sidestep her silly mother but Roxie...heavens to Betsy, not to sound like a starlet, but sexy she wouldn't mind.

"Oh, Ros, will I ever grow breasts?" whined Kay sliding off the bed and posing sideways to the tall mirror. "You've got the most perfect body, lovely round titties, beautiful legs. Why will boys ever look at me given the likes of you?"

"Kay, don't be daft. We're only fifteen and still growing. Someday it'll all be fine. You'll see."

Even then Roxie half believed what she was saying. Her parents' was the only marriage she knew of. There had to be other ways.

Eight years later, at twenty-three, Roxie essentially married her mother, not her wonderful dad. Harold was hand-picked for her by her mother aided by the women in her circle of "proper" families. Harold too, like her father, was upper-crust, but oh so different. His relatives were principals not in an ordinary bank but an *investment* bank. Dealing only with clients who were "loaded," her father's term of contempt which she never forgot. It was easier to follow the system and not fight it. Besides, her mind was engaged otherwise. For two years after Wellesley she worked at an inner-city day care center, one of the first of its kind. Worked, well, volunteered; the pay was a pittance. Her father happily helped her become ensconced in an apartment in a quasi-proper part of town, which she shared with Jill, another ex-debutante-in-waiting for betrothal. With Jill she felt like two she-peacocks strutting about an estate, all of it sanitized and barricaded from the world beyond massive stone walls. The sharing was obligatory, a baseline charade to appease her mother, outraged by her job — not the child care but the neighborhood. Jill, graduated from less of a convent than Wellesley, was mostly cohabiting with her boyfriend ten years her senior. Roxie was thriving with her independence, an avid reader of world news and fulltime student of how poverty cripples.

"Do you realize these kids come to us with barely a slice of the lousiest white bread in their bellies? Peanut butter, forget it. The unmarried or beaten mothers go off to scrub hotel toilets with a cup of coffee if they're lucky — coffee they scrounge at work." Such sentiments Roxie hurled at Jill early on. Jill grimaced in pain at Roxie's pronouncement but not really. A dubious

English major, she was thrilled to be a secretary at a prestigious law firm, its lackeys and mating material recent Yale and Harvard Law School grads.

Roxie bedded some boys and agreed to be bedded on several occasions those years. Her chum Kay had been right about her good body. She enjoyed discovering it, despite diaphragms and the lot, with as much relish as she took having a life apart from her parents. Paraded through the odd family and social event, Roxie knew her luck could run out, she could become pregnant, and lose it all.

Harold, from the right side of town although all wrong for her, was exceptionally adept in bed compared to the run of the mill. He'd been a preppie, of course, and got into Harvard by the skin of his forbearers. Somehow it was overlooked that he did not graduate, was briefly an officer in the Army, and soon swaddled in "the financial sector." He thought his family and hers were making a stellar match, and she never quite roused the energy to correct him. In fact, she appreciated the padding of their lovely penthouse overlooking the Boston Public Garden: all the more opportunity for her to re-charge before confronting the inner-city battlefields of her work.

"You're the most beautiful girl in Boston," Harold would swoon. "You know that. It's no wonder you stop them dead in their tracks and can manhandle those little monkeys, the riff-raff, oh my dear Roxie." And so they would rip off their clothes and copulate—she loved that word, it being closer to the truth, of course, than making love.

Harold was very cute and sporting a great body himself, which he should be, given the hours of racquetball, squash, and tennis with the boys. But he and she those years were like two adjacent tide pools that sometimes overlap but are more often distinct, the sea withdrawn.

The day care center flourished under Roxie's supervision. She was able to both manage the chaos and spend most of the day with the rambunctious tots and then counsel the exhausted women at collection time.

"Now you do know about a diaphragm? Here's the card of a free clinic that can outfit you." She shoved packages of condoms in the pockets of their aprons. "And there's always withdrawal. Even for the Church the rhythm method is fine so with all this other stuff... well, the priest will never know. And don't you tell him! For God's sake," and Roxie winked.

Harold would read the sports section, attempt the crossword—of course he'd interrupt her every two minutes—while she devoured the Sunday Times. She appreciated his instigation of their social life. His doing this as well as breezing solo through cocktail gatherings permitted Roxie more time for her reading plus frequent drop-ins to support a political upstart, a moneyed sort but progressive and concerned. During visits with her parents she maneuvered herself into a confab with her father, the two of them huddled in one corner of the living room in dovetailed wing chairs delighting Harold and her mother so they could wade into society gossip, perched like Kewpie dolls on the settee.

She heard of a group organized around the nascent but emerging crisis of population control. She attended meetings, next passed out leaflets to her friends leaving dinner parties. She half-expected the looks of bedevilment if not outright scorn. So she focused on women high school teachers, finding a more receptive audience, even when the leaflets included a carefully-worded paragraph addressing teenage girls on "How and Why Not to Have That Baby." This being the era of Irish Catholic entrenchment, she had to skip parochial schools but public schools were fair game.

And then Roxie became pregnant.

To give him his due, Harold was a devoted dad. If Roxie could follow the tenets of her craft, Abigail would be an only child, as was Roxie herself. Harold was smitten with their girl from the very start. This suited Roxie. Her work in the field could continue, by this point leaving child care to others while she procured serious jobs for single mothers. It became her passion. She kept this covert, the whole business suspect in her and Harold's world. It needn't be an organization, just an organizer. Harold was vaguely aware of her comings and goings, facilitated by their nanny Bernice, a black woman terrifically able-minded whose children had passed through the day care center and were excelling in schools despite the neighborhoods. Bernice had them reading kids' classics each night! Roxie inspired women, one at a time, to upgrade to a better job, to get their tubes tied, to teach high school English with *Madame Bovary*, tragic but at least with a mind of her own. She found lawyers willing to waive fees and help women get divorced so they could marry more appropriate gents.

There was one relationship at which Roxie was increasingly unsuccessful: that with her daughter

Abigail. The tiny, beautiful baby girl was locked eye-to-eye with her mother from day one. Silent and serious. Not irksome, ever. With her father she would cavort; Harold was a natural at that. He gave up hours with the guys at the clubs, rarely showed up at his job in the upper echelons of finance, orchestrated by his parents for appearance sake. He escorted Abigail to dance class when she was three—a playgroup for dainty daughters of her bearing. Once Roxie had to pick her up. The place was like Santa's workshop run by mincing elves, all pink and glittery and make-believe. Roxie shrugged; the child was happy, until she was back under her mother's aegis.

For years Roxie thought this was good. Abigail was very much her own little person. Good for her! Of sterner stuff than her father. Yes, Roxie had tried to varnish reality, so absorbed by her work. She had to acknowledge the child was hijacked by the bloodline of her birth certificate, Harold's surname embossed on the family coat of arms. The mother's maiden name? Of no consequence in this case.

Roxie began calling her Abby, ostensibly to distinguish her from Harold's prim mother, also Abigail, matriarchal imperative accommodated as well with this set. Harold thought "Abby" had cache for his milieu, and so it stuck. With the girl's nickname Roxie was also prompted to irritate her mother-in-law, the woman lock-jawed with resentment at Roxie's obvious disinterest in mothering let alone her choice of work. Charity balls in support of the homeless or whoever they were, that's one thing. Running around all day in the ramshackle ghettos, this was the worst possible reflection on her son as well as her. In time, after the nanny years, Abby was fobbed off to her grand-mother's after private day school, her house a cornucopia of flouncy dolls, delicate pedestal dishes of tissue-wrapped candies, an entire room full of toys.

Abby came to tolerate Roxie, worship her dad, idolize her grandparents' lifestyle — cruise ships, ball gowns, one of the city's first television sets!

It was about this time, Abby aged eight and proficient at the flute, Harold ever-so-slightly balding and often attending parties without her, that Roxie one night in her early thirties met a Tibetan man at an underground fundraising for his fellow refugees now sequestered in Nepal. For Harold and Abby and herself, life was never to be the same.

Up to then, Roxie never suffered guilt. She would later be amazed at this: the near-neglect of her daughter while she, Roxie, felt empowered, almost entitled as she saw her own birthright, to pursue the course of her choice. Yes she was lectured by Wellesley to take herself seriously, though primarily to marry well. More to the point, she was fed by her father, day in and day out despite the demands of a heart surgeon, to reach out to those in need if, and only if, this coincided with the nurturing of her soul's deepest desire. Drip by drip, like one of his catheters forever connected, she was infused with a quiet resolution to follow his lead.

Her father said he didn't believe in God as it was bandied about, but he did like the supposed teachings of Jesus. He said God was something inside of you, but that confused her for years, until she got outside of her world, the first step being at a talk by a man from half the globe away.

"My name is Wangdu. I am Tibetan and one of a few people to flee our homeland and settle for the time being in Nepal." Roxie squirmed on the rickety wooden folding chair in the basement of the Unitarian Church. She strained to follow the speaker's excellent English accent as he documented his peoples' anguish. She found herself, however, studying the serious man's mocha frame—Oriental, best she could recognize—but with an obviously sturdy build beneath his ill-fitting khaki shirt. She'd been invited to this lecture by Joyce, one of her colleagues aiding single mothers with indigent or absent men. Roxie knew the varieties of urban black skin, the rainbow of colors, the variety of skulls, lips, gestures and speech. But she was fascinated by this speaker as an almost alien creature. What did she know of her planet with its infinite array of human beings? Impassioned, this man was, as she finally focused on his words.

"...in spite of the centuries of Manchu emperors and Mongol rulers, then many Tibetan kings, the neighboring Chinese forever looming over us, assuming us simply another of their provinces, we Tibetans have persisted in holding sacred, inviolable, our native soul. And American people, with all due respect to each of your many religions, here is the bulwark of Buddhism. It matters not what encroaches upon us materially, from the outside. We are free, every day, to follow the Dalai Lama, our living god, to enlightenment and inner peace."

He paused. Roxie perched on the edge of her seat, willingly treading further into new terrain.

"And the world for all of history thinking of us as 'up

for grabs,' as you say, Mao Zedong has announced that Tibet is to be reunited with the Chinese Motherland." He went on to flesh this out.

Why am I here? Roxie thought as he rambled on.

"The blood of the Chinese revolution is drowning our people. Land left untouched for generations out of respect to our gods is being bulldozed by the Chinese for their own purposes. Our families are being separated, children made to accuse their parents of imaginary crimes, tenants to denounce landlords, pupils to revile their teachers, some children now being shipped from their homes to Peking to study Mao's revolutionary goals. My own father, a Buddhist scholar whose entire life was teaching our philosophical texts and scriptures..." and here Wangdu was choked by tears. "My father was forced to fornicate with a whore, in public, and then was beaten, spat and urinated upon. No one would speak to him. His books were burned by the Chinese invaders. He waded into the river until he was washed away."

Roxie's heart sank, looking closer at the defeat in his eyes despite the clarity of his convictions.

"We have lived in wide open spaces," the man carried on, "and now we are crammed into the steep and narrow valleys of Nepal, fighting for land and water with the natives plus their strange animals, the cattle and sheep, all of us groveling in the dirt." He started waving his fist at the group. "A third of our men are monks but the Chinese are condemning our monasteries and temples. Those of us who have managed to arrive in Nepal are now beggars in a foreign country. Many Nepali hurl stones at us. We are fighting for our lives let alone the saving of our culture. There are wives among us wandering in a daze, their husbands having stayed behind to fight the Chinese. We watch our supposed saviors, praying over their statues covered in yellow flowers, worshipping the incarnation of their Hindu god Vishnu, all the more dehumanizing to our destitute people seen as intruders, violators, and lost. With no immunity to the local diseases we are dying as the final insult. Yes we escaped through icy winds, following trails of blood in the snows left by the wounded feet of our yaks. But we must get back to Tibet! We are a separate race and rightful owners of our beautiful land."

Roxie strained to picture herself in this predicament. Damn it, I'm justified for leaving Abby and Harold yet another evening, was her reaction. She was clenching her fist.

"We are trying to survive in the wickedly hot Kathmandu valley…I myself must bury the dead while organizing others. Crying children whose parents died of frostbite somewhere along the nineteen-thousand foot pass into Nepal…"

Roxie lingered to engage Wangdu after his talk.

"I learned English from a British ex-Army officer," he was explaining to a small group. "That's why I've been sent to seek help…"

Joyce interrupted. "My friend Roxie here has been amazing at raising money for underprivileged families…"

"Money, yes," said Roxie, "but how can we help? How could I?"

"Don't be ridiculous, Roxie," said Harold a few nights later. She had met with Wangdu in earnest over lunch with a few others. Harold re-filled his pipe; Abby was upstairs finishing a book report three days in advance.

"It would only be for a few months. It could all be arranged by the Swiss Red Cross."

Harold hoisted his eyebrows, glanced aside. "If you'd like, my dear."

As usual she could not read his reaction. Annoyance, eagerness, indifference? Likely the latter. "Even your mother, Harold, will approve. What charity here rivals the urgency of children starving to death?"

The absence of electricity and paved roads was the first shock to her system, more so than the tsampa, the barley flour porridge which she forced down as if saw-dust. She was housed in a tent in a field on the outskirts of Kathmandu, the city itself, despite its being well-known as the significant center of Nepal, was no more than a medieval village. At first she was relieved by the native men in white jodhpur pants and women in their colorful saris carrying woven baskets heaped with tomatoes, onions, and carrots from their fields to the town pagoda for sale. Shriveled old men and women were laughing in the shadows as girls washed clothes in water gushing from the mouths of stone dragons. But she quickly learned the facts from her handler, Tashi, the Tibetan leader of the refugee encampment.

"Two of every three Nepali children die. Their life expectancy is twenty-five, maybe thirty years. I wonder how long we homeless can last before we can return. Look at these scrawny dogs! Like the natives in the hills. But believe me, Tibet is rugged, high terrain. We are tough!"

Tashi was vainly attempting to persuade a fellow Tibetan burying his valuables in a hole to trade them instead for flour, cooking oil, lentils and salt. This man like the others, first thing in the camp, buried for safekeeping an ancient family hand-painted cloth, wooden bowls intricately carved with silver threads, turquoise and coral jewelry of all sorts. How could their most precious possessions possibly be worth a few bags of rice?

Roxie was on a break from directing children to and from the nearby forest to collect firewood. She had gagged upon confronting the putrid smells of yak cheese and rancid butter in the campground. These poor people had lived on nothing but dried barley and butter-salt tea for the months in passage over the Himalayas in their escape. Now in Nepal surrounded by mud brick houses with thatched roofs, the Tibetans fashioned their tents of stinking woven black yak hair. Accustomed to the bitter winters of the Tibetan plateau, they wore heavy wool robes and did not bathe. Their skin appalled Roxie, often oozing with blisters for which there was no local remedy. They hung raw yak meat inside their tents to dry and even ate meat that had rotted. Roxie's tent was one of the few from the Red Cross, luxury quarters by contrast.

Initially she followed Tashi through his chores, besieged at every step he was by recalcitrant, befuddled countrymen. One minute he was pleading with them to accept the powdered milk, rumored, they cried, to cause tuberculosis. Next he was distributing spoons and beseeching women to wash their wooden bowls instead of licking them clean.

He sighed and wiped sweat from his forehead. Tall, angular, his skin glowed like an oiled tangerine.

"Roxie, you must take every care. I worry about you and Peter." Peter was an Austrian mountaineer recruited by Sherpa friends to assist refugees in their crossing. Peter was so overwhelmed by the chaotic squalor of the camp that he agreed to stay for the time being. He and Tashi, the only educated, English-speaking men, had become a fortress of two amidst the horribly sick and utterly confused refugees.

Peter was single, late twenties, clearly a born and brazen adventurer, visually, unabashedly feasting upon Roxie from the onset of her arrival. Perhaps by way of deflecting him she found herself increasingly compelled, within a few weeks, by the widower Tashi, his wife having miserably died en route. As such he was safe, she figured, from her own desire for him by the single-mindedness of his mission. Maybe it's not lust on my part, it would occur to Roxie, organizing children to pick lice from each other's heads. Maybe it's unalloyed sympathy for him in his grief. She offered extra help to his two young boys as they cut long hair from the men and women to get rid of the bugs.

She began losing track of the time for her commitment, the vague planned schedule for her return. She became near-drugged by the heat, the incessant effort of washing her clothes and flanks and her hair cropped to inches like the others. She dreamed of sharing Tashi's tent next to hers; she woke in the morning wondering if in fact she had, and what could possibly be wrong with that? Home was a million miles away if not a blank altogether.

More urgent in the morning was burying the dead, a ritual she now took for granted. It was no longer alarming. Nor reports by Peter of the Tibetan trekkers' dysentery, TB, diphtheria, even death by anthrax, ordinarily common to cattle and sheep.

She did whatever Tashi suggested. She attempted to teach them with sign language to plant not eat the seed potatoes. She unbundled a shipment of denim and loose clothing to replace the stifling and rough woolen garb that was rubbing and infecting their skin. She arose hours before dawn and gathered children to avoid the day's heat, leading them to collect the firewood. "Why aren't we using yak dung for our fires?" Tashi translated their puzzlement for her. She hugged them and sang to them as they struggled to be patient, waiting an hour on line to collect water from the meandering stream. She drew funny faces with a stick in the dirt to amuse them. She forgot about her own child, forgot about her life up to now, it making no sense relative to the agony of these people. But how could she possibly stay in this place and be productive, even remain healthy? At least here she felt sane, an island to herself, one task at a time.

Despite the mud, the feces, the filth, each evening the poor people would pile much of their precious food in a little heap outside their tents. Intently they would light their crude yak-fat candles and pour melted butter into their lamps, lowly chanting "Om Mani Padma Hum," their throats cracked with thick dust. Roxie, looking on, was stunned into silence.

"They're calling up forces within themselves," said Tashi. "We can only be effective if we're free from selfish desires."

As if not wanting to starve to death is selfish, marveled Roxie.

She had been digging trenches for the latrines, sup- posedly illustrating for the women labor they could manage, working side-by-side with them nevertheless. She collapsed that evening in her tent before sharing supper with Tashi and Peter. By morning there was nothing more to vomit or defecate. Her guts ground to a halt. They found her unable to stand, to move. It was a miracle, the doctors said, that she endured the journey back to Boston, arriving at the ER with no pal- pable peristaltic movement. The surgeon was incred- ulous there was no gangrene. For two weeks she was prostrate in the hospital, various tubes entering and exiting, Roxie losing nearly thirty pounds.

She recovered. She resumed her former routine but as a ghost. She would hear of the escalating savagery of the Chinese in Tibet, their torture of the rebels, the vast flood of refugees into Nepal with their soaring epidemics and pleas for help. She read of their valiant effort to weave their beautiful carpets, to pay their own way and reclaim their pride. But she was as far removed from this news as she was from her own rea- son for being, a dust mote casting about, of no conse- quence where it might land.

Her life tripped along but evermore detached from gadabout Harold's. By the time Abby was twelve, surly and self-absorbed, she was not so much not speaking to her mother as genuinely independent. My mirror image! Roxie would chortle in a fleeting moment of levity.

"Harold, we should divorce. Really."

"Oh, my dear, why bother? The fuss."

"I know you're fine, you have your women."

"Actually it's just Estelle nowadays."

Roxie sighed, gripped the wine glass. "You're right. Divorce is beside the point. What is central is that I'm leaving our daughter. For real. I'm going to Africa, no, I'm moving there, to Rhodesia. It's about to become Zimbabwe. I know Abby will never forgive me. I'm willing to sacrifice myself as her cutting stone. It's a price I'm willing to pay to…to save myself." She bit her tongue, forced herself not to apologize, not to waffle, not to admit this was the height of selfishness and lunacy, especially after Nepal.

Harold raised his glass of Bordeaux in a toast without leaning forward so their glasses didn't have to click. Roxie swallowed the rest of her wine in one gulp, ideally her residual guilt along with it.

"So you're leaving," said Abby straightening the folds of her pretty dress. "And you're divorcing with Father. That's nice, I think for you both."

Roxie was speechless. I must not cry. I will not. It flashed on her that this separation might strengthen them both, perhaps even someday resulting in a bond.

Abby stopped tidying her clothes and made direct eye contact with her mother. Ever so gradually, she smiled.

Roxie's parents, now deceased and free of them, too, had been High Episcopal, meaning her mother went through the motions while her father would tell his little girl stories, one in particular embedded in Roxie's backbone.

"Now you've heard of the Last Supper, but they may not teach you in Sunday School that at the conclusion of this momentous event so heralded in Biblical liturgy Jesus got up from the table and, one by one, he washed the feet of his disciples. He said to them: 'As I have been a servant to you, may you go forth and be servants to others'."

Chapter 4

FRED, EARLIER

THIS IS AS GOOD AS IT GETS, FRED THINKS, glancing around the sparkling gallery packed with hundreds of people—friends of his, friends of Eleanor's, the gallery owner, and the most loyal of his patrons. The gleaming white walls are enhanced by several skylights, emphasizing the pure colors of his paintings. He often fears his work too subtle and pale to be taken seriously. For himself as onlooker he's pleased by the overall restraint. On the other hand he longs to paint big and bold, someday. To what end? His art is who he is. And for now, his paintings are mellifluous, palatable for sure. What's the rub? Finally, Fred addresses the fellow waiting patiently for his attention.

"Hey, Fred, these are beautiful. You know we've expanded the law offices, nice new reception area."

Fred's pulse quickens: another sale? Jerry is athletic, forties, an all-American good guy. Fred holds his tongue, allows Jerry to continue.

"The water scenes, mountains, I get it." He hesitates, looks down. "You ever include a sailboat, some seagulls?"

"Oh, I, ah..."

"Now that farm picture, mud season and all, boy I can identify with that one! Maybe..." He presses his lips in a tight grin, taps Fred on the elbow, and shuffles off.

A third of the sixty-some paintings already sport red dots. He's especially happy for Eleanor, now scooting about with her assistant Meg. And it's only the first hour.

A short bubbly woman is enthusing about his watercolor of apricot roses, the intertwining petals so soft but with "an erotic intensity." Over her shoulder he catches a glimpse of June orchestrating her hors d'oeuvres which Freddie is passing around with a charm Fred recognizes from his own youth. Is the smile sincere? At twenty-one, to his dad Freddie is midpoint between child mind and adult body, going through inherited motions his son has yet to revise, reject, or not. Bursting with ambition and about to enter business school for an MBA, Fred both admires his pluck and shudders at the carbon copy of himself at that age.

"Oh, Fred! This is fabulous!" hisses Eleanor, brassy spangles as earrings and swirls of Technicolor Indian cotton to which she's graduated from Presbyterian cloth. Fred is enthralled by her mad dash from a boring marriage. Don't draw the parallels, Fred, he admonishes himself. Not now. He himself chose a plain linen shirt not tucked in for the occasion; a modest bid to let the paintings star.

"It's that second of your prints, the press release in The Boston Globe," Eleanor adds breathlessly, eyes swiveling to ensure she's not missing the signal of a buyer. "It's blowing off the roof!" She hustles off, a mother hawk, wings outstretched to enfold her flock.

Fred joins a small cluster, to listen and evaporate, not an easy feat given he towers over most folks. A New York printmaker of note propositioned Eleanor and himself to reproduce six of his signature paintings — florals, landscapes, waterscapes that had been featured over the years on gallery announcements — on high-quality velum to distribute nationwide. The gentle pebbles of the stock even fooled him into thinking the paper identical to his finest French cold-pressed. If only his father Al was alive for Fred to say, See, Dad? And you were so distraught by my ditching the agency to paint fulltime. His mother Rose, more recently passed, could have cared less as long as her boy was happy, he perpetually faking it for her benefit, his success her only source of satisfaction.

Again he scans the scene. Thank goodness these watercolors have a life of their own and stay eternally fresh, he thinks, while he, their perpetrator long after the fact, can get weary as a professor listening to himself deliver the same lecture the two-hundredth time.

"Sweetie, I sent Freddie home for extras," gushes June at his side. "Lucky I made more! This is so exciting," and she squeezes his arm before stepping away.

Fred allows himself to be led to two paintings by a woman who politely asks his opinion of which he prefers. He speaks by rote, fixated by his June, pretty as a picture. Pretty as his pictures. A link there best shelved but no: I go for sweet over sour, contained over reckless, diaphanous over dirt. June here with her simple navy shift, she's never one to shout. Fred's girlfriends were the clever ones who gave him lip. They seduced him, nice guy, big guy, shy guy, but he still got in their pants. And so when the time finally came for him to choose, the awkward gentle giant, she was the most undemanding, adoring of girls who asked only for his smile, the meeting of their eyes forming a calm pool dammed against the roaring tides all around. For over twenty-five years they've made love barely touching bodies, his learning and placating her tender pathways to arousal, or so he hopes is the case. His careful ministrations are calculated to satisfy her before him. Every so often she would seem agreeable to please him orally, but signaled with tightened brow, never so much as a word, her discomfort as his ever-readiness to reciprocate, to postpone his penis and offer his tongue. Even when supposedly lost in his painting Fred can obsess over June, their evolution from sealing off the world as bonded, hormonal teens to their linkage now, well into their forties, circling on the dance floor, elbows at right angles in a foxtrot versus belly-to-belly in a tango of limbs. Am I attracted to Eleanor and her ilk? he wonders. Of course, he answers himself, especially for her balls, so to speak, even more than the possible hot sex. She's like the spitfire lasses of his youth, a place of exotica fun to visit but not where he'd want to live. June has always been his bedrock, far more solid than him in her way.

More recently Fred has realized his instability is shared by their daughter Nell, nineteen, college dropout and that just for starters. Since a child she expressed contempt for her mother's quietude, a vassal to her husband, daughter and son. This has crushed Fred, believing June positively not the doormat as was his mother Rose to his bellicose father Al. June exudes happiness, or at least has herself so convinced. Every bit the product of women's call to question their roles as Fred, she forged despite her working-women friends her desire to be an at-home mom, ignoring the darts of disparagement. Sometimes to Fred his wife has been like a beautiful gilded box of gourmet chocolates tied up in a ribbon on display, saved for a special occasion that never arrives. Is this my fault or hers? he frets. She's not complaining. Is Nell doing that for her mother's sake more then her own? Isn't any child shaped for good or ill by the parents' dynamic: another issue drilled into him by the damn women's magazines in the dentist's office. He can picture June and himself like soldiers marching in tandem rather than grunts in the trench, surviving battle, tasting joy. He knows for certain that he and June have something they cherish, they've worked hard to achieve, the envy of a sea of misshapen souls connected to a spouse or otherwise, dulled by pain, blinded to their own inner strength which has to be one's ultimate salvation. And so Fred paints, on and on. For this he does have passion.

June and Freddie are offering canapés at a pace more relaxing, blending in. Freddie is a handsome devil in white shirt, black jeans, black-watch plaid vest; he could pass as a bartender at The Plaza. Big and fair-skinned like his dad — his dark hair, piercing brown eyes and high-sculpted cheeks make him downright pretty like his mom. June doesn't need adornments, Fred thinks, mingling, letting the praise wash off while thoughts of June continue their grip. Her basic good looks speak volumes, perhaps endow her with uncanny poise, her lack of capacity to flirt, to convincingly please people without a motive of her own. What bullshit, she's a robot, sneers Nell, likely objectifying her mother to sculpt herself.

"Tell me about this one, Fred, the carpet. The tapestry?" says his friend Howie. "I like it but it seems unfinished. Know what I mean?" It's the single painting in this show that unmasks an edgy striving, a vacillating, nervous fluidity.

Fred lights up. "It's actually my favorite piece here. When I get going sometimes I can't keep the whole thing as defined as when it starts. I got carried away with the intricacies of the pattern, the texture, as if I'm rendering an illustration in a medical text. And then I lost interest. It just bled to the other side. As if the highly-articulated half had to be balanced, almost a violation to have become so explicit." He pauses although Howie has stayed engaged. This is the most Fred has spoken during the entire affair. "It's like the body and soul of it, neither one complete without the other."

"Left brain, right brain, maybe," says Howie.

Fred nods, delighted his friend catches his drift. Howie is his closest cohort from the mixed bowling league most offended when he left the ad agency to paint. Howie, the extroverted and avuncular entrepreneur, a gutsy mentor in fact for Fred to take this leap, has saddled himself at midlife with a successful insurance agency, a horde of employees with payroll to meet, the very opposite of where Fred was desperately aiming, to go off on his own.

Fred is further buoyed that Howie buys the painting, hopefully proof the guy's offbeat streak is still intact.

At home Fred is in T-shirt and shorts, a cold beer in his hand having not even sipped the gallery Champagne. He sinks into the family room's plush

sofa with its forgiving coffee-colored corduroy compared to the eggshell linen gracing sofas in the living
room. There the down-filled cushions require fluffing,
so they're rarely sat upon but look perfect. Here he can
flop and unwind his huge frame, although it was he
who selected their fabrics, commandeered the seemingly eclectic but conservative mix of contemporary,
timeless furniture and Oriental antiques. He sips and
sighs, the take from just his show heading straight to
savings. He's made more than enough for years now to
pay off the mortgage of their low-clinging, architectur-
ally stunning home so far removed from his and June's
original ranch. He loves the way the dry stone walls
embrace the house then meander down the several
sections of lawn to his English-worthy flower beds.
He thinks of the curving paths, the widest one to the
brook, all of it to frame their coveted view of the rolling
hills, the glimpse of mountain which unfailingly entertains him, shifting from violet sunrise to often crimson
at cocktail time. What is my home, my yard, he keeps
reflecting, if not another work of art? Where do the borders of the watercolor end and my physical surround
take over? Isn't it all the same? Yes, but how can one
peerless painting after another thwart complacence?
"Oh, you've done my favorite meadow by the Jackson
farm!" someone cried at the opening, as if this was his
sole purpose. "Isn't that May's Harbor?" said another.
Well don't blame them, Fred, for your depictions of
nature like crown jewels in a showcase. How are folks
supposed to know of the fistfights underneath these
idylls? A clump of hydrangea in pale blue? Hell I had
to grapple with all my might to keep it from coagulat-
ing into a stagnant swamp. It takes my clenched breath

and biceps to hold that pinpoint of a brush and place a single drop dead-center to outline one edge only. So they look "facile," according to one stinging review. So I "churn them out, greedy to ride my acclaim," according to another. Probably all true. I can live with that, for now.

He slugs down the last of his beer.

Nell did not come to his opening although she shares an apartment nearby with her boyfriend Suleyman, sounding like a storybook genie but in fact Sudanese. It is not a nice part of town. Fred has always thought Nell brighter than her brother, but she's followed a rocky path to say the least. It started with the innocent lies at twelve. "My parents took us to the Bahamas over Easter," she'd tell her classmates when hers was a bottle tan, let alone his income that loose those years. By junior high began the minor piercing, in defiance, June acquiescing, Fred withholding his feelings, thinking but never saying: While you're under my roof, young lady, you subscribe to our rules. It went from tongue to eyelid but, thankfully, those are sealed over. The forearm cuttings followed the petty thefts, the shoplifting of scarves, makeup, escalating to shirts and jeans, coming and going in her simple frock then shoving her loot into her handbag in the dressing room, the wire-cutters for the tags secreted there too.

Fred reassured June. "I've engaged this highly-recommended psychiatrist." His initiative helped compensate for his guilt, his believing it was he, not June, who empowered their girl, gave her unspoken license to rebel which he never did but should have, given his father's abuse.

Fred arranged for Nell's abortion when she was sixteen without telling June, which Nell insisted upon although it was and remains another source of guilt for Fred. I'm more open with my daughter than my wife? "Yes it would break her heart, Nell. Even though you know she wouldn't show it. She'd support this, too."

The more Freddie became a replica of his father's schoolboy goody-two-shoes, the deeper it seemed to Fred that Nell waded into the abyss. He agonized over Nell more than he did June, June kissing his forehead when presented a bunch of early daffodils, warming her feet on his hot but idle calves in bed.

Fred is having lunch at Nell's request, out of the blue. The diner is midway between their worlds, the place considered gourmet comfort food but Everyman enough.

"What's the deal, honey?" he says over his salad after small talk about his art show and Nell's new, paid job as helper at the women's health center. He knows something is up; there never not is with Nell. She wants to go back to college having only lasted a year and a half. Can he pay the tuition? Wishful thinking that she wants to return to school. She's driven to adopt a foster child, can legally do so. Still, a silver lining.

Nell swallows and flicks long strands of her knife-straight, brown hair behind an ear, securing it with the hand not holding her fork which she finally rests. He's always loved this head-tossing gesture, unconscious to her in its frequency, vivid for him in a righteous assurance of her claims.

"I may be splitting up with Suleyman."

Flood of relief. He seals his lips, feigns neutrality;

hopefully he's learned something in twenty-some years as a parent.

Nell had met Suleyman at the meth clinic, his coming off heroin, she there as a staffer with a drug history of her own, although marginally less toxic and fatal.

At the time it was Fred not June who could not disguise upset over this latest leap into lunacy.

"Dad, addiction is a disease not a choice," said impassioned Nell at the time, correct as only the untested can be. "He was even stealing from the homeless who had been scavenging in trash cans, Dumpsters. He once grabbed a cup full of cash from a legless vet on the street!"

Fred knew not to argue, to listen.

"If we just ignore these people it's making the epidemic worse, isolating the addiction, adding to it."

He nodded, truly meaning an affirmative response, while also seeing how she utterly missed the irony of becoming the twin of her bleeding-heart mother whom she rejects.

"But you love him?" Fred offered.

"I love caring for him. I love helping the helpless. Maybe it makes me less so."

Although Fred bemoans the lack of respect for June by their daughter, on this occasion of Nell's broaching the subject of her druggie boyfriend it was to him that she confided, could trust, even though he plainly expressed grave doubts.

They've finished their lunch and catching up but remain seated in the diner booth, each leaning towards the other. Nell is yet to disclose her reason for the break-up. He hopes for Nell it's not an inquisition although, once again, it was he, cool Dad, whom she summoned. Nell wedges back first one and then the other side of her lank hair. A nervous habit or a gesture of stalling? If the latter, Fred thinks, at least she does eventually say what she thinks, unlike June. Nell favors his looks more than her mother's: his Irish nondescript-and-tall but still fine-boned like June. Although only nineteen but having been through the mill, she is her own person he wants to think. She's healthily individuated, as the shrinks say, free to sally forth from loving parents instead of the reverse, hanging on, insecure.

"Suleyman is doing the leaving," she says wanly. "He wants to go it alone. Maybe I've become clingy." She readdresses her empty plate.

Nell was caring for children, babysitting and dog-sitting as a very early teen. She volunteered as an escort at the regional abortion clinic after her own procedure, fending off the screaming naysayers with their go-to-Satan placards nearby. Instead of studying freshman year she manned a hotline in the city for bullied teens. One of the very first ways she got into serious trouble was wrapping a loaded pistol in her handbag in seventh grade for her buddy, an effeminate black boy, taking the gun he'd swiped from home, neither of them knowing it was loaded.

Fred lets her take time with her story, just his sitting here empowering her, at least letting her vent the latest of her traumas. Look at me at forty-eight. Whatever am I up to next, empowered by her.

"Dad. I'm pregnant."

He lowers his chin. "By him, of course."

"Of course." The bangs have resumed their mission

to hide her forehead, half her face. "And I'm going to keep it. Unlike last time. That's why he's leaving."

Fred has been here before. The several of his recollections during this visit — those are just on the surface. Those just actions, literal events. He's been looking her in the eye, like now, since she first arrived on earth. She was not like him. Not like June. Not like her brother, god knows, and a welcomed relief at that.

"Nell, that's okay, that's what you're thinking now. Maybe you're mostly reacting to him, his decision, not your ultimate one, what you want for the long haul."

With two hands she shoves the hair behind both ears and holds her gaze to his. She needn't say another word, and doesn't.

He sees his daughter at this moment hardly in isolation from her family for all her piss and vinegar. June steadfast and himself at loose ends and Freddie the Wunderkind and she, Nell the determined fuck-up, are absolutely connected like a herd of skittish antelopes, anxiety rippling through them and taking flight in sync. Nell created herself in opposition to her brother and mother but upon her father's misfires and who knows how many chapters lie ahead. He fervently hopes Nell will find her true center. And, ideally, abort.

June and Fred are lingering after their typically light supper. They are both so well behaved. He takes pride in that. What has he ached for all his life but an oasis after the misery perpetuated by his dad? Like encircling planets, he and his wife have plenty enough warmth and shine cast from the son of their making, their beautiful home, four-squared Freddie mostly cancelling the chaos of Nell. June's being everlastingly content cancels a day in his studio ending with a watercolor ripped in half, at his worst, or lobbed onto his reject pile, a small square possibly redeemed some-day as the most personal of greetings cards. June is presently chatting about the lovely new napkins she's found, stylish enough for a dinner party while foldable straight from the dryer, no ironing needed. He is think-ing of himself and his wife as no longer the sum of their parts. Allowing each other such distinct space, their twosome is drawn with blurred lines. They've become like formerly zesty herbs in a stew overcooked, flavors completely lost.

Fred is evermore on an island with his freight train of watercolor outpourings, his formula found, but increasingly anxious that at the core they're turning rancid. He was expected to soar after the ravages of the world war which shaped his parents. He was the reward for their scrimping as well as enduring Al's hot tempter, Rose's meek forbearance. With Fred they won the lottery, his obedient, workaholic self capped by the full scholarship to college. Have I ever let go of some elusive rage shuttered from birth that has me slam like I did last week a whole bucket of filthy rinse water over the attempted commission, my fourth try at a lucrative rendering of a patron's grotesque mansion in ethereal watercolor?

Fred is tapping a leg under their kitchen table and scratching his scalp, the most insidious of his spasms when thinking this way.

"Fred," says June musically. "I've been toying with something different for next Thanksgiving. It's just us and Nell too and her friend." The merest wrinkle at the mention of Nell hardens above one eyebrow and then she brightens. "We can have Freddie ask his pal Mike, not Freddie's girlfriend, yet, not to add pressure, but a small gathering, small enough to let me sort of experiment. I saw an article about tender turkey breasts, no skin, no bones, pounded and rolled with cranberries and nuts and herbs, then sliced nice and pretty, on an angle..." She carries on.

She so rarely does. It's always me and my nonsense, Fred thinks, while June keeps herself under wraps, my shit showing, never hers, exacerbating my guilt.

June is selfless but not in a laudatory sense. Selfless implies sidestepping one's own agenda. Does she have one beyond wife and mother? Lay off, Fred. Forget about what you want for her, but he can't turn it off, like her having so few women friends. Fred was praying she'd accept the invitation from a book club but June declined, telling him, not the friend, it sounded "too serious."

Fred lightens the moment, avoids what is brewing in his belly. He recalls a quip from a colleague in his ad agency days on managing a marriage like a brand: every now and then it has to be "new and improved." Of course to Fred that begged the question of what sort of dregs customers been swindled into buying all along?

He can almost swoon beholding sweet June as she reviews prospects for Christmas. She's unchanged from the college cafeteria to now, a Miss Universe then compared to the smart-aleck, bespectacled coeds he was expected to date, and did, until he met her. Embarrassing, his occasional birthday gift of a sexy dress or piece of chunky, hip jewelry he'd foist on her, things she never wore. Sexually gentle was good, had worked forever, him adhering to the original counsel from *Playboy*, thereafter the reams of women's magazines vilifying hoggish, clueless men in bed. He'd actually hurt the high school girls who lured him so they could lose their virginity. A married man in midlife, enlightened by the women's movement? Easy does it.

And so have gone too many years, ostensibly pleasant but Fred fearing that infrequent, less greedy sex signals his losing interest, possibly prompting June to question her attractiveness, all such polar opposite to his being horny nonstop...or his becoming less of a man for not initiating regular sex...or his often prior masturbating to prolong her pleasure and his restraint...or his resulting in unreliable erections when he suspected her merely tolerating him...or their settling down to a snuggle feminizing him. So much self-absorbed drivel.

Bottom line, he wants to stay faithful to June, mated for life, each to be witness to the other's demise.

"Oh, and Fred. How about I go alone to the movies, the James Bond a must-see according to Freddie? I know this weekend is the last time for that Turner show at the museum you've been hounding yourself to catch."

He sits upright, having been slumped. What am I about to say? That nearing fifty I'm admitting the darkening of my dreams, potential rightly claimed by people half my age, but for me? The errors of his youth he saw as detours; an error now is a dead end. Do you believe she's too fragile to hear the truth? This is my problem, not hers. And a disservice to June not respecting her god-given resilience. He could add coward to his litany of shortcomings.

"June. We need to talk." He hesitates, she's rapt. "I

think I need to rent a place, nothing but a studio, well, actually live there...fulltime...for a while...see how it goes. I—I need to do this, June. Sweetheart. This is so fucking hard. Help me if you can. Let's just think about it. I know I'm out of my mind."

June gets up from the table and clutches Fred from behind. She squeezes him, the most of a hug he can remember. He wrestles himself up, shaking, to face her and return her grasp best he can. His eyes are blurry but he sees hers, clear, open, both alert and at ease.

Chapter 5

ROXIE, EARLIER

SHE WOULD AMBLE OUT OF BED PRIOR TO DAWN, even before the roosters began their matutinal blasts. It was before the children cried their complaints, before their big-bellied mothers shook the ground plodding about their pole and mud huts, before the few menfolk in the village coughed up the effluvia of dust lining their lungs.

Roxie drained a cup of water from the big jug on its low stool. She allowed it a minute for the sediments to settle, the tiny flecks that made it through the filter. A far cry, it was, from the brackish red drink upon her arrival—a year ago, was it now? She gazed at the sea of elephant grass surrounding her substantial, wooden hut. The grass was starting to undulate after its night-time stillness as the screaming orange-red ball of sun splintered the gray reeds, the gray sky, even the packed red dirt gray at this instant when all the elements were as one.

Actually, how many months? wondered Roxie, as if that mattered. Her life here was reduced to one day at a time. Time itself was devoid of forward or backward movement, every glance a photographic image with no story other than its own. She spread the sour jelly of malala fruit on a dried chapatti. She sipped the cool water after stepping outside and relieving herself in the grass. Back inside she got a whiff of the cow dung her housekeeper Chimenya used to scrub the plank floor the day before. Not bad compared to the ointment of goat dung, Roxie's last resort to ward off horseflies. She became spellbound by the brightened grass as it assumed a deeper auburn from the rising sun. She paid no attention to the heat, brought to a boil by mid-morning. She like everyone was saturated by the heat but oblivious, going about their chores and swatting at the flies. If at all distracted it was by the beating of the insects' wings, her partners she'd think of them, performing a dance. Meanwhile she savored her morning ritual, the ephemeral quiet into which she evaporated every dawn, her moment of gratefulness at being so accepted, productive, ultimately invisible — apart from her shell — to all those around.

She straightened her bed and simple linens, her "European" bed, as they called it, for the white lady, with its wooden platform so unlike their straw mats. She recalled the effort it took Mama Milly to rid the mattress of its fleas and lice and other varmints at which Roxie had initially shuddered, the bedding a cast-off claimed from the days of English Army officers. She brewed bright green herbal tea as she ate millet porridge, much improved over sadza, the coarse, polenta-like paste preferred by the natives. She held the glass of water and swallowed her daily ration of glucose tablets and vitamins Milly had insisted upon, Milly still with contacts with her time as an ex-nun near Salisbury.

Roxie slipped into her light cotton frock which Chimenya had scrubbed on rocks by the river and set out to dry in the sun, the cloth becoming cardboard-stiff. Best for her to continue in her simple but American clothes, according to Milly, to remain apart from these lovely people in, to her, their near-tribal rough garb, for generations unchanged.

"Rux, you are the teacher sent from afar," Milly had intoned. She tried for Rox with her excellent English compromised by her indigenous Shona tongue. "The gods have sent you as the reincarnation of Nehanda, the great woman warrior first to attack the English the turn of the last century. She was murdered but vowed to return." Mama Milly clicked her teeth, her exclamation point. "Rux, these people barely have maize to grind for their meal but their spirit is boundless. So is their strength. You will see in short order, my dear."

Milly, or Millicent Sakuta—the English usually giving their Christian names to their subjects, Roxie learned, was a lucky one from the mass of orphans to be "rescued" by a Catholic charity and given an English education. "I was taught the fall of the Roman Empire, then the supremacy of the Anglo-Saxons," Milly had regaled Roxie at one of their earliest, frequent tea breaks under the shade of a eucalyptus tree. "Then all about the stupendous British Empire which we were so fortunate to have been embraced by. Of course, we were never taught of the 'primitive' people, our legends and gods and healers and special history. But that bubbled up from our own stories. You cannot keep black people disconnected from what circulates in our very blood. *Is* our life blood, because what else?" And she would rock around on the low tree stump of a stool, the fat of her flanks cascading over the edges like candle wax.

"If I can teach the children," said Roxie clutching the tin mug—another legacy of the colonial infantry, "so the mothers can work..."

"Collect the children," Milly interrupted, lowering her huge chin and collapsing the fat there like an accordion. "You will not teach them English, maybe simple words here and there, but the numbers, yes, that will be good for a start. Just to hold the chalk. Just to give them paper."

At such moments Roxie would regard herself the student, absorbing so much in just a speck of this continent. Her own education, her supposed privilege, were as marooned as mere islands in an archipelago of multiple thousands.

The village had come to life. Acknowledging her reddened forearms she quipped to herself that she wasn't such a white woman after all. Red dust was ground into every pore. Her hair was cropped almost to her scalp, the remaining brown frizz hidden by her kerchief. Even the simple straps of her sandals—practically barefoot like the villagers—turned her out, she hoped, as opposite to the white ladies and their gentlemen occasionally roaring by in Land Rovers. They were overseeing the recent African Purchase Areas established by the minority white Rhodesian government to break up the old tribal system. Roxie understood from Milly the tradition of sharing land, cattle and food reinforced the regional network of extended families. No one man was ever a stranger but a relative to someone or other, and welcomed with open arms. The soon-to-be independent, fledgling and autonomous Rhodesia, declaring itself done with its British imperialist caretakers, could better "protect" small pockets of natives, and undermine the tentative but emerging drumbeat by blacks for recognition of their legitimate rights.

Emboldened by these recollections Roxie left her sturdy shack with its glazed windows, tin roof, screen reinforcements against the snakes and stinging flies, to begin her day. Reddened skin or no, teacher in cotton dress or otherwise, Roxie's life was becoming indistinguishable from that of her tribe, and this she relished more each day. So she had a housekeeper, a European bed to boot. All the women helped each other with every task. Tending their children was the toughest job of all.

She greeted and hugged a mother struggling with the cloth harness Roxie had ripped and fashioned from an old sheet. The women could work in the fields or separate the stones and dead bugs from the rice with their infants more securely strapped to their backs. She showed them how to make diapers of old rags to keep them both from being splattered. A few of the men lived on their own, the enterprising ones as laborers trucked to the copper mines or to the vast fields of the white farmers. The native men slept there, too, to protect the crops of potatoes and pumpkins, beans and peppers and maize from being crushed by hippos, buffalos and elephants. A life could be lost to the odd lion or crocodile when crossing a stream, but such was their world. The less-motivated men drifted off into groups, sucking stems of what Milly called semi-hallucinogenic weeds, telling stories, rollicking with laughter, whittling wood to pass the day.

"You are in a woman's world, my dear Rux," said Milly early on. "What are these big round breasts for, plus our wattles," and here she jiggled her gargantuan thighs, "but to keep us low to the earth where reside both our spirits and the roots of our food!" She clicked her teeth twice before heading off to help gather the children for Roxie's classroom--"playpen, but call it what you must, white girl." She sucked her enormous lips into a rose, blowing Roxie a kiss, and waddled off.

Venus of Willendorf, it crossed Roxie's mind as she bent and placed small pieces of paper and a chalk for each child about to crash in. She snickered at such seepage from her archaic past and then thought about what kind of faces—people or animals—she'd have them draw for today.

The large school hut she had built for her was at the base of a kopje, or hill, so it was shaded to better cool the children under the oppressive heat. She assumed they'd become restless, want to queue up at the village spigot with their cups, chase butterflies or each other with twigs, giddy with relief. But no, even the littlest ones shot their big brown eyes up to her for hours at a time, watching her every move, smiling when she did, holding and smelling and licking the chalk, in no rush to plunge it to the paper as she expected. The children were wondrous at the effect of the chalk, staring long moments at the magical mark before making another.

A few men had recently slipped into their village of twenty-some mud huts with their thatched roofs, the men welcomed as usual. One of them, Amos, spoke English as well as Milly. He quickly befriended Roxie. Amos began organizing the men and many of the women to dig trenches for latrines. He told them to collect the usual roadside feces when dry for compost piles that would eventually help produce more abundant harvests of their tubers and corn—surplus that could surpass the needs of the village and be sold at nearby town markets. He corralled the lazier men to gather the wild herbs Milly identified which she applied as ointments and dried as teas to cure the myriad of their ailments almost overnight.

"These things bring a good price in the city," said Amos to Roxie as they knelt over a clump of rhodiola, working side by side. "The whites may think of us as uncivilized inbreeds but that only enhances their esteem for our native medicines. Whatever do the English know beyond the quality of their Smith and Wessons and their silver plate tea service here in the outback? Now the Dutch, the original invaders from centuries ago, they too know this sansevienda dilates the birth canal and that aloe greatheadi cures gonorrhea, but they fear us blacks down deep. They know this land is ours! They're terrified at the thought of being left the sole white landowners without the British military." And he flashed a grin revealing brilliant white teeth, likely, Roxie guessed, from chewing some or other gnarled root.

She kept her focus on the plants while savoring, she couldn't help it, the sweet oil smell of his skin. No she would not compare herself to him, this man of the world, be it urban or here in the veld. Weeks before he was dressed in khaki shirt and shorts, proper boots and floppy cap, but seemed to make a point now clad simply as a villager. About this she asked.

"Later I will tell you more. For now please just help

me be like you, a do-good outsider." She flinched then took it in stride. They continued to collect the herbs, nodding approval to others doing likewise, but in silence. Obviously he was younger, exuding vitality. She assumed he saw her as ageless, another shoulder to the wheel. He was very agile but so was she. However I mustn't seek his approval, she told herself. Not the goal.

Roxie wanted to learn everything about Amos with his wild hair and wire spectacles, his pierced ear. He was exploding her universe of the spoken word with only Mama Milly heretofore. But this also threatened to upend the peace and quiet of her steady work, tending the children, teaching the mothers to string extra beads for sale in town beyond those they wore at their rituals. She wanted to keep sealed her thirty-six or was it – seven years of her life before the one she now cherished in her Africa, yes, now hers. This man Amos seemed to embody the breadth, the legacy of half the globe in his tensile limbs. I am coming to qualify as his partner. And there is Milly, Roxie thought, the black queen of this country, grafting me onto her implacable stock.

Weeks went by. Amos was as eager to talk to Roxie as she was to listen. They were making progress in coaxing the villagers to adopt higher standards of hygiene, nutrition, gradually accepting habits associated with the white intruders and their evil ways. Amos and Roxie were making more time to visit during and after their many teas, even to share the local beer brewed by and for men, so for Roxie it was on the sly and well after dark. He and she sat on the step of her hut, the kerosene lamps extinguished as this was not a night for her reading.

"I was a teenage waiter in a European café in Salisbury," Amos said, craned over with elbows on knees, collapsed as they both were after another day of hard labor. "My father Josiah had worked there forever, really ran the place while the fat old Greek owner slumped at his table in the corner day and night with his cronies. Indifferent, really, to the goings on. My father ordered about the staff in the café as well as the kitchen, but when talking or rather listening to the owner, he simply bowed his head and nodded.

"It was always jammed with young whites flocking in after parties in noisy, drunken carloads. They made fun of my father who'd become slow by the wee hours. To make sure their girls didn't think of them as softies or sissies they'd hurl insults at Josiah.

'Hey you, madala,' they'd yell at him, which meant old man in kitchen kaffir. 'Bring us a Coke and six straws.' This one night I'm lurking in the background, as usual, collecting trays my father had loaded and me taking them to the kitchen. Father was struggling to wade through the crowd with a tray of coffees. As he passed a table one of the boys grabbed the tail of his white uniform. 'Those coffees will do fine,' he slurred. 'Hey you, put them down, boy,' said another. 'You deaf?' another shouted. Father didn't change his expression. He remained calm as ever after a lifetime of servitude which never really broke through the quiet of his inner world. He leaned against the pull on his coattail and towards the table he was aiming for. The youth said something like he'd hooked a big fish. Suddenly the boy let go, Josiah lurched forward, the tray rose up from his hands as the coffees crashed to the floor along with him. A loud cheer went up as Father got up from the floor, collected his cloths and knelt back down to clean up the mess. I gripped the edge of a sideboard, frozen, God help a black man who dared strike a white, this was all I could think of as my body released my grip on the table. They were yelling 'bob-bejean' this and 'bobbejean' that—baboons just come down from the trees. Josiah was groveling to gather the shattered ceramic. The Greek owner peered over, not moving a muscle, just another trivial item in the café. Then one boy poured his ice-cold drink down my father's back. At this I thrust myself through the wild crowd and grabbed this boy by the throat, shaking him like a chicken that refused to die. And then I punched him square in the face. Blood spurted over my fist. All I can remember is the sudden stillness, absolute quiet in the café, no one making a sound. It must have been long enough for me to dash through the kitchen and into the night.

"I never returned, but my father Josiah went on as usual, as if nothing had happened, never complaining about the bashing he took, the blows to his head and shoulders and backside, before he crawled to the kitchen doors, through them on his hands and knees, finally helped to his feet by the kitchen kaffirs, them holding ice to his bruises until he was able to return to his work, the café soon empty, the owner finally rising to his feet to lock the place up for the night with not so much as a word or a glance to my father.

"If the crowd knew that I was his son they would have kicked him to death, crushed his skull with their boots, and sauntered out to the street."

Roxie went about her work, her attention not compromised, she refused to call it, but rather evenly divided between the mothers with children and impassioned Amos. He revealed for her an ever-deeper knowledge of this land and her people, the better equipping her for saving these children. Wasn't that her bedrock purpose? They talked—meaning he spoke and she listened—continuously, whether tea breaks under the shady mucha tree or pauses in his demonstrating to villagers the proper way to anchor a fence post. He interrupted his garden work to check in on her school, attaching four bottle caps to a hunk of wood so the kids had a make-believe Land Rover. He did all this while fielding constant queries from the men, in Shona, as well as her prodding more of his stories, in English.

"Roxie, beyond this peaceable kraal of huts the country has turned into a police state. It's totally illegal for blacks to organize. A mandatory hanging clause just for anybody suspected of being a 'terrorist.' They keep banning the next attempt for a black government party, so the leaders are in exile. But these leaders' plans are stupid! Amass hundreds, thousands of us to march on Salisbury. Like the colonists! We'd be gunned down in a flash."

"We?" Roxie offered modestly but insistent that Amos say more.

"Look. Roxie. I can trust you by now. I know where your heart is or you'd never have risked your life like this."

"I've never thought of this as risk, Amos."

It was after dinner, the lights of the lamps long since turned down. She never thought of being deprived of electricity, running water, wheels, any of that. She had come to crave the sheer simplicity, profound and unalloyed as the red setting sun.

"You are naïve. You know nothing of the white police, even the black constables or informers slashing with a broken beer bottle the face of a villager they think, just think, may know of a terrorist harbored in their midst."

She struggled to stay sober from only a few sips of the strong brew. She said nothing so he would gladly fill the void.

"I have cousins rotting in jails, sentenced to death but dying from starvation and lashings."

"You're an activist, Amos. I understand. They've never caught you."

"I joined a group sent to China to study the theories of Mao and his revolution. I was there three years. Paid for by the Russians, too. I was trained with machine guns, bazookas, anti-tank mines, all this sophisticated assault weaponry. My colleagues and I kept our mouths shut but supported each other until our return, but to the leaders here we didn't agree with. And so we've formed a commando group, all split up, to meld into the bush and eventually, hopefully, stage hit-and-run raids. With petrol bombs! That's it. Here we have thick woods and split rocks in the mountains for caves to hide in." He chugged his beer, his taut chin thrust out to the night, Roxie no more than a witness, hardly a helping hand.

"You're hiding now in our kraal."

"Not hiding. It's essential to our plan. Earn the support of the locals. Rile the whites, terrify them with the possibilities for havoc. Incite the blacks, always simmering under the tight surface of their compliance. Seething! Everyone is, if you allow yourself to see it!" The glare of Amos's eyes illuminated the night. "You will have to leave someday, Roxie. You have the respect of a handful of natives but you are white. The government will not be able to protect you. This village is a cocoon. It could be razed any day, any time a simple black man lets slip that an organizer may have snuck through not just his village but a white farmer's cornfield miles off."

As he carried on, plus a few more sips for her, Roxie found herself agreeably engulfed by Amos's rhetoric and the heat of the man himself. The color of his skin, and hers, was of no consequence in the aftermath of sunset, the insect chorus punctuating his speech and leaving her mind a blank slate upon which both Amos and the insects played. At some point she realized he'd enfolded her in his long, strong arms. There was not a flicker of resistance on her part.

A month later, Amos absent for three days, he returned to tell her of his whereabouts. His gang was ideally to be the first cell of its kind, duplicated nationwide. They had carried rocks into an isolated stretch of road used only by whites at a late hour coming home to their farms from cavorting in town. She knew only blacks carrying IDs could travel, strictly in daylight. His gang had written placards that read: "We will soon kill all the whites. Beware." "We will wait no longer for you to give us back our land." Amos as leader made last-minute adjustments to the wicks of their petrol bombs, eight bombs, two each for the four men. Amos had stolen a pistol and bullets from a military vehicle but decided this would only be for personal protection. After hours of waiting the operation would take five minutes. Finally a car approached, the gang hidden in roadside ditches along the narrow lane. One of Amos's bombs missed its mark of the car, all others failed to ignite. The placards were left in the ditch but only Amos and one other man escaped into the woods beyond the lamp immediately flooded by the driver onto the scene, the other two men handily shot dead struggling to scale the rock ledge.

Dear Abigail,

I know since I left, you had no choice but to leave me. I am proud of you if this is the case, or will be in the future. Hopefully you will come to mother yourself in a way. You can be strong and learn at an early age to unearth what resides in your soul without undue interference from your parents, at least from me. Despite your not answering any of my letters I trust your father Harold remains steadfast in his role and obligations. Your grandmother, as well. I'll be forever indebted to them. In no way does this exonerate me. I am addressing you in your preferred name of Abigail instead of Abby. "Abby" was born of my ill-mannered nature not to submit to the formal stance of our families.

If it might be of interest, here is something that happens every day in my adopted family.

The people are guided by their great spirit Dambunzo whose story the men in our village tell weekly around a fire as they dip their fingers into a pot of ground maize (corn). There was a man named Goredema who had sixteen wives to sleep around him to protect him from his many enemies. He was sought after the Shona rebellion he led against the white invaders from Europe. He'd killed many, but was ultimately defeated; there was an informer among his wives. He became a legend and a substitute on earth for Dambunzo. Dambunzo is their mythic warrior who was captured by whites and repeatedly stabbed to no avail. Dambunzo's body kept rolling in the dust though he was skinned and alive. His heart was cut out, his wriggling body finally at rest, the heart locked away in a grain bin. When the whites came next day the heart was still beating, wrapped up in a coiled, venomous snake which immediately shed its skin. It's said that black people will never lie down, will shed their shackles and strike like snakes until their home is once again their own.

The re-telling of these fables is accompanied by drinking black tea brewed from a mysterious otherwise poisonous dark purple plant found only here with the people of this special place on earth.

Dear Abigail, I cannot tell you my story after all this time, but I can share the tales of this, my new family, which are timeless.

Your loving mother,
Rosamund

A stockpile of arms was found in an abandoned, now obsolete British fortification. Amos refused to use this material. He was adamant that guerilla warfare was the only effective way to unsettle his country, incident by stealthy incident, under cover, protected by increasingly sympathetic natives learning of the prison tortures of their loved ones. In addition to fear of the ever-anxious white police, there was the theft of the natives' cattle and fields by evermore fraught white farmers, formerly content on their individual acreage but recklessly claiming more land as auxiliary defense.

Amos became Roxie's life. His cause was her own,

she and Mama Milly fully aware of Amos's mission. Their goal was to keep the village calm and concentrated on its many new ways to eat well, provide for their young, plus leisure to tell their stories and bury their dead with full revered ceremony.

Milly was no innocent, having fled the nunnery in the first place in her late teens to follow the lessons of Christ—whether or not the stories were fairytales, she said, they led to good aim. She joined a new unit of the Catholic Society, well apart from the Peace Corps becoming established in other nations but not her own. By her late twenties she'd organized a major orphanage on the outskirts of Salisbury, toddlers carried by children barely older streaming in from the townships where parents died in droves, from disease, from merciless treatment by whites. By her late thirties she'd headed deeper into the bush, to this village which was desperate for help. Her and Roxie's histories were identical twins. It was a black woman in Boston whose son had gone to Rhodesia to teach in a school who knew of one amazing Millicent Sakuta. It was through him that Roxie made contact with Mama Milly and led to the adventure, the calling, that seized Roxie as had nothing ever before.

"We are trying again," whispered Amos one night as they huddled in the narrow bed in her hut but well apart from the others. Although under cover of darkness, this was nothing new in their habit of constant companionship. He was another "English" to the Shona-speaking; he may as well himself be a white. "We've stolen so much petrol from the tractors on the white farms. We have more than can be stored for the bombs."

"And you're better with the wicks?" she whispered

back. "None of the gang too young who might flee if things go wrong? You, the panther, my love, can slice through shadows let alone thick woods." But of course she was fretful, she and he now as one flesh. Her nerves, however, could not rattle his. Fifteen hundred soldiers, twelve helicopters, and three spotter planes it was reputed had recently scorched a nearby region where a terrorist had been disclosed by an unwitting kaffir. White supremacy was fueling widespread African horror and anger, Amos hardly alone in this land.

Amos was gone for a week. Roxie was beside herself, Mama Milly her only balm. "Child, you are here and one of us but do not forget that like me he has sprung from this very soil. Think of the animals, eyes ablaze and seeing through the night. They lie in wait for their prey. Amos, your man, our man, is one of them."

Roxie could no longer ignore the reality of Rhodesia, her world as well. It was creeping with a caterpillar-like imperative to reach its destination of Zimbabwe, let no white man, or woman, be in doubt.

Dear Abigail,

I am living in a woman's world. Yes there are men but their lives are so limited! War, work. I feel sorry for them. The women watch over all of it, saying little, accumulating wisdom. Our village is run by Mama Milly — Millicent Sakuta — but the older men believe themselves to be the authorities. They sit all day and polish their spears and axes and muzzle-loaders dating back to the ivory-trading days of the last century. They confer upon one of them to be "nganga," or Head Man, who leads their circles and invokes the spirit mediums. He's a kind of magician mostly to cure impotence. They sacrifice a goat but the women very soon skin and butcher and cook it. Meanwhile it is Milly who administers herbal concoctions for pain, fever, blisters and gut ailments, tends to the mothers and children, oversees everything from the slaughter of guinea fowl to the collection of income earned from extra crops for tractor repairs and new tools.

One man recently came to her complaining he wasn't able to satisfy his wives. He said he was miserable having to decide whether to dip his cattle against disease, which cost several quid, or to save up for a bike. She roundly scolded him for neglecting his cattle, his wives dependent on him for their livelihood, and soon all parties would be happy.

Milly is blessed with tenfold the education and experience of the villagers. She was raised in English Catholic schools in the city. But she was taught in the Bible about countries her people had never heard of...the white tribal spirit called Christ who wanted to obliterate all other native spirits, especially her own. In time, with talk of Civilization and Christianity and peace, what she saw was racial hate, police who beat up her people, the rich whites, the black servants treated like dogs to obey and never bark. She upped and quit the Church, the convent, her enslavement. Bilingual and benefitting from multiple points of view, she's had impact way beyond our village. Women from afar travel to see how she's helped people rise from squalor and oppression.

Although she's an ex-nun, she says "I don't abdicate to God, but I check in now and then. As for Mary, fertilized by the wind? The woman gave birth!"

I questioned Milly about the men having a dozen or more wives. She said the men say "What good am I if I only make one woman happy?" And she rolls her big black eyes and clicks her teeth — no more to be said on that subject.

I wrote to you several letters ago about the spirit gods for these people. But it was a woman, Nehanda, who begets their deepest respect. At the end of the 19th century she rallied her tribe to fight, not just resist, the British. Entire villages had been riddled with deadly maxim guns; captives made to hang themselves by jumping from trees after shots of buckshot in their buttocks. Their land was burnt. She knew the British were too strong to defeat but that they would become weakened by fear and hate if the Africans dared to stand up for themselves. Better, she said, the land be drenched in her blood than cower on, defeated and humiliated. The British called Nehanda "the witch of Mazoe." They hanged her in public which lionizes her to this day.

The menfolk may sit in a circle around the fire but they fall into the spell of a lovely young woman celebrating Nehanda, dancing to the music and singing to the whole tribe gathered around. She is wearing a flimsy, flowery dress stretched tightly across her shapely breasts. Multiple bands of colored beads are tied across her forehead and draped about her neck. She clutches small "hakata" or divining bones which clutter along with the dozens of bangles. Several of the men are wearing masks; some have a lion's tooth fixed to their chest to ward off evil spirits.

"Advise us, Ambuya — grandmother. Tell us what to do!" There are high-pitched shouts. The drums beat ever louder. Silencing the circle, speaking with formal politeness and sweeping her eyes to the sky, she calls upon Nehanda to guide her, whereupon she declares the answer to the most pressing issue of the day: any freedom fighter must be looked after by the village.

There is a man for me here, Abigail. His name is Amos. The women of the village already know what Amos is about. He would have been captured and killed by now if the women were not complicit in his cover.

He is, in some ways, still a servant, if for an honorable end. It's the women who empower him.

Maybe Wellesley was not so far from the mark. Funny to think, at first arriving here, I bristled that a woman was an object given to a man...

I will forever wish the very best for you, looking out for yourself and others but not for me. You are to be as you've always been – a strong and valiant soul.

Rosamund

This is how she was told that it happened, one of the gang having slipped into her hut one night, placing hands over her mouth, frightening her but achieving her silence. His English was identical to Amos's.

"My name is Damba. There were twelve of us, Rux. We were each perfectly hidden by boulders. We chose the spot of narrow road, narrower especially for approaching a bridge. No shoulders. Plus the giant rocks for cover. We each had several Molotov cocktails and ample matches. Amos could light these with his eyes shut and he taught us to do the same."

She was propped up in bed, her heart as if unable to beat allowed him to go on.

"A car approached and the angry man got out, striding up to our rock barrier we had made in the center of the road. He picked up a small rock and hurled it blindly into the darkness. And then our shower of stones pelted him from all sides. We could see he was bleeding above an eye. Bewildered he scrambled back into the car as we threw our bombs, all of them igniting, several landing atop the car's roof which burst into flames. The man had not closed the driver's side door, leaning over his seat and grabbing something in back. We could then make out the woman in the front seat clutching a child. He emerged with the rifle blasting in all directions, hitting a few of us but most of us heaving more bombs which exploded into a wall of fire. He was cursing 'bobbejean,' baboon, non-stop, taking aim at any motion in the shadows. From nowhere it seemed Amos leapt out with a dagger and plunged it deep into his back. The man spun around and shot Amos point-blank. He fell and the man kicked him into the ditch. We could hear the woman and child screaming. The man managed to stumble and slump behind the wheel, jammed the accelerator to hurtle over the rocks. He lost control and the car flipped into a steep gully, all of it aflame. Within a day we learned the dead man's name, forty-five, like most Afrikaaners a father of eight on his huge farm. The man was burnt to a crisp but his wife and daughter slightly injured somehow staggered off. Amos's village here has been kept a secret so far, but the government has strafed a dozen villages well removed from this one. Amos made sure the site for the bombing was nowhere close by. But a dozen kraals targeted as possible safe havens for terrorists have been blasted into dust."

He finished but had been holding her, squeezing her to keep her upright. She was speechless. This he understood and so she didn't have to ask.

No, Amos did not survive as had most of the men of his gang. And so would she, Amos made Damba promise to assure her, in case he did not return.

Roxie was bearing his child. This she knew all along, even the likely night of its conception. She had so violently shuddered, unlike anything she knew her body capable of. It was not the first nor that last time they had fused. She did not think of a baby as hers, or his either. It would be a blend of them both, a sublime shade of brown, but not belonging to anyone, its parents included. Nor would it answer to itself, in time, as had been the single-minded pursuit of her own journey before landing as just one more being Africa embraced by the millions, outliers and all.

But she nursed her baby Amos as her own, until she released him to the careening, motley gang of village urchins. Even by the time he was two he was his own little man, seemingly oblivious to any notion of mother-and-child which she too had to relinquish. The essence of his land and the seed of his father gushed through the veins of his beige robust body, jolly with her, with Mama Milly, to every big-bellied woman at hand.

"You have got to leave, Rux, my white girl," said Milly, "but you know that. And you've got to leave him."

Yes, this too she'd known all along. She tried to steel herself for this, which was surprisingly easier a process than she feared. There were rules enforced by the ever-stricter authorities. No child could depart Rhodesia let alone with a white woman claiming what she might. Her word and her years of work as a kaffir sympathizer in fact led to her ouster. Even the Afrikaaners did not want a recalcitrant white woman's blood on their hands. If it were known the baby was Amos's, him now a notorious hero nationwide, she would be expelled with the boy possibly seized and killed in captivity. She had no options.

The day arrived for her leave-taking which Milly

arranged through her connections. She didn't hand little Amos over to Milly, the waiting Austin idling, so much as allow him to scoot readily into the big woman's grasp, nothing different from her assisting Roxie with his birth and all the days of the two years that followed.

There were tears aplenty streaming Milly's face while Roxie's stayed bone-dry. She had rehearsed this moment too many times. She didn't touch the boy or Milly, backing up a few steps at least permitting one final look at them to be branded in her brain.

And look hard at that mucha tree, just the biggest one, she told herself as the Austin packed with her few belongings inched along the rough, people-lined road. The tree and the people are rooted in their earth as I've been, the roots drawing strength from below as they all stand tall and stretch to the skies. I don't speak their language, nor they mine, but that's not been necessary. In fact it's been better than words, beyond them. They look alike to me. To them I believe what mattered was my honoring the spirits of their circles. I slept on their dirt and swallowed their food, Roxie thought as the dusty road gave way to macadam. On wheels these years I'd have missed the colony of strange orange insects under that rock. I too was absorbed by the thick, ever-saturating heat, the heat incessantly swirling and cradling from without as does the blood of these people pulse under my skin.

Traffic both ways now on the road.

These people, Roxie smiled to herself. That means the three of you, one gone but two here for good.

Chapter 6

FRED, EARLIER

HE WEDGED HIMSELF UNDER SCRATCHY needles of the tree, but the heavy, low-hanging branches were perfect for concealing him in their game of hide-and-seek. At seven Fred was bigger than the other kids making it harder to find a good spot. His heart thumped as the distant voice got closer. This place was practically a cave. He tried to hold his breath and lie absolutely still, but he was distracted by a crawling winged-thing. He was fascinated by the wing, its intricate lines crisscrossing and making neat patterns like the windows of his mother's church. Oh how he wanted to pluck one of those wings, to examine it right up to the tip of his nose. He could make a drawing of it in school! Maybe even at home when his father wasn't there. His best secret hiding place was under his bed where he stored his art supplies. His father didn't like him spending so much time with his pencils and crayons and poster paints. Fred especially loved opening a new box of crayons and uncapping small jars of paint. These he would inhale, instantly picturing an island overloaded with gigantic jungle flowers, a riot of wild colors and aromas he could only imagine from his storybooks.

He was glad his house was close to these woods. Their own neighborhood had no trees, just sidewalks, not as much fun as getting lost like this. His house was like all the others. Sometimes the littler kids couldn't tell them apart and find their way home. But he knew for his parents their house was very special compared to the ones they had come from.

He forgot the creeping bug and picked a tiny flower. Boy what a beautiful yellow. His colored pencils weren't good enough to make a color this bright. He squinted at the little blossom, carefully detaching one petal at a time. He smelled it. He squinted at the wavy lines thinner than hair that made a heart-shaped circle on each leaf. The green was duller. This he could do with his crayons.

A loud voice reached him but it was muffled by the thick evergreen. He figured Jerry was real near but still he felt safe from everything outside his secret cave. He shoved the flower and its leaves into a pocket of his short pants. He'd sneak them into his room. It would have been wrong to kill the insect just so he could see it up close. He knew from the look on his mother's face when he'd done something wrong, when his father walloped his behind with the back of her big hairbrush. She never spoke to reprimand him. She didn't have to. She was the one who went to church and so she knew God's rules.

"Ali-ali-in-free!" he heard it screamed.

He didn't want to leave his wonderful hideaway but finally crawled out without the needles prickling too bad.

"Fred! You jerk!" the others hollered. "You

cheated!" "You big oaf." "There were two more turns and you never came back in!"

The teachers always tacked his artwork first onto the bulletin boards. He was the class artist. It made him feel important. It also made him sad that most other kids never had their things selected.

"I can't draw a straight line," said Susanna, the prettiest girl ever. She didn't really sound disappointed.

"I can't either," said Fred hoping to make her feel better, although he sensed she just wanted the chance to talk to him.

He would often recall the thrill of finger painting in Kindergarten, smearing the sticky stuff, his hands like the paper a crazy mess of amazing colors, the miracle of purple exploding from mixing red and blue. Now, so much older, on his hands and knees on his bedroom floor, he strained to get the flower the exact color yellow, the lines in the leaf a perfect picture of the real thing.

One Saturday morning in junior high he stepped out of the shower shocked to have his father standing there with one of his buddies from work.

"He's gonna make a helluva lineman, Al," the man quipped, leering at Fred all naked and fumbling for the towel while his dad stood there grinning. Fred had a few hairs over his prong but was embarrassed that there weren't near as many like some of the other boys. He'd seen his father bare-assed plenty of times and knew that soon his stuff would also be a handful. He already knew the facts of life from the other guys let alone his dad who repeated how much of a good time with this equipment was in store. Fred wasn't worried.

He already had to wear two jockstraps to the sock-hop dead-bulb dance when you were allowed to grab your partner up close. His boner was plenty big enough so he didn't want to frighten the girl. But it was great fun like his father promised. Before long he was wearing underpants under his pajama bottoms, rinsing them both out so his mother wouldn't get upset.

His mother Rose was Irish, kind of plump, with very white skin. Every time his father Al yelled at her, her face turned red as a Christmas bulb.

One morning getting dressed, even though his door was closed, he could hear every word.

"Goddamn it, Rose, buying him a shirt from Butterworth's! Jesus Christ I'm the manager now of my goddamned sweatshop, I wear that suit and tie to keep those asswipes in place. I need swell clothes. But take the kid to Filene's basement, bargain day!"

Fred hovered next to the door. His mother, as always, was speechless but he knew what she'd have said, like she would to her boy but never to her husband. "You're outgrowing everything so fast, Fred. I'll see what I can find on Two-For day."

His father had left for work. As she made Fred's lunch he could see red rings above her wrist where his father had gripped her and squeezed her soft forearm, harder and harder to make sure his message got across.

By age twelve Fred had several yard accounts in a fancier section of town. He cut the lawns, raked up the clippings, raked the fall leaves and shoveled their driveways and walks all winter. He'd earn a dollar, often a Hire's root beer to boot.

"Do come in, dear Fred. Please sit down," said the

sweet widow lady. "You're ringing wet. How about a Pepsi Cola this time? It's a bigger bottle." And she would fetch her dish of peppermints, each wrapped in tinfoil, thrusting a handful across the table to him. "Don't be shy, sweetheart."

He opened a savings account and gave the teller his wad of bills and pockets of coins.

"Attaboy, son," Al would say when shown the passbook with its increasing tally of deposits, his father's neck veins temporarily hidden. "You're gonna be somebody someday, kiddo. No driving a filthy truck for you." His dad had been one of the drivers for the fuel oil dealer but probably yelled at the other truckers so much that the owner made him manager in the smelly highway office, Al now in a tie. He still drove a truck, for UPS on weekends and holidays, to make ends meet. Al counted to the penny what Rose spent for the household, sometimes cussing her in front of their son. "A damned mop with a handle? Since when did rags go out of style?" This made Fred work all the harder and save all he could.

In his middle teens and a starter for junior varsity football, Fred discovered an art school on the other, nicer side of their town. His bank account was getting hefty. After practice, once a week, he dashed on his bike to the art studio, him the only kid in the room full of women. They would beam at him and be astonished at his pastel chalk rendering of the jug of iris one week, the still life of oranges in a pewter bowl the next. Fred was suspended in a kind of heaven hunched over his work. It was so peaceful, so perfect to be here, he thought, like sealed inside one of those glass globes that you shake to have the snowflakes float down on the little snowman, but after the storm, all silent and calm.

"Goddamn it, kid!" his father stomped into his room one night, Fred finishing and proofing his math homework still with time for vocabulary before bed. Al was waving the savings account passbook, shaking with rage. "What in God's name are these withdrawals?"

"I — I'm setting aside for Christmas presents, for you and Mom. Oh, and I had to buy a new rake for my yard work. Plus some other stuff." Fred was learning to be fast on his feet with his father.

"What other stuff?" Al was still quivering.

"Workgloves..."

"Workgloves? Damn sissy," and he slammed the passbook onto Fred's desk, strutting out.

Fred completed his vocabulary and re-read the O. Henry short story for extra measure. He understood his father was German and Germans had a temper. He wasn't soft like Rose "and her kind, holy rollers and puppets of the Pope." He rarely went to his Lutheran church and let that lapse for Fred, too. Fred well knew that any kids had to be Catholic if one of the parents was, but "no way in his family." He decided his dad was a victim of sorts with the misshapen knuckles on his left hand, the hand his drunken father had smashed on top of the kitchen table with a really big bible when Al forgot to take out the trash. Fred thought his father was better off Sunday mornings, Rose at her mass, him slugging down beers at the nearby tavern. It would leave Fred free to avoid the actual worship service so he could deliver the printed church bulletins for that Sunday to neighborhood shut-ins. He was pleased by his own scheme to skip church but also receive smiles, hugs, often a soda.

"Fred, you are the nicest boy ever. You must make your parents so proud," from crippled Mrs. Cowan.

"Son, you have a girl yet? She's going to be a lucky gal with a lad like you," from Mr. McSweeney clutching his cane.

By high school lots of girls had crushes on him. They said he was cute. They said he was sweet. They said he was shy. "Ferd the turd," said jealous teammates in the locker room. "Ferd the Nerd" was common, too, he being "the class brain."

"Fred! Thank goodness you're here on time," exclaimed Marjorie. "Are you out of practice early? These posters for the fall foliage dance, just look at the sloppy ones I did!"

He fingered the rainbow of Magic Markers, every conceivable delicious shade splayed across her dining room table. He wanted to finger *her*. He'd done so lots of times with various girls at the drive-in but it was Marjorie Olenhouser he coveted. He got down to business with the posters, Marjorie hovering near shoulder-to-shoulder. Even her aroma was intoxicating, like everything in Upper Hillview which made his own town seem more of a dump. He drew with his usual steely penmanship but saw perfectly well the shiny, honey-colored woodwork, the massive chairs padded with velvet, he supposed. "Hey, Ferdy, what's the rush?" one of his pals asked as he whipped into his street clothes after the workout without a shower. Now he worried about how he smelled for Marjorie.

She, too, was one of the smartest ones in school.

Increasingly Fred was drawn to the girls beyond his reach—best-dressed, best spoken, but who would tease him like the guys. Only in the case of the girls, he'd get aroused. Marjorie, especially, was quick-witted and sassy. She was so much more of a challenge than the girls who had given him a hand-job at the drive-in, willingly slipped off their bra and let him fondle and kiss and prod but never below the belt with his hard-on, just his hand. Marjorie here was untouchable. Her family had the only swimming pool in Upper Hillview. He was desperate to get invited; he'd rather jerk off than tamper with her and wreck his chances. With the likes of Marjorie Olenhouser, her talk of Ivy League schools, her own teal blue Mustang, there was no hurry. He could take his time. By senior year Fred knew what he wanted.

"You shudda smashed him, son," barked Al who was now considerably shorter and leaner than Fred. "So who gives a shit you broke that kid's teeth last week, the jungle-bunny from the city team? Use your bulk, your power, that's what you're good for." He chugged the last of his beer. "Of course don't forget those grades," he added, subdued. He reached into his pocket and produced a packet of Trojan-enz. "Don't forget these, too, Fred. I know what goes on in that drive-in, I'm not as dumb as I look. For shit's sake if you go all the way, you better pull out if you're not wearing one of these. Knock her up and you're dead meat. Most of these little cunts, it's just what they want, drop out of school and have a kid for Christ."

Fred won the Halloween window painting contest.

His idea for a mural for the lobby of the new town hall was accepted over dozens of others, two local architects included. The settings for his boyhood puppet shows had been so compelling he had charged admission, neighborhood parents coming, too, with their kids. What Al liked was Fred pitching soapsuds commercials during the intermissions. "Go into sales, son, you're gonna wow 'em." Back in junior high Fred asked for his birthday to be taken into the city to a particular art supply store, one made famous by the television show hosted by a fantastic artist in charcoal drawing. Al declined to accompany Fred. "That's your mother's thing." By senior year of high school Fred could render bodies in motion, gestures of hand, every variation of facial expression. The accumulation of prizes for artwork shared space on a cramped kitchen shelf with his football trophies. In fact Fred had no complaints that he was a trophy himself, the way his dad would sometimes beam. Rose stood there at his bringing home the latest award, hands folded over her cotton housedress, lips sealed, Fred assured of her deep-seated delight.

Yes this was all for his father's approval, but fine with Fred if it meant a ticket away from this hellhole, to use Al's reference to his own, foul boyhood in the slums. It came as no surprise that Fred was offered a full scholarship to each of the four Ivy League colleges to which he had applied. He'd already accepted, at seventeen, the Upper Hillview Princeton Alumni Club's gift of a hardbound Roget's Thesaurus inscribed to "the most promising boy" in his school. So long ago, Fred thought nearing graduation, were the days of sneaking out of neighborhood touch football with the gang, slipping off to the ladies' art studio instead, dirtying the knees of his jeans with mud before he got home so there'd be no reason to suspect his transgression. One of his first attempts with oil paints at ten or eleven still hung in their living room. Forever daydreaming of pastoral vistas, nothing but trees and meadows and flowers, he had ripped off the cover of a *Vermont Life* magazine in the town library. He folded it carefully inside *Treasure Island* then faithfully copied the scene onto a small canvas block, having purchased brand new supplies from his first snow shoveling jobs.

In time his savings passbook was of little interest to Al, as was Fred's outpouring of art. As long as his kid was intent on making money and good grades. And grabbing at girls. Very early on during a raucous wake at the home of one of Rose's Irish clan, Fred lingered with a cousin in her bedroom, cocooned from the fracas. Soon they were fooling around. All of a sudden she goes screaming off to the living room of plastered adults. "He made me touch it!" she bellowed, instantly silencing the mob, Fred shell-shocked at her side as his father Al winked.

Fred spent his college years uncertain of his role, as if he couldn't tell the difference between himself as the caged or the jailer looking on. By way of not fitting in, it wasn't so much the preppies whose intellect could take a back seat to their sleek sports cars. Nor was his inferiority due to their having learned three languages at an elegant school in Switzerland while their fathers were attached to embassies or corporate boards. It wasn't the classy girls still acting like debutantes; he'd gotten over lusting after Marjorie in high school; the girls of lower breed were surely far better lays. It was the hurdles he constructed for himself. How could he make millions if he was studying Dostoyevsky instead of statistics? He could not make up his mind, so he majored in "American Studies," a little of this, a little of that, no focus in particular, destined to leave him unemployable without a male relative on Wall Street. Pining after the trappings of privilege he did enroll, while blithely taking for no credit, all the painting and drawing courses on campus. But however to support himself someday as an artist? He stewed in this quandary.

"Fred, my good man, you've got to join us for Thanksgiving at our place in Cleveland. No views of the steel mill, I promise! Mum and uncles simply own it."

He looked like he belonged but that was a ruse. Over this, too, he agonized. Until June.

Part of his full scholarship was a token shift in the school cafeteria. June, a local girl, was employed there. Her smile demanded nothing more than its being returned. Her beauty was for all the world to enjoy since she didn't own it nor claim it to be of her making. June was as common, uncomplicated yet breathtaking as a full moon against a star-studded sky. She was his haven, his real teacher from the real world, and so Fred could flourish with his studies.

They moved into a cheap, downtown apartment on her meager earnings while he delved into literature, art history, the litany of humanities not worth a nickel. It was about this time his dad Al died of a heart attack at age fifty-five. Fred, so detached from his background at this point, felt little emotion. Mostly he was amazed his father's neck veins hadn't burst long before. It was June who helped Rose settle affairs, to get her a job as a waitress until the time came, years later, to find her a state-run nursing home, marginal at best. After college Fred and June married, Fred commuting to a prominent advertising agency as a graphic artist, June working night shifts at a nearby greasy spoon.

Fred was more or less, mainly less, in the "creative world," his cubicle flush with every manner of paints, pencils, markers, brushes...but in service to the latest version of floor polish. Each night he scoured the city trash cans for frequently-discarded canvases, actual paintings albeit factory-fare which he could gesso over on the weekends and paint anew.

"I'm getting a raise, June! They've asked me along on so many agency presentations at the clients that they're not only letting me flip the charts I've designed but I'm speaking to the marketing points, the graphs, literally giving the sales pitch."

"Well, heaven knows you're handsome and tall enough to be persuasive."

"The fact is I'm nothing more than a flip chart myself," at which she squeezed him by way of reply. Whether with hugs or endearments, June was unalloyed affirmation. She could not mollify his lingering sense of inadequacy. Floor polish an outlet for serious talent?

It didn't take a degree in psychology — although he had snuck that course in, too — for Fred to realize he'd taken on so many of the wounds of his downtrodden dad plus his mother Rose's unyielding self-effacement. Everyone is shaped by their parents, but isn't that all for the good? Hold dear what's right, ditch what isn't? Fred thought.

"Hey, son, why don't you paint one of those metal wastebaskets with the numbers so the damn birds and plants look real?" Al once offered in a rare bid of acknowledgment that his boy was hell-bent on art. And so Fred did just that, to please him but primarily to carry on with the sketchbooks hidden under his bed. Rose nodded approval at the paint-by-numbers handiwork, clutching the waist of her apron, Fred without a clue as to what she really thought. Maybe she didn't just endure her husband's cussing but let it flow off her plump, rounded back, satisfied her boy was big and strong enough to withstand the verbal tirades.

Fred often puzzled over his parents, anchored in his young marriage. He remembered running away, at ten, and took his father's beating like a little man. "Now don't be a freakin' fairy," Al would react to the elaborate, handmade birthday card Fred had concocted for his dad, complete with the lid of a beer bottle popping off when the card was opened but dolled up with turning maples, pumpkins, cheery sunflowers and other saccharine notes of the season. Of course Rose would melt at the hearts-and-flowers Mother's Day card he'd made from his finest, most colorful construction paper. Now and then she could not squelch spontaneous joy which more than cancelled Al's ongoing splenetic tongue-lashings. Once his outburst was actually amusing to Fred, amusing in retrospect but crushed at the time. It was the occasion of Fred's fourteenth birthday. Fred grandly paraded out in his fantastic new pink high-collared shirt and black bell-bottomed pants. "Jesus H. Christ. Pink!" "Dad, it's like Elvis, it's all the rage."

The further Fred got from his father's death, the more often the odd, affirmative if not affectionate item would filter through the fog of memory. Fred was constructing his latest puppet theater when his dad said "Now lemme show you how to hold a hammer." And he craned himself around his son, an arm over the boy's, not touching until his hand actually clamped upon Fred's. Forever Fred recalled the intense warmth, a sudden immersion into a misty dream utterly unreal, a storybook magic kingdom, a sensation unforgettable because it never happened before or after. Fred would make mental apologies for his dad, the grimy jobs he'd slogged through so his boy could leap ahead. He slept in a homeless shelter the first four months of his son's life because "the little bugger wailed all night long, off to work with barely an hour's shut-eye."

All this has faded for Fred, eventually to be with kids of his own, no easy task. He could forgive his father for beating him, for slapping his mother, for his being unable to keep his anger from erupting, constantly brought to a boil. But was it true forgiveness? Fred understood he had spun himself inside a silken web, a silk he could see through but impenetrable to others. He first beheld this chimerical state as the big loud clock in their threadbare living room struck six, the evening of his sixth birthday. Fred can inhabit that child to this day. At each of the six strikes of the clock, he wove another layer around himself, like an Egyptian mummy preserved intact, eyes forever open. He could come to no harm. He could, in an instant, transport himself to wherever he wanted to be, nothing beyond his imagination. He seized so often upon this image. It was only violated by one act emblazoned on his brain. He could gloss it over, he could dismiss it for ages at a time, but still it's encased like scar tissue in formaldehyde, dead but indestructible.

"Go on, son. Grab ahold of it by the neck."

The two of them were squatting at the toilet. Rose had fled. Fred, named after his father Alfred so the man could lay claim beyond their surname, had rescued three kittens in a box by trash cans on his way home from school. He was eight years old, well into artwork his father glanced at with a grimace.

"Chrissake, no animals in this house, no pets, goddammit you know the rules."

"I can save some of my lunch money."

"Just do it," Al shouted, "like this!" And he shoved one of the squealing kittens into the water of the bowl. "And hold it under so it can't breathe, until it's still. Like this." He tossed the lifeless, soaking kitten onto the tile floor.

Fred was thunderstruck with fear. Finally, gently, he picked up a kitten, he swore it was purring.

"No, grab both of them, one in each hand. It'll be quicker since you're being a pansy. Do it! *Now*," he hollered.

Young Fred did so. And as an adult he could confront not avoid the impact of his father Al. Fred could pride himself at the quantum leap he had made of his own, otherwise middling career so far, at the least his forging step-by-step those few things to which he clung as guideposts. But this outrage he could never forget. If it had any merit it would remind him, when he came to be a parent, that to teach his kids kindness, to care for others not so fortunate, such would be his obligations above all else.

Chapter 7

FRED

IF I COULD LEARN TO STOP THINKING, WOULDN'T the art take care of itself? Fred ruminates as he faces the blank paper taped to a large, flat board. He would like to plunge in, helter-skelter. Jab a stiff dry brush into a barely moistened cake of — close your eyes and just do it. Dare you. Make a hue that will stain like ink. It will lie there, defy you to deal with it. It's the complete opposite of his lifetime of watercolor building from light to dark, safely, one step at a time. What's the point of leaving June, on his own a year now, rules and protocol out the window" Fuck the floral still-lifes that sold like hotcakes, the meadows, the whorls of wildflowers. Forget nature itself! With eyes pressed shut he fumbles for a brush, whichever, and grinds it across his palette. Why settle for one color, why not a friggin' rainbow? He lifts his arm. The baby cries.

Fred slumps, rests his brush, rushes to the crib a few feet away. April's eyes are wide open. She's smiling. She knows all. He lifts her up and nuzzles his nose with hers. "You stink," he says and sets about the chore. The baby gurgles; she's not complaining. Never has, all these months of Nell now living with June, the both of them working fulltime. June is as bubbly as ever, in a craft shop collective, cashier/clerk by day, creating ornate costume jewelry off hours.

"It's you, June. It's you," he remarked during one of his frequent trips to her home, previously theirs, to retrieve some tools. She displayed her latest assemblage of rhinestones and sequins and little brass bits. "Hearts and flowers," said Fred. "You never let yourself get so dolled up. This is great."

June flushed pink.

"It's a little Zsa Zsa, though. Stuff women would wear in Las Vegas or as if they were," he teased, the formality of their separation far outweighed by their intimacy of a lifetime. If they were still celebrating anniversaries, he thought, the commemorative material would simply be a rock.

"Oh, Fred. This is so much fun," and she clipped a grape cluster of sparkles onto an ear. "And I never had my ears pierced. Nell says I'm so retro. Maybe it's not too late for me to catch up." She pranced to a mirror with two of the crazy things clamped onto her lobes, looking ridiculous. But isn't that because of the box in which he—and she—had kept her captive all these years?

Fred once thought of their marriage as a compost pile, sometimes steaming, sometimes inert, a heap of indigestibles yielding in the end a loam from which anything could grow, for good or ill. Now, living apart, it was all up for grabs.

He is pacing with the baby, pleased to be distracted from being stymied by his painting. His thoughts shift to Nell who has morphed from renegade to single, working mom. Fred watched from the sidelines as his daughter charged ahead with the new one of her own, honoring June by naming her little girl the month of her arrival. Meanwhile Freddie, off to graduate school for an MBA with dreams of moneyed nirvana, suddenly dropped out. Is he finally taking cues from his sister? There was always Nell's ongoing addiction and its multiple offshoots prior to Fred's departure from June. He figured Nell's transgressions in fact solidified her as a buttress against the smug, predictable, law-abiding world to which her brother aspired from first grade. Or did until last month. Why should my children be any more decipherable than me? Fred wonders.

He is presently amazed at a rubber nipple being able to replace human flesh. It portends stainless-steel knees, artificial kidneys, an internal penis pump.

Nell was meant to command others, to be a mother, Fred concluded early on. Even more so than June who, like himself, was playing follow-the-leader. Everything about Nell was so intentional. She like April here was eagle-eyed from birth compared to her docile, cherubic brother. Nell's heart is dead-set on her work at the single-mothers' day care center. She loves tending children but her focus is helping women, especially ex-addicts, find better-paying jobs, specifically arranging computer instruction and wheedling grants. She herself barely earning a living, Fred reviews, strolling about with April, Nell now housed free with June at his former, suburban sprawl. He'd cashed in everything to paint fulltime and bought this tacky little ranch in the next town, closer to the city. He wishes he didn't have to keep mowing the damn miles of lawn back there to save money. What was I thinking, all those years of creating an ersatz estate? Have I lived half my life in reaction to my parents and that threadbare block of row houses?

He steps outside with the baby. Maybe she's asleep, he prays, picturing the brash slashings of watercolor he was on the verge of painting. The square of backyard is lined with chain-link fence. He's stopped pruning from its bottomside the collected detritus — plastic shopping bags, McDonald's cartons, burst birthday balloons. The mustard clapboards have faded to batdung brown. The sliding glass doors rock and roll like a toy train about to derail. I love this place, ravaged as a war zone, he summarizes, rubbing the baby's back. The bleaker the better, so maybe something brilliant can compose itself on that spread of pristine paper.

April squirms a little protest back in the crib. She knows. She knows her dada is a gift of the gods. Her mother Nell has probably been reciting the sermonette to her in utero that children who are wanted, children who are loved, children who are man-handled as well are the fortunate few.

He presses a finger onto her belly after tucking her in. She squeezes it and lets it go with reluctance. Fred returns to his table in the same room. It's the largest, formerly a living room. This unlikeliest of studios is a beginning to my reinvention, he thinks. Now what about the watercolor? We're good to go for maybe an hour if I'm lucky...

Fred is slumped at day's end at the Formica kitchen table starting on his second beer, Nell having long since relieved him of April. Nell had rattled like a machinegun with a volley of her day's accomplishments. "Shaquelle has been hired by a law firm!" He knows he has to clean the kitchen floor some day. He's tossed everything he inherited here into a Dumpster — plastic curtains, Mickey and Minnie Mouse bunk-beds. Plastic flowers! Start from scratch. Whatever did Rothko do when he began? Certainly not as he ended, the canvas distilled into a block, alright, two. Big, though. Enormous canvasses as if his mission was so momentous, so obviously urgent, that it could not be contained on a mere slip.

Fred tries to sip but he's finished that one.

I'm forty-nine. Like being told one has terminal cancer with a year to live. Yet I'm only my parents' age when I graduated from college. They were haggard, finished; I was just starting off. They had no options. Things were simpler then — the last century?

But Fred and June: work, marriage, make it. Maybe he's the victim of an errant gene, Fred's mind continues to meander, popping open another brew. A single cell — "art," of all things — compounding itself into a tumor, not malignant but dividing unstoppably. Like a baby born into the wrong body, a boy's instead of a girl's and vice versa. What about this body, he goes on. Fatter. Evil processed foods. How could he live to be like Picasso, no, his a monumental ego. Maybe more like the Sardinians and Okinawans and Caucasians you read about, average age one hundred…

Okay, so he left the paper blank today. That's alright. That's a start, in its way. Why should I have to accomplish anything except for myself? Relish the beauty of mistakes, the riot of colors instead of me personally leading the charge. Fred is sick and tired of queuing at the supermarket checkouts facing the racks of scandal sheets that trumpet one movie star or mogul or pol after another, reminding him of his insignificance. You matter to yourself, attempts his internal cheerleader. Isn't that the height of self-indulgence? the naysayer replies. Like Nell on Facebook with April's every slobber, her very own Grade B movie.

Fred downs the beer and realizes he must do something about food. He's reverted to his and June's feeding Freddie and Nell as gross grammar school rascals with Spaghetti-O's and Ragu. He lets himself be serenaded by the posters of Diebenkorn and Frankenthaler, his only nod at accessorizing. They tell him to shut up and get going, just because he feels these days worthy only as footnote in the longwinded tome of his life.

Day after day Fred peels the next botched watercolor off his 18 by 24-inch block, or board, in the case of the taped-down single sheet 22 by 30 inches. He does this calmly with no regrets. That's progress. Maybe baby April is drawing him into the simpler, shallower tides of her own easy breath. One time he tried to copy the rambunctious Helen Frankenthaler poster, whirling without restraint. His version, a mud-pie. Next. Did she give a shit about ending up in a museum? And so what if she did? Why not let this inspire him? What's the matter with being in a museum before you die? Aim higher, out of your reach.

This latest of his watercolors at midpoint after a near-hour is all pale yellows, barely perceptible spidery lines of ochre, just enough to create a few clouds, amoebas, dollops of definition to suggest not even say there is life throbbing where you'd least expect it... Dash of umber, reckless, sabotage sublimity, dead.

Next.

"I thought you'd get a kick out of these kids' draw-ings from the center, Dad," exclaims Nell sashaying in with armloads of Pampers. Making an entrance into his set of drab cubicles does not take much. Nell outfits herself from thrift shops, wildly mismatching blouses and skirts and scarves that make her father jealous of the carnival bravura. Today's pyrotechnics remind him of his own rollicking Kindergarten finger paintings.

"I love these two," says Fred. "All four edges busy as the middle. So eager to cram it all in," he addresses Nell's back, she bustling with the baby.

Fred's mind flips to a scene, height of his realis-tic watercolor days, sprawled in a rural village by a bridge, willow trees, babbling brook. Not Hallmark sticky-sweet but close. At one point he hears whispers interrupting the efflorescence of colors, two brushes clenched in his teeth, four others in his elevated left hand as his right is executing the jagged cracks and their violet shadows in the stones of the old bridge. He looked up to behold a gaggle of children on their way home from school. They are hypnotized by what they are witnessing. He smiled at them, nodded acknowl-edgment but can't stop his work. Oh, to capture that propulsion in a new medium, he thinks, admiring the chaos of colors in the drawings Nell has tossed on his table.

"How's your work going?" Nell says clutching April and shoving all manner of baby do-dads into her voluminous tote bag. She checks the fridge supply of formula, pulls aside her curtain of long brown hair so they can make eye contact. "I like this one. The reds and purples. Vivid for you."

"It's blackened into sludge. See here?"

Nell frowns, dismisses April slurping onto the sleeve of her dress. "You okay, Dad? Not much in your fridge." She notices the beer cans piled on the counter. "You're not drinking during the day, are you?"

"With April? Good god, no."

"You started that weekend art group you mentioned?"

He knows what she is saying, not asking, her eyes and mouth gone all serious, bearing the weight of her responsibilities at work plus concern for him.

"I'm thinking of it. Maybe soon," he says.

"Maybe good for a change of pace, Dad." Finally she smiles and wrinkles up her nose as if erasing any note of mothering him, as well.

She dashes off then looks over her shoulder. "Mom made a mountain of lasagna. Bring you some tomorrow." She can't help herself.

For the past few weeks Fred has abandoned his watercolors. He knows he's subjecting them to the opposite of their very nature: soaring transparence. Watercolors at their best, whichever the colors, whatever the subject from which the painting was launched, are wings that take flight. If oils are prose, watercolors are poetry. And so he hammered away, abruptly, with a new box of pastels. The fragile chalk crumbled in his tight grip. Besides, they were pastel, inherently limp-wristed and pale. He did no better with bigger chunks of charcoal. It's okay if aggression is his urge of the moment to unleash. But it is not, nor is anger, nor any one thrust about which he can make up his mind.

He has come to a standstill. I'm not even moved

by little April. I'm glad for every nursing or change of her pads. Less time sitting like a doll at an amusement park waiting to be shot off the shelf.

He sips the aromatic bourbon, his shortcut to shutting down. Maybe less caloric than a six-pack, he thinks. It's got that going for it, too.

Fred is used to solitary confinement, by day. Then, by late afternoon, there has always been with June the mindless but loving return to—chatter, dishes, impending social dates, the pablum of his life to offset the bitter pills of his art. Here in this bungalow he's become oppressively alone long hours, with or without tending April. The baby in her crib or in his arms does not prevent his thickening obsession, as now, with June. He cannot picture her survival without him. More accurately, he cannot picture his without her. Yes Nell and her baby keep him a link in their chain. And Freddie, of course. Freddie has always favored one-on-one, father-to-son weighty conversations, as if he Fred was the goal zone towards which his son battled yard by yard to reach.

"Dad, you're my role model. You're your own man. I really respect how you've kept stretching into new directions." His were the bright eyes of youth, unclouded by multiple points of view. His thick brown hair was styled every-which-way, his energy exploding like popcorn in the making, reminding Fred that he himself was over-the-hill.

"Thanks, Freddie. But it's so important to look beyond your parents...to other ideas, other inspirations." Fred knew this counsel would amount to light rain running off a metal roof. It was as if his boy was genetically programmed to duplicate his father's fierce clutching at convention for years and years before confronting reality: the resentment, the sham, the truth of what he should be about.

So Freddie has dropped out of business school but to take the fast lane to big bucks. Must every generation try to one-up the old man? Fathers are the roar of winds but mothers the pull of gravity. They should carry more clout.

As for me and June—forget wife, this woman side-by-side since their teens, how can we truly sever ourselves, knowing each other by heart? I can move to Alaska, what would it matter?

He is slouched at the pedestrian kitchen table, this becoming a habit.

His love of June he is supposed to suspend, to see how it was based upon his now obsolete notions of him as her provider, her protector, and, just as unseemly, her own excuse to remain dependent, typecast upon arrival, his still life of a forever-blooming flower.

He can't believe her cheerfulness since their split. She's on automatic with him, wouldn't want him to feel any guiltier than he does. All this is unspoken between them, the more potent and subversive for being so. Maybe she's relieved, released? It occurs to Fred that it is he who is borderline despondent, and not for the stagnation of his art.

No, June too must be suffering, he wants to think despite knowing that this reinforces his neediness for her to be defined by him. Yes she is so effusive and sunny by nature. But that's just on her surface. That may be essential for her survival and well-being. How does even he, her longstanding mate, know if her surface was shaped in response to the possibly dark, twisted crevices in her childhood...untranslatable passages that we all, thank goodness, for the most part gloss over?

He misses her, or them, at his depths.

But he loves her. It's that simple. And it's the source of his pain.

He reaches again for the bottle of bourbon.

"Oh dear, this is so difficult, changing poses every minute!" gushes the middle-aged lady to his one side. "But that's good, isn't it? Forcing us to..." She makes mad strokes on her pad while jabbering on. "I thought it would be another woman, I mean female, it was the last two times. But this man, well, it's another matter!"

"Shouldn't be," mumbles Fred to be polite.

"I know, it's just limbs and angles and... I hope the instructor switches to five minutes, then ten, so I can concentrate! Golly."

The twenty-some people in the figure-drawing workshop are flipping pages, furiously sketching. He ceases to hear the woman's patter. He likes the rhythm, the loosening of his arm muscles, smudging the spine one minute, fleshing out a thigh the next.

The white-haired, elderly woman at the desk to his other side has been drawing ever so gracefully, he's noticed out of the corner of his eye turning pages. None of the slap-dash of himself and the others. He sidles over to this woman during the break, mostly to avoid the motor-mouth. The lady smiles up at him, fine bones of her upper chest exposed by a stylish boat-neck sweater.

"Can I have a peek?" he says. "I'm going like a whirligig by comparison." She's lots older, he realizes, her thick mass of short-cropped silver hair so luxurious that at first he thought she might be prematurely gray. There's an unforced vigor to her upright bearing.

She lets him page through her sketches.

"You've only made three or four lines," Fred remarks, "but you've captured the whole. I'm straining to get the arm angle, the elbow, just right."

"There is no right," she says, sighing, "is there?" She's folded hands loosely in her lap. He's struck by leathery-brown of her face defied by the radiant mop of hair, sleek as satin.

"Well, I agree with you," he says. "It's not actually a body but a gesture."

She shakes her head, the hair glistening like a jostled Christmas tree of tinsel and distracting Fred. "It's not necessarily a figure. For me," she offers. "It could be the twist of a vine. And not even that."

"How so?" He's hunkered down his looming frame to better level their positions.

"First off, it's a Rorschach test. What am I seeing, feeling, at this moment? If I'm tense or upset, I think that would show itself on the paper." Small but classy gold hoops pierce her earlobes, yet another disconnect between her apparent age and hip appearance.

"You must be quite mellow," Fred chuckles, instantly flagellating himself at the presumption.

But she chuckles, too. "You know, it's not always about simplicity. Thank you for saying what you did about my sketches reduced to a few lines, but it could just as well be thousands. I remember that one of the Austrian emperors told Mozart he had too many notes. That they obscured a clear, clean melody. Imagine!"

"No hard and fast rules, you're saying," replied Fred.

"There are, what, a few dozen of us here," she says, "and likely no two drawings the same. I'm glad many people pin work up at the end so I can delight in all the difference."

"I better sit down. Nice talking with you — oh, I'm Fred."

"Roxie." Again she smiles sweetly, crinkling her eyes which seem fixed in a mode of amusement. "Now, Fred. Relax. Enjoy. Let your hand be limber, your mind taking a break."

He delves back into the longer poses for the second half of the session. No, don't delve. Flow. Listen to the lady. The guy's neck, the nose, it's not necessarily a man. It's a mood, express that or not, but let go. Be a medium through which stuff deep down gets an airing for a change. No destination, just some art taking place. Who knows? This detour in his home studio routine might unchain him from acting like a rat caged on a lab wheel.

Finally he gets lost in the moment.

An hour later they are gathering themselves and their materials, paying the instructor, signing up again. Several of them are perusing samples of today's outpouring voluntarily posted, the Chatty Cathy among them freeing up Fred to have a final word with the amicable lady.

"Excuse me, Roxie," Fred says and bites his lower lip, indicating the final page of her pad. Although just a few lines, the sketch is unmistakably a penis.

"Well," she sighs. "He was so enormously endowed. I suppose that's what caught my eye this time."

Fred's face is immediately aflame but he laughs.

"Fair enough. Not the whole but a part."

Roxie shrugs. Her beautiful smile eradicates decades. "I'm not usually so literal. His business end…that's all so long ago. Maybe I needed a refresher course."

He flushes again, more sparked than embarrassed by this perspicacious dame. "See you next time, Roxie?" asks Fred, he hopes not too expectantly.

She shakes her snow-capped head in the affirmative. "Maybe it'll be another man."

The female model at the next workshop was truly a woman, Fred thinks, poking about with the baby April, a slight lift to his gait. He reviews how he did not stop fantasizing while drawing her cleavage, the sumptuous roundness, the seductive drape of her rug of red hair.

"Sorry, Roxie, but guess today's it's my turn."

She laughed. She'd wrapped her elegant, petite figure with a flowery shawl, not unlike his daughter Nell and her preference for loose clothes with an ethnic flair.

Fred was hesitant to tack up or show Roxie his figure studies, too specifically detailing the model's buttocks and flanks.

"How about a cup of tea at that nice café around the corner?" suggested Roxie without warning.

And so they did, Fred trying unsuccessfully to pose as many queries to her as she did to him. Women, he always believed, were hard-wired for that, interviewing to unearth the man. And rightfully so: whose seed would she select? Nevertheless, peppered with her questions, he felt diminished but still he loved it.

"My whole thing has been nature," said Fred.

"Never the figure, a face."

Roxie gently encircled her mug of ginger tea as Fred sipped his latte. "Nothing wrong with nature," she said. "Beauty. If you live in the city maybe you paint buildings. Or abstracts born of urban angst. At least the trees and mountains and what not allow an artist reprieve. Goodness, all the pollution and strife in the world. It's important, I gather for you, to assert your gestalt—flowers, fruit, sunlight. Think Cezanne! Monet!"

"Yes, but my things have been so bloody literal."

"You know Charles Demuth, I'm sure." She slapped hands to her chest. "Ethereal. You absolutely look through his flowers to—the universal soul. Connecting everyone and everything." As quickly her face slid back into its habit of composure.

"I do love Demuth. I'm trying to get someplace else but I've no idea where that is. Nature is so...feminine."

"Thank you, Fred. I'll take any credit I can. But I do disagree. Feminine to me is forceful. The primary one, Mother Nature."

"True," said Fred. "She's in charge. Isn't that why they name the hurricanes after women?"

They laugh.

"But watercolor, Roxie. It seems so feminine-receptive?"

"That's a problem?"

"I'm a man. I need to be bolder than I've been."

"Doesn't it take strength to restrain yourself with those soft brushes? Otherwise you'd make a mess."

Fred could see she was enjoying this banter, tweaking him, taking side-swipes. To him this visit was a postponement of the return to the muck he was making of his life. He described his trashy, cookie-cut-ter house and how he hoped it would catapult him to a new realm for his work.

"You're absolutely right about nature, Roxie. It's always been my inspiration. You said the source can hold solid but interpretations can go wild. I should be living in a cabin in the woods," he said, trying not to sound glum to this feisty lady. She may be old, he thought at that moment, but I detect the blush of eye-liner, the palest strokes of pearly lipstick.

"Funny you should say that, Fred. I live in a cabin in the woods. My neighbors are evergreens, mountain-tops, the whims of clouds. I do adore it after a lifetime of humanity on edge and all that. Don't give up on nature, if that runs in your blood. You're a young man. You've only scratched the surface of your art. Who knows where it will lead?" And here she withdrew the grasp of her mug and tapped the top of his hand.

Chapter 8

ROXIE

"**O**H MY GOD, THIS IS MY DREAM," SAYS FRED the large man emerging from his too-little car, swiveling his mop of reddish hair as if assaulted by a plethora of visual delights and unable to choose any one for focus. After several more workshops of sharing their sketches and comments, she'd suggested this visit.

"The figure drawing," offers Roxie, "got to be more disciplined than energizing, don't you think, Fred?" She leads the way to her cabin, barefoot over the trodden wild grass of her former lawn, not that she ever took her initial forays at grooming the place very seriously.

"This is heaven, Roxie. Thanks so much. I've tried to pretend the chain-link fence around my postage-stamp yard doesn't exist, but no luck." He's watching his step, she observes, as if a rattlesnake could slither upon him here in the wild.

"Drop your things on the porch. Goodness, you're a hefty man. Hope all my floorboards hold up." She fetches her supplies, the old blanket to perch upon, what else? Leave the tea for later.

The ever-curious chipmunks scurrying about upon

his arrival are now in hiding.

Soon they're settled with their sketchpads at her home base, she calls it — the bank of the pond overlooking its rippling surface, the looming mountaintop, the restless sky, the smorgasbord of trees. They're squabbling for attention which she loves to thwart, often refusing them all, suitors at the ball, she flitting about and feigning indifference.

"Sorry, Roxie, your lotus position, no way."

"Oh my dear. Grab that tree stump. Hollow and light as a feather, old as I am."

This he does, setting it just off the blanket. Each of them shimmies their sketchpad to near level on their lap, sighing, ready for action.

"I have an idea," Roxie states.

"Oh, no," says Fred. "I thought there'd be free-ranging here."

"Let's face the same direction. Alright, that dead elm over there." She points with her pencil. "Now shut one eye and draw. Whatever."

"I can't close my right. My eyelid is vibrating. Yeah, the left I can do."

"Go for it, as they say." Funny, that remark she thinks as her pencil begins its calligraphic leap. As if I'm from a distant generation. More like, despite his bulk, he seems a boy.

After a bit Fred says, "Can I peek and open them both?"

"Just close both eyes and rest. Then start again." She attempts not to be distracted by him and simply draw. Maybe that's not the point of having a friend here, she thinks. Let him float, him the kite, me holding the string and watching from below. He's so dutifully silent and stern. "Well now Fred," she interrupts after a while. "What have we done?"

He gives her his pad.

"It's the dead elm!" she cries.

"I can actually see sharper than usual. Like having binoculars."

"Oh but Fred, you've gone beyond realistic. It's the Medusa, all head of writhing serpents. Don't tell me those are twigs."

"Remember you said, during our second chat…"

"You're counting?" she beams.

" —that realistic or abstract doesn't matter. It's the reaching down to our depths and yanking stuff out."

"Don't listen to me, dear. I have another idea."

"Wait," he says frowning, still so serious. "What did you draw?"

She hands over her sketchbook and elevates her forehead.

"It's all a jumble," says Fred. "Circling squiggles." "I must have seen the mass of branches all entangled, like a woven basket, all interconnected, no end or beginning."

"Cool! Roxie, that is so cool. You're amazing."

"Just you wait. Now turn to our left, the evergreens. They're a black-green wall, yes? Don't sketch any object, only shadows and very broad strokes. Not a single trunk or limb. Go."

What fun, she thinks. Like the children in her makeshift African classroom, her supposedly the teacher when she was every bit as much at the starting line. Fred is as riveted as those tots by the task; as eager for escape. In their case from the obvious, desperation and danger all about. In his case who knows? Not her business, she should be on guard against that.

"Lovely," says Roxie several moments later of Fred's flowing lines. "I half-expected shadings with the side of the lead, like mine. Good for you! Haunting vague lines leading nowhere."

Fred sits tall on the stump. "Next," he says brightly.

"I have to think. I know I'm not supposed to think. Okay, about face. Towards the cabin. But don't draw it or the porch or the compost piles or any of that. Just draw the negative space, what the hard objects are not."

"I should have worn sweat pants," says Fred wrestling with the snug grasp of jeans on his upper legs and crotch. "Is that a sarong, Roxie?"

"A dashiki, technically. Same thing. Loose clothing, Fred. You men in our culture have a long ways to go."

"Dashiki sounds like an African tribe."

"Very close. But let's get to the drawing. You must be expert at negative space with your watercolors. More of that later when we talk." She tries to dismiss him—this big, attractive man, suddenly planted in her isolated Eden. She tries to concentrate on her own assignment, its purpose of formlessness and habit-breaking. But this silent admonition, too, is counter-productive. She knows, let it all go, at this she is well practiced. Take deep breaths and with those she draws.

An hour later they situate on her porch with a pitcher of iced mint tea she's made for the occasion. She asks Fred to fetch a chair from the kitchen; visitors let alone gentlemen callers are few and far between. Roxie chortles to herself at labeling him as such. But a man at her side let alone a true gentleman like Fred? She surprised herself at having donned this colorful wraparound instead of her smock.

"That last one, squinting. I liked that best," says Fred shifting his massive frame on the flimsy ladder-back chair. He is all decorum, she thinks. God forbid he crashes my silly antique flat onto the floor. "Fogging over my view," he continues. "You know, Roxie, I think that describes the best of my watercolors. Nothing too exact."

"Well, like the Impressionists," she says. "I've always thought that's why they're so popular. Invite the viewer to wade around, not spell it all out with easy access to concrete objects. All blurry it forces the eye to participate, to get involved in the mystery, the miracle of whatever in a different dimension."

"Exactly. I know this. But still I struggle against putting in too much detail." He's sitting upright as a soldier on guard, hands grasping the glass of tea between his thighs as if the vessel, too, is a precious antique.

"Keep drawing with me. Maybe you'll change. It's such a change for me to have company. I just may go in the reverse direction with you here, Fred. Render that maple leaf by leaf!"

She sets down her drink and stands. "Come. I want you to see this painting inside." She leads him to the large piece hanging in her bedroom; he probably can't tell that, the room a tumble of pillows and fabrics strung about. "Now this, Fred. It's a head and a hand and torso and what not. Actual things, you could say. But then what?"

Fred's eyes widen. "Wild. A huge hand, a tiny head. Genderless body I guess. But the head is black, the body white. It's — troubling."

"Good," Roxie says after a lingering silence. "It

still has that effect on me. Let's go back to the porch. I just wanted to make a point. Things may start off as literal objects in the mind's eye, but then the mind takes off." They sit again, Fred's long legs splayed jerkily given that chair so darn low. "I'm sorry," she says, "you say you're going nuts with your work right now. But I've come to the conclusion that our creativity is always there, butting up against our roadblocks. And it gushes through any openings we allow, intentionally or otherwise."

"I could try painting with my eyes closed," he remarks unconvincingly.

"Fred, bring your watercolors sometime. I'd love to work with them again, it's been ages. You can teach me!" She has crossed her legs, the loose skirt leaving more exposed than she'd realized which she hastily corrects. Honey, the legs are the last thing to go, she recalls Harold's uppity but sassy grandmother instructing her a lifetime ago.

"How long have you taken up artwork with such enthusiasm?" prods Fred.

This could lead to unsettled ground. "I've been playing with my chalks and colored pencils forever. I don't think of it as art, not at all. It's mostly to trick my head into shutting down. A sleight of hand." She's amazed at these thoughts. Compiled, even unbeknownst to her, and filed away...or merely prompted by this man, a self-proclaimed artist?

"I like that idea of avoiding calculation," Fred says. "I should sit or stand in my studio and tell myself it's time for meditation. Tune out. Just happen to be holding this brush, dabbing it into the paint, letting it have its way on the paper." He gulps the iced tea, finally.

"You know I'm joking. Sort of. I don't mean to belittle your intriguing suggestion."

"There's this saying: Be creative but not the creator. I suspect the process takes a lifetime, Fred. There's no rush."

For a while they slide into silence. The tinkling of leaves in the breeze shifts from background music to the forefront, agreeably lulling them both.

"I keep dwelling on the masters, their output," Fred says.

"And so must have they been hacking away. Why are you any different?" She's re-crossed her legs, open slit and all. Harold would have been shocked back then in the Dark Ages, she as well.

"I'm thinking right now of those Warhol portraits," says Fred. "Trippy DayGlo faces of Marilyn. Jackie O, Marlon Brando. Obviously higher than a kite he must have been, blazing, a hero as a heretic to those around him. And now he and his art are icons and sell for millions." He's hunched forward; they're in a huddle.

"Yes he was a rebel," she says, "but he was playing the game, too, I gather. Hanging out with those celebrities. Look, Fred." She sits up straight, she hopes not to lecture but isn't she entitled at this stage? "There's the culture that dictates parameters to define and perpetuate itself. You say you've done all these landscapes which are so adored. Fine. You're trying for otherwise now. But back to Warhol. What would be his irreverence, his sticking up a middle finger, so to speak, at conventional art without that smug status quo there for him to butt up against? I'm trying to say that all this revolution, this utter innovation you're judging yourself by, or reaching for, is really one and the same thing."

"Two sides of the same…" He doesn't finish but echoes her, like a tidy disciple. Let him be.

"Pioneers," she takes up her theme once more, "and yes, they are that, in due time they become a bastion of stability the next crop of artists will rebuff. I mean, Warhol lionizing Liz Taylor, John Wayne? Picasso his mistresses albeit with their crossword puzzle faces? They're still movie stars, it's still these women as the objects of Picasso's obsession. It may appear revolutionary — or loving, adoring representation — but it's all on the surface. I think the interesting thing is what happens to the artist. Is there magic in the making?" She sits back and grabs her now lukewarm glass of tea. "Goodness. Sorry for all that, Fred. Random thoughts, they say more about me than these artists!"

"Wow," says Fred softly. He's folded his hands which are wedged below his knees.

"We'd best stick to drawing," Roxie says. "Talk is cheap."

He's practically swooning at her, bug-eyed, as if a dazzling butterfly positioned itself inches from his nose.

"Let's go for a stroll, Fred. You've got sneakers. I'll put on mine. I have paths here but mostly I go over rock ledges and duck under trees. Would you be up for that?"

Of course, he nods and grins.

She changes into shorts. Soon they are off, her leading him alongside the pond, across a field of wavy yellow grass, gradually twisting uphill into raw woods. She's appreciating the silence after her unleashing all those theories of art. He too must need a break. But isn't it the commentary that has led them this far as new friends?

After a half-hour she stops, wipes her forehead, and Fred follows suit. "Gets a little steep here, my dear."

He shakes his head "yes," slightly out of breath. He's tied his blue chambray shirt around his waist, she noticing the dark circles under the arms of his T-shirt.

The dramatic incline forces her to take deeper breaths. She grips a rounded rock with her left hand, assists herself forward by clasping a dead limb with her right. She knows he's fallen a bit behind but she must forget him and maintain her momentum.

Roxie then Fred arrive on a ridge. She's enjoying the sweep of blue-black to pale purple mountaintops more lavishly displayed here than the vantage point of her pond.

He is forcibly breathing, sidling to her side to share the view. His T-shirt is drenched. "Whew," he manages.

"This may have been too much. Forgive me, Fred. I do this every day."

They are standing in her kitchen. She's selected a salad bowl and plopped it onto her butcher-block. Next she's scanning her fridge. "How rude of me, Fred, not to offer you a bite. I'll just toss this leftover slaw... forget the limp celery, okay the onions. And maybe chop up this apple, would that be okay, my boy? Pinto beans! Protein." She throws it together with olive oil and a dark ruby rice vinegar. Next she crinkles some of her hanging dried herbs on top. "You probably just open a can of tuna in a rush. If I didn't saddle myself with all this homegrown..." Fred has himself propped up on her old wooden stool, still appearing pooped. Not that I've given him a second's chance to help, she thinks, spinning about like she's making wait the King of Siam.

Back on the porch they munch away. Crude pebbly bowls from the craft collective—she felt sorry for the man at his idle little booth, are balanced on their laps.

"You sure have lots to inspire you here in the woods," says Fred.

"As I've said, that can be a challenge. I draw to isolate myself but there's such a spectacle to take in. Notice me! seems to call every tree and twist of cloud."

"I gather you're alone here but it seems like a universe. All your homesteading projects."

"I must say, Fred, it's becoming too much. I do have Hank for the heavy lifting, the tilling, tinkering with my old jalopy. Goodness, you've probably never heard of that word. Plus ladders. I don't trust myself anymore to change a ceiling lightbulb. Honestly I'm ready to live in a single room."

"Oh come on, Roxie. Obviously you're wonderful company for yourself. All your books. Me, I feel like one of the city homeless, I'm that out of sorts."

"Just a stage, my dear. A launch-pad. Good for a start at this next chapter of yours."

"You have a family, Roxie? Can I assume you may be widowed?"

Watch it, she tells herself. But his pink cheeks and broad forehead are so unfettered, now, unlike his sergeant-at-arms the first workshop. He's so open, so clearly wounded, how can I not assuage him?

"I've had children, Fred. I'm afraid they've not had me." *Stop right there.*

"I'm sorry. Didn't mean to be nosy."

"But of course you are. Don't apologize. You don't

hack your way through the Sturm und Drang because of art alone. You have a wife and grown kids you've already mentioned. No one leapfrogs beyond all that."

He's wolfed down his salad, rested his bowl, declined more. "I should get support," Fred says, "maybe from a group of like-minded folks. Like yourself, Roxie. Other painters but, I don't know, maybe a book club. It's still weird on my own after all these years. I've been pretty stir-crazy without adult conversation. The baby! You...this has been great. I don't want it to be an obligation for you. I know what that's like."

"If I may say, Fred, you need to breathe. Keep hiking. Join an outdoor club."

"I know, I've gone soft." He pats his belly.

"Long shallow breathing," she goes on, "that's when I'm drawing my best. But link up with others for fun, for diversion. I've been in communities which I've clung to because of a greater good, so I thought at the time, ignorant of my neediness for connection. Groups are composed of incomplete individuals, like oneself. So looking to others—it can be tricky."

She can see he's been riveted by her every word. She can also tell, as a gentleman, he's aware of the impact of his presence in her vernal, becalmed hideaway.

He leans forward, about to rise. "I must get going, Roxie. You've been so kind with your time. But I have to ask you one more thing—about that painting. The small black head and the big white body. Boy, such a powerful image. Reconciling opposites but not really. It almost looks like a child, someone unformed. And it's your painting. Did that just pop into your mind, out of the blue?"

She hesitates, fearful to expose her rapid breathing. She stands and so abruptly does Fred. If anything he's been too delightful, too appreciative, too easy to have around.

"Each painting I imagine is a story, a story without words. Beyond them," she says. "Leonardo said any painting is a painting of oneself. You see, I studied useless things like art history, so I was convinced at the time—thought it was useless." She's lost eye contact, her gaze unfocused on the floor. "Oh Fred, that's plenty for now. More idle chatter the next time."

He places his big hand quite tenderly on her shoulder by way of farewell. Thank god he doesn't kiss her or shake her hand. Even worse.

Fred drives off before Roxie slowly turns to face her modest home, the chipmunks darting about for their daily feed, the coast now clear. At least I didn't offer him a proper meal, a slice of ham, a bottle of beer. *Next time*, however, she reminds herself. I think those were my very last words.

Chapter 9

FRED

NELL TOOK THE DAY OFF FROM WORK TO bring April to a scheduled check-in with the pediatrician. This allowed Fred to suggest that Roxie and he have their weekly at his studio for once. They'd long since quit the art workshop, finding ample ways to engage themselves on their own.

"This is a wonderful big space, Fred," Roxie says upon entering the former living room, the baby's things organized in one end but the lion's share available for his art.

Roxie does a little swirl, almost a dance step, not surprising with her being so agile for an oldster, Fred thinks. She whips off her star-patterned fuchsia scarf and stretches it broadly as if it's a jump rope and she's about to commence leaping.

"The table's large enough," says Fred, "so we can do watercolors side-by-side." He had sulked at the prospect of introducing her to his depressing quarters compared to her lush, woodsy retreat, but her constant cheerfulness cancelled that. "If there's one thing you've helped get through my thick head, Roxie, it's that surroundings don't matter." He shows her about the ramshackle ranch house. "Now don't look in my fridge. If you really are what you eat, that's half my problem right there."

She sets a picnic basket atop the kitchen table. "I brought a few things. Why should you fuss with food, your family dealings and all?" Today Roxie's outfit is navy slacks and a snug, white-and-blue striped jersey making her look ageless, Fred reacts, leading them back to the studio. Well, contemporary, he modifies. What workaday woman of any generation wears a dress any more?

"This is exciting," says Roxie fingering the various samples of watercolor paper Fred has displayed. "I love this bumpy, textured one."

"High rag content. It can absorb so much but the colors fade to practically nothing."

"Then you can start dark and daring!"

Such optimism, Fred thinks. Is that set for life at birth or could it become second nature, like finally walking a tightrope, perfectly balanced and without fear? He tapes a single sheet for him and one for her to the table and assembles his largest palette and jars of multiple brushes between them. "You can perch on the stool. I'll stand."

Roxie is lightly stroking the paper with fingertips as Fred fetches four tubs of fresh water, two each. For some of their last sessions at Roxie's cabin she had set up a still life on her kitchen table, "as a catalyst for whatever ensues." "Okay, Roxie. Here we go," Fred now says. "Blank room, blank paper. This will put us to the test." He wets a large round brush as they exchange smiles. Roxie pokes about and chooses a slender sable.

"It may be hard to make more than a tiny line with

that," Fred suggests.

"Maybe with you I'm a contrarian. You inspire the opposite. I just may start with little dots, not even a line!"

And so they begin, Fred with massive swirls over his paper which he has first thoroughly soaked to paint wet-on-wet for a broad, vague background. Hold dark in reserve for his usual, limited, initial commitment. Roxie is dabbing her small pointed brush into one discordant hue after another, alternating pokes at her paper with rinses in a water tub which soon becomes muddy blue-black. Fred catches her attention with a look of mock-alarm. Roxie returns that by curling out her tongue to her upper lip as if painting is delirious fun because of her trashing the orthodox watercolor rules. Fred is enjoying himself immensely which happens with each of their get-togethers. It's as much about that, he surmises, as absorption by any one work. Fine with me, he thinks, if it leads to a breakthrough with me trapped in this place. His work has been going nowhere for months. But, thanks to Roxie, he doesn't particularly care.

They are silent and focused for the better part of an hour. Fred has changed the rinse tubs once for himself, four or five times for Roxie with her slapdash plunkings of bright color. Each of them is now still, their duet having come to a rest. He sighs.

Roxie abruptly grabs a fistful of tissues Fred keeps at the ready to blot up mistakes, unfavorable intensities, a runaway flood of paint in the wrong direction. He is gaping at her: what will she do next? With the sleeves of her jersey shoved up to her elbows she's frowning now at her painting, best he can tell, as he

135

expected, a carnival of mismatched hues, a disconcerting zigzag of lines in search of a theme.

Roxie's pink-tinted lips suddenly twist upwards. She takes the cleaner tub of water and pours it over the whole of her work, rapidly wiping up the overflow streaming onto the table.

"Ta-da!" she exclaims and faces Fred, setting the dangly beaded earrings, a first today at such a length, into a tailspin.

"Oh, boy," says Fred. "A masterful turn!"

"My dear Fred. You've taught me everything I know about watercolors. What to do, what not to do, and all in between."

"When that dries it's going to be a wonderful grounding for perfect dollops of detail," he says, her comment about his influence on her not sinking in, as usual, until much, much later, not spelled out and burrowed under the skin where it can resonate even without his compliance.

"Let's see what you've done, my dear. Oh, Fred. That's beautiful. It takes my breath away."

He's hardly noticed the confluence of gray-to-cinnamon variations now drying and leaving residues of marble here, smooth velvety spans of alabaster there. "It's like rock," he whispers, a stranger to his own painting, whispering as if not to disturb it, to let it go. "And yet it's all air, translucent."

"Just like you've told me so often, dear Fred. Your painting here is — is that mystical balance between the obvious and the implied. You've drawn something solid from down deep and made it one with — something else that could never be physically held." Roxie reaches over and squeezes his forearm.

It takes all Fred's wits to not pick up a brush, to avoid the temptation of one more accent. Don't be a diamond cutter cluttering the gem with a last, superfluous slice!

"Oh look at this glop!" cries Roxie, her painting reduced to befouled bathwater. "But golly it was fun."

Fred decides he's becoming fat. No, he revises: I am fat. I have been for ages but never before leaving June. My diet stinks. Even without so much beer these days, Roxie still outpaces me on our walks.

Roxie is so sly. She'd never say it outright but keeps offering her healthy fare, suggesting he might like to join her in her yoga practice sometime.

April gambols in her playpen as Fred feeds her little fingers smooth and pliable toys for her to suck. Occupied as he is does not forestall the ever-sharper recognition of his horniness and his physical decline. They are totally at odds with each other. He can barely picture having sex let alone immersion in making love which is based upon the dissolution of oneself. And him getting so lost is based upon a confidence that he's good at this, it's natural, he needn't be dwelling on himself but solely on her.

The baby is sprouting with added vitality each week like Play-Doh pinched and bounding into bold new shapes. Just the strength of her chubby legs shoving against him changing her diapers mocks his slack muscles by comparison. He's alone late afternoons and evenings, all weekends, he has no excuse.

"Hi, I'm Stratton. Welcome to our new Sunset Pilates class!" She looks like a model with more flesh—tall with cascades of beautiful brown hair pulled back into a lush ponytail, firm as hell but not overly buff, and, in that leotard, tits and ass to die for. If this doesn't inspire me to get here three times a week, Fred thinks, forget it.

First they limber up on a mat besides the reformer bed doing squats, high kicks, jumping jacks. Fred is sweating within minutes, aghast at having to view himself full-frontal in the damnable floor-to-ceiling mirrors.

They climb onto their beds, more to him a medieval rack for pulling apart limbs, and set about the routines. There are seven others, but it is for him the instructor is constantly reducing the tension and resistance of his coiled springs. He doesn't mind, not one whit. She flashes her perfect white teeth at him while bending her lithe, fragrant body about his machine, never losing a bat of breath as she instructs the group for the next position and simultaneously giving him a wink.

Fred, you are here to lose flab, he barks to himself, eyes pressed shut and enduring the burn.

On it goes, an endless hour.

"Fred, you did great," says Stratton, arms akimbo, slim hips cocked. Well, what else is she going to say?

Fred is wiping off the equipment and then himself. "I haven't exercised like this since..."

"Oh, come on. You were clearly a jock. There's muscle memory. It's all there, okay, so a few layers have to go. We'll melt 'em off!" She's at the counter computer, scheduling others, dispatching encouragement, waving folks off.

Why am I idling here? he asks himself but can't answer. He is trying to think of her as another machine, a robot, really, with programmed lines like the automated verbiage insulting you when dialing the electric company or the IRS. And yet here she is, free of the others, facing him bright-eyed as baby April ready for the next thrilling adventure in Wonderland. He has nothing to say. But she does.

"I'll admit, Fred. You are a big man. We have to be careful on the bed. Just move as slowly as you find comfortable. You don't have to reach the full range of each position just yet."

Is she flirting, or is this for real? My body size…the stuff my muscles are supposed to remember from… high school football? What's my bio got to do with a Pilates class? She flashes her killer smile in farewell, Fred signed up for months ahead and paid in full.

Fred soldiers on with his experimental artwork, presently limited to creations with a new set of charcoal on a giant pad three-by-four feet, his compositions in stark black and white. He carries on with his family—June, Freddie, Nell, all at arm's length. Each is uniformly smiling and supportive of him but he can't decide if that is masking a crush of disappointment at such disruption in their little family, all his doing, or vaguely disingenuous, in truth more immersed than ever in their individual pursuits. He himself goes through the motions during his care of the toddler, for which he chastises himself at not being truly present, but Nell seems genuinely grateful. Freddie, blessedly, blasts on, a steamroller of ambition. And with June now fully employed at her crafts center five days a week, his guilt that is mollified at her distraction can't begin to outweigh the blunt fact of him deserting his wife. These conflicting thoughts buzz about like a single, circling mosquito preventing deep sleep.

As for Roxie, Fred and she keep religiously to their weekly workshop for two, alternating between her place and his. Their expansion into oil sticks, cardboard cut-outs, collages with swatches of exuberant native fabrics from Roxie's "years overseas" keeps them fully compelled, if more by their far-flung concoctions than by each other.

Meanwhile, Fred has not missed a heartbeat of opportunity at the Pilates class.

"I hope you can see the results," says Stratton in electric ice-blue tights one early evening two months into this routine. "I can," and without hesitation she pinches one side of his waist.

"I hope you're right," he says. "I try not to look in the mirror, at least naked." He is speechless at his gaffe.

Stratton doesn't crack a smile, remains cold sober. "You're probably eating less crap. Always happens when people start taking an interest in their bodies for a change."

"Drinking lots less beer, no more booze," he says. "I just wish I could make time for, you know, fixing salads, preparing veggies..."

"Are you free to grab a bite, Fred? The Green Grocer's only three blocks away. It's mostly a sit-down deli. Great tempeh and avocado wrap."

"If it can spring one into shape I'm all for it."

They have a delightful time, Fred listening to the history of her boyfriends, her earlier triathlon career, the explosion of microorganisms in a much healthier gut, one's "microbiome," from drinking kombucha plus daily doses of fermented foods. Once determined that they're both single and available in general—Stratton between disastrous affairs, soon the after-party at the Green Grocer becomes a Friday night given.

Fred has just polished off an unsweetened kefir shake without gagging. Fine, since it was "dessert" after the Waldorf tofu salad which he enjoyed.

"You know, Fred," says Stratton after sweeping bits of green residue from her lower lip. "You're fucking cute for almost fifty." Her full but unpainted lips are absolutely neutral. "I don't mean you're not handsome...in your way...I can see you twenty years ago. Your peachy curly hair, my God, no wrinkles and just a trace of dimples when I'm embarrassing you like this." She unfastens her ponytail, unfurling a majestic sweep of hair constrained like an opera curtain now barreling closed to conclude the show. Slowly she slides fingernails from his elbow to his wrist, his forearm like the rest of him flash-frozen. "When's the last time you had sex?"

"I—I'm... Stratton, my mind's a blank."

"Let's go. I get the bill this week. You, next. And there will be a next, whether or not we're about to have a good time."

All Fred can remember is her lissome body but never in any one configuration. His own body did not exist. Of course she was in charge. That was clear from the onset. That said, he could not recall ever having been so active himself at joint sexual pleasure.

"No, wait," Stratton teased, "I'm not finished with you yet," he remembers that one.

And "Touch me here. You're too low."

"Nice, isn't it, stretching it out...no rush? You know, we're going to come together, it's really the best. Now lie over here, like so."

"You're a big boy, Fred, but we're evenly matched, don't you think?" He was about to utter something but she shut his mouth with her lips.

They were sweating, made sliding easier, this too he recalls, incapable of making more of it cohere, of making any sense whatsoever to him, this Stratton and their tangle eclipsing all else, spinning itself into an orb circling so far apart from his life and routine. It was like stepping all alone into an exotic new movie theater, a beguiling rainbow of light bulbs adorning the entrance, and watching a flick of him with her and then leaving the theater and returning to his dull matchbox of a house in the duller-still suburbs.

But they coupled again. And again.

"Well, you're all bouncy-bouncy with my little girl," said Nell one afternoon.

"You're awfully quiet these days," said Roxie at the usually-loquacious summing-up of their most recent session.

"It's the drinking, Roxie. I've stopped cold turkey."

"You're looking so well, Fred. I'm pleased you're succumbing to my healthy lunches."

"Yes, that's it," he fibbed which was not much of a stretch.

Fred has become addicted to the thrice-weekly Pilates class. No question he is gaining strength and agility. This is true also at exploring sex with Stratton. "I'm not ready, sorry Stratton. You first. You're teaching this old dog new tricks. My turn to watch that gorgeous face of your seize up tight as a fist." And so she goes along for the ride, his call this time.

Alternately, Fred is fraught with doubts of his virility. What am I but a sex object for her? And her for me? What we're about is hardly the real thing. What is supposed to be exhilarating I've turned sour. Typical, he tongue-lashes himself.

One night, limp in the morass of wet sheets, Fred says: "I can't thank you enough, Stratton. You've..."

She cuts him off with a kiss. "Time for you to get back in the field, to free-range."

"I will never give up the class. I'm on a roll."

"I wouldn't let you. I'm not done with your body. That way," she adds. "But this is cool. I'm seeing Brad again."

He doesn't believe her. Something unsettled, tottering in her voice, Fred thinks, her fishing for a saving grace, Brad having been her latest, his mentioning likely business at the tip of her tongue.

"So all is good," Fred says, the two of them now flat on their backs, the flesh of their toned biceps making contact but that doesn't rank very high after this month of blasting his life into smithereens. Time to pick up the pieces.

"It's hard to comprehend, Roxie, that I've spent all these years competing at art with others, and then competing with myself. There's no difference. I've gone from one little triumph to the next, no one of them lasting. You have opened my eyes to a much better approach."

They are at Fred's this week. Each has done three watercolors simultaneously, taped vertically to the board. This is Fred's idea.

"What a nice thing to say, Fred. I guess if you fall in love with one piece it just sets up disappointment for the next. Or the next dozen." Once again Roxie is looking trim even in a baggy violet T-shirt, incapable, Fred assumes, of abandoning fashion outright. But those playful rolls of oscillating white hair — he thinks of smooth billowing foam at the base of a huge waterfall, plus whatever her outfit, grace her with an insouciant glamour of which he assumes she's entirely unaware. "Oh, look," she says, "it's so dark in this one of yours and light in the next and the third, on the bottom, is a blend. A triptych!"

"No, now Roxie, it's just work-in-process, no finished thing. I'm beginning to sound like you after all this time." Fred relaxes back on a similar stool he found at a yard sale, his shoulders slumped. Stratton streaks across his cerebellum, as she will. How sweet with Roxie, he muses. A meeting of minds instead of bodies, that so transitory.

"You know, we could do some yoga beforehand right in your studio, Fred, like we've done a few times on my porch. We have to stay limber. You've no hills to hike."

She adjusts the small but sparkly cluster of stones, one earring having slipped out-of-kilter.

Good grief, Fred thinks. She's like June with her outlandish costume jewelry. But no. Whatever Roxie wears doesn't shift from encountering her, on terra firma. On Roxie the earrings are festive, he ponders as Roxie puts a few finishing touches on her work. On June they're sadly disjointed, her straining to try on a new mask, the last one also failing to enliven. These women do, however, share a common thread,

Fred continues. A reserve that has helped enormously to calm me down. But as June is docile this Roxie is serene.

"Are we ready for the veggie wraps, dear Fred, that you got again from that nice green grocer take-out?"

They're enjoying their day, every Wednesday that Nell now takes April to a toddler play-group. Between munching, perched atop their studio stools, Fred says: "My father did all the talking. My mother stood there. It was his harping — make something of yourself, make money, meaning make him proud, live better than him as a near-squatter, do it for him, all about Al, and so I did. Taken me so long to move beyond."

"Yes, you've moved, my dear," says Roxie. "And not to this humble spot. Not by any means. You know that."

"I'm beginning to see my mother Rose as less of a victim and more of a woman. She had her family. Especially she had me. It took resilience to shut up and let my dad think he had his way."

Roxie has left half her wrap on the plate. She'll say she's filled but Fred knows it will be for some of his supper. "There's always a tension between a man and a woman," she says. "I've never thought of it as domineering father, inhibited mother. It should be a struggle, for both parties. She's grounded, he's in flight. They need each other. I know that's stereotyping, Fred, but goodness we can't refute millennia. Reaching for something steady in the perpetual chaos of uncertainty." She pauses, deep in thought. "In a positive sense it's like the churning well of creativity we keep talking about. Or rather, we gnaw on like an old bone!" She's crossed her legs and faces the window-wall, as if to change subjects or give him space. From the back-side, plus her cascade of silky white hair, he's startled to think she could be a woman half her age.

"I still get flavor from that old bone, Roxie." He's tempted to gobble down her half of the sandwich but he remembers why she's left it untouched.

"There's this Egyptian king, an early pharaoh if I recall, who's immortalized as a hero-son never weaned from his mother. I can picture this image from my visit there clear as day. And she's the vulture-goddess, all teats, and he's depicted on his throne with a spear held high while sucking on her voluminous breasts. An early rendering of the Great Mother. You see, my dear boy, you're not about anything new here, balancing the male-female tug of input."

For a second Fred pictures Roxie naked, rendering him awash in shame. I've weaned myself from sexpot Stratton, let us hope!

"You are fathering yourself, Fred. Can you see it that way? You're mothering yourself, too. Both."

"What about your mothering, Roxie" he retreats. "You're a mother for real. Where are your kids? Who are they?"

She pushes back from the table, the visit nearing conclusion. "I've told you some about Abigail. We've not talked in years. Her choice, mine too, I guess. The other, my son, he's in Africa but I don't know him. Another story, Fred my dear. A very long one. The telling of that will keep us going for months!" She takes her folded hands—hands pockmarked with brown spots—from her lap and rests them on the table edge.

"I love it, Roxie, that you still have depths to plumb yourself," says Fred.

"Still? Are you implying…"

"That you're the most interesting person I've ever met." He stands to retrieve foil for her leftover wrap, a gesture mainly to release her. And he does want to release her, this last of their chat he sees as having bordered on discomfort for her.

"I have an idea for our next, my place." She taps the tabletop spritely, her nails uncolored but impeccably groomed like the whole of her. "Let's try portraits of each other. Just the face. That's better even than so much sharing of our pasts. The face tells all."

"Not full figure. Only the face. And fully clothed," he can't resist. Maybe a little jest but is there anything in this world Roxie has likely not touched upon? he wonders as she gets up and gathers her things.

They loosely hug, as always, before he opens the door. On this occasion, she pauses and turns to face him. "One more thought, dear one. About strictly dropping the past. It's always there, of course, not to be unheeded although not to be the source of one's forward march." She raises a finger, smiling to the sky. "I often think of myself as a grain of sand, once much earlier coalesced as a boulder before it was ground to bits. Like me. The littlest bit. But I know I'm essential to everything amassing once again. Not past, not future, just little ole me but part of something so vast it's incomprehensible." She addresses him squarely. "So we all can relax, my sweet Fred. Make every minute a blessing in disguise." She strides to her car, lifting her arm in a little wave but not looking back.

Is she a foxy lady or what? Fred thinks, stepping lightly into his studio. How did I get so lucky?

Chapter 10

ROXIE

"I
WAS RUNNING HEAD START PROGRAMS FOR YEARS
but I kept reverting to being a teacher. I just loved
the little children...their innocence and openness."

They are hunkered around the old wooden kitchen
table in Roxie's cabin for their weekly, but in no rush.
It's too brisk to work outdoors but cozy inside, the
woodstove long standing idle. Roxie has fixed them
steaming mugs of lavender-mint tea. Fred is gobbling
up her plate of buckwheat shortbreads laden with
toasted pistachios, orange zest, dates and cardamom,
a long-ago Indian recipe. To say the least, his appetite
has rekindled her paging through dusty cookbooks.
He's starving, she thinks. All the exercise. But this is
good. Change is definitely taking root.

"My Nell is a chip off your block," says Fred.
"Tending tots at the center plus her own. I've told you
about her self-destructive teen years. Child care has
saved her life."

She almost rises to fetch more cookies but resists.
He's on a journey, don't insert yourself.

"My dear Fred. I know you well enough to know
you have fostered kindness in your children. Nell

for sure. You've remarked she's the antithesis of her mother—which I doubt. All these things are so on the surface. Even if she's rebelled against the role model of your wife..."

"June," he interrupts.

"—that's made her trust and respect you all the more. I've spent my life raising children of all sorts, but you've been a true and very present father. And now grandfather!"

Fred pauses to inhale the fragrant tea. He stares at his hands dwarfing and circling the mug as if it's the crystal ball of a psychic looking back. "I used to bring the Sunday church bulletins to shut-ins. I shoveled sidewalks even for old ladies who couldn't come to the door with a dollar bill and a soda like my 'customers.' I thought I was doing it to earn and save money—my father yapping about being broke and all—but now I'm not so sure. I wanted to help the old folks, especially lonely widows who made me so sad."

Roxie squirms. She does not think of herself as old, as a lady, a divorcee, widow, mother, nor alone for that matter. Those labels no longer apply.

Fred fills in the gap she's unintentionally allowed. Ground into women of her generation and now by instinct she's always rapidly returned a comment in any conversation to keep the spotlight on the other person, her innermost thoughts to herself. For safe-keeping...maintaining the upper hand? Rusty I am with a man!

"You're an inspiration, Roxie," he's saying. "How do you handle it, grown children you no longer see? Don't you miss them?"

She looks him in the eye. Sun is now streaming

through the windows igniting the cobwebs as if they're icicles. Why aren't we engrossed in artwork by now? "So I've given birth to two children, but that never imposed upon me any more obligation than I felt for any children, of whatever origin — the orphans of Tibet in Nepal, the beleaguered tots of Rhodesia..." Fred, on the other hand, is fighting his need to let go of family and take flight, but with this thought she remains silent. "My wonderful father," she continues, "you see he was a doctor instead of his birthright as a banker and he instilled in me..." and she fleshes out that part of her past. "I fervently believed this back then, less so now. I don't feel fervently about anything anymore."

"You don't make that sound depressing," says Fred. "It's sounds liberating in fact."

"When I was so full of myself I was convinced that dwelling on others, not on me, was the path to freedom. Of course it's not so simple. We're all connected, part of the whole."

Lips sealed, Fred nods for her to go on. The rare man! damn it. He's waiting on me to get beyond the sermonette.

"Look," says Roxie emphatically. "I lost custody of Abigail when she was twelve, when Harold and I officially split. When I returned from several years in Africa I wasn't appropriate to be her mother. Mothering, yes, but not in the ordinary way. Oh, Fred. I was obsessed with — peoples' misery, orphans that were destitute. My head at the time was wedded to Siddhartha... renunciation of comfort, tradition, family, royalty in his case although I'm arguably of American aristocracy. Boston bluebloods! For me the goal of humanity was and still is to lessen suffering. If I keep myself central it diminishes others. Compassion for all is the point. Any suffering of my own dwindles to dust." Roxie tosses hands in the air, realizes she's raised her voice.

"Phew," whispers Fred, a sweep of placid, star-struck wonder composing his usually stern and tight-ened face. "Please say more."

Get it over with, his fascination. "Before Africa right after college I went to Tibet. The Chinese had invaded this peaceable sanctuary. They were razing monasteries, slaughtering innocents with Buddhist icons in their shacks. Then the flood of orphans. It was before the Peace Corps. I became quite ill—I was dig-ging latrines!—but I never regretted my linkage with the Red Cross. Constant urge to do more of that sort." She lowers her voice. "Indeed, I came from an afflu-ent family, Harold's even more so. I didn't resent it so much as seeing it as an opportunity. Imagine these vast societies with utterly no material well-being. With spir-itual guts is how they survive, I learned. If I could do something on a personal basis…giving was a reminder of my wealth by comparison. Giving gave that a pur-pose." She draws in a deep breath.

"Somewhere in here you had a son you've never seen," says Fred.

"When Rhodesia became Zimbabwe soon after my time there I was blacklisted. My baby's father was con-sidered a terrorist, killed in the rebellion and a hero to his people. But he was treasonous even to the emerg-ing black government. And then Mugabe, the horror, the evil of this man. I don't dwell on it. And still he reigns. Fred, I've had to let it go. Even though I can picture Amos to this day at two years old when I left. Oh yes, I used to imagine a life for him, emboldened by the legacy of this father but smarter. Smart like Mama Milly whose wonderful care he had."

"He's a grown man," Fred says. "Kids of his own. Maybe he'll seek his birth mother someday. Not for your sake, I gather, but for his. This happens nowadays, true?"

"Dear Fred. It's hard for you to fathom. I don't mean to patronize. For decades it's gotten worse. Despite foreign aid. It all goes to Mugabe and the elite. Same old story in any dictatorship. I've had to accept all this and move on."

"You must have been a kid yourself at the time, twenty or so? Of course we move on."

He's demolished the shortbreads, every last crumb. Their tea is ice cold. "Actually I was thirty-five. Knew quite well what I was about."

With his pinched forehead Roxie can tell he is doing the math. "Golly, I dated Aaron, a Jew at Yeshiva Medical School just to yank my mother's chain. I brought him to a Christmas formal at Wellesley! Wearing his yarmulke! He was working some at a clinic in Harlem where I got my first dose of desperate mothers and orphans. I was more compelled by this clinic than Aaron. We use each other like you did your father to jump-start a new trajectory, but that doesn't mean we necessarily harm others." Roxie pauses and beholds this man. "Now look at you, Fred. Swallowed your father's agenda and then tossed it, but that didn't mean you stopped caring for your loved ones. You agonized over your mother's ill treatment by her husband. And you shepherded her at the nursing home until she died years after your father had passed. And here you are supporting your daughter no matter the cost to your fledging independence."

"I never encouraged June to take herself seriously. Totally self-centered."

"Nonsense. You're both onto new paths."

Fred shakes his reddish curls. Slivers of gray around the ears, she hasn't noticed. "Roxie, you've been a wild woman."

"Been?" She laughs. "Don't pin me down."

Finally they address the business for today, squaring off at the kitchen table with the pads and pastels Roxie has assembled for facial portraits of each other. She's appreciating the silence, this chance to fully absorb her friend from a supposedly-impartial perspective. Fat chance, as they say. Yes his countenance is a dozen corkscrews, the myriad of muscles about the eyes, above the nose, the mouth alone—where to begin? Look inside. She sees him as a little boy, equally serious, the freckles, the one dimple, the darting gray eyes. He's big but less fleshy since she's first met him but still soft in his way. He's an oddly sensitive man, she rambles on to herself as she smudges the pinks, the shadowy blues, the darks and lights initiated seemingly by her fingers on their own. Her reflections flow in tandem with the chalks, as if she's hovering above it all, a genie peering down, a momentary escape from the players and play on the stage.

She gathers Fred saw himself a klutz as a boy—too big, too clumsy, power that had to be stifled, held in check, warped to abide by the rules. And so he largely remains despite the elegant streaks of his art. All this is warring on his forehead, and look! I've dashed it with a vivid ultramarine. Yes, there's a cauldron bubbling away. Of course the shame, the loss of his wife and the sadness affixed to his actions. But those flared nostrils now as he concentrates; it's a fight. This thrills her. He is a coiled spring of contradiction that, as best she's discovered, is essential to make art, to combine the conscious and unconscious so neither holds sway. Something brand new just for the moment before it's replaced by the next. Her fingers are working more rapidly than her mind, thank goodness. She beholds Fred as diving into his depths, struggling to stay under without oxygen and glorying in those rare glimpses never before revealed.

She stops. They've made fleeting eye contact between frenzied bouts of breaking pastels, attacking the paper as indestructible. Alternately they are gently grazing patches of color with fingertips, as if the paper is delicate and downy as a baby's skin.

As Fred is soft in the best sense, Roxie pictures her daughter Abigail as she cannot help but do on occasion. Abigail, older than Fred, was hardened and self-sufficient as a child which she as her mother never took credit or blame for. How can any of us outfox our inner nature despite our eagerness to claim it's all our parents' doing?

Fred is now ripping his work off the pad and starting another. She does not want to intrude. He is clearly upset.

"Not good enough," he mumbles. "Too reverential. Too loving. That's me. You're more complex."

"Nothing wrong with loving," she replies but to his bent head.

Recklessly, to her, he is scrubbing broad strokes with the sides of his chalk. She sits back, addresses her portrait of Fred as if she's still cocooned and not influencing him with concern for his distress.

He tears off the sheet and starts another, his forehead glistening with the effort. She wants to see the positive for him in this, that he can't get it 'right,' that he's carried away and perhaps climbing onto a higher level, a more expansive version of himself, not her, Roxie, other than as a medium for mad dashes. Not even that. Skittering between multiple options, a maze of uncertainty, all exits blocked.

"Shit!" he roars and slams his fist on his pad.

She senses her shoulders relax as the whole of her evaporates. She remains silent but bathes him with her eyes. Don't speak, don't touch him, above all.

"It didn't work," says Fred, now slouched over his lap.

"But you did," Roxie offers.

"Oh please. Don't give me that crap."

"I've given you nothing. Just observing."

"Forgive me," Fred says. "I'm just so frustrated. I wanted—not to get you literally—but—capture your peace. It's so special, Roxie."

She hesitates but proceeds. "It's now time you're taking yourself seriously, Fred. What have we been doing? The art sessions, yes, but the probing into new ways. Me, I'm just dabbling. Alright, it does lift me to a sublime outpost. But you, it's your work, your passion. It's not work unless you're relinquishing that nasty habit of depicting what you see. I've come between you and that process. We should call a halt to this for now." Whoever said this, whatever the source of these words, she has no idea.

Fred has shriveled to his scolded little boy. His

brawny body, his rosy face, ordinarily bursting with expression have collapsed in a heap.

"I'm nothing but a bridge to your own best self," says Roxie. "Just look at my outline, not what's underneath. Don't dwell on me personally, Fred dear. Just leap off all the lines in my forehead, the crevices and cracks." Stop preaching, she cautions herself, but carries on. "If you can cut loose with your palette it won't be my face...more the crepuscular surface of the moon."

With effort Fred lifts his large head. "Roxie, I need you. For now. Don't dismiss our get-togethers outright." He brightens. "You've said yourself, this rot of mine today could be a breakthrough! So you've been down, I don't know, this well-travelled road, warts and all. You're leading and I'm following. For the time being. They're just roles, just on the surface, not where it's really happening. A-ha!" And he points a finger at her as if he's caught her in the act of trying to pin them each into a box.

Roxie tilts her head, lowers her eyelids. "Time for some yoga. Enough of the art. And way too much of the words."

"Now remember in the triangle the upward hand reaches high, the lower reaching down, yes Fred, that's good," she attempts to correct without criticizing. "And don't forget to breathe."

Fred grunts to extricate himself, stands tall, tries again. "But Roxie, my upper arm is parallel to the floor! No way will it aim like yours straight up as flag post..."

She refrains from comment on that one. "Let's slide

to our hands and knees, the Table, on to Downward Facing Dog, lift the butt, feel that lovely stretch in the calves..."

He's using her yoga pad, she's on a throw rug, the both of them swallowing the space of her tiny bedroom. She moves them to Warrior one, Warrior two. "That's it, keep the upper torso straight, not bent forward...breathe and fire those strong legs of yours for support, friendly fire...feet rooted to the earth, drawing strength..."

"Ow!" Fred cries. "Charley horse!"

"Look up and breathe. Breathe, Fred. Crown of the head to the sky. Let's lower to hands and knees, all comfort and grounded there."

They stand again and this time she steps to his side and tenderly raises his rear arm, gently presses his side below the armpit to coax the upper body to a more vertical line. He is massive but solid, she reacts, quickly withdrawing her hands upon noticing the sudden ease of his face, the calm brow, the faint smile.

Roxie does her best to verbally guide him in a whisper, next positioning her back to his front, the easier for Fred to follow her example...without nay-saying on his part, his bemoaning his lack of limberness or the lockjaw of his joints.

They complete the moves he's formerly learned and practice a few new ones from today. Tree, balancing on one foot. Cat and Cow, alternately arching and lowering the spine. He promises to try them on his own. "I won't attempt to look up at my hand for now. Lost my balance completely."

"Balance is one of the beautiful benefits of yoga. Elders like me die all the time from simply falling over."

"Elders like you," laughs Fred. "My friend, you break the mold." Fred stands with his arms akimbo. "How many years, Roxie, did it take for you to become so nimble?"

"I don't count the years."

He looks about. "You've worn that skirt, that jungle-flower wrap." She has it draped from one of the many hooks on the inner cabin walls.

"That's from Mama Milly. In Rhodesia. She was my—mentor at the school where I worked. She actually was the village leader, but she wouldn't acknowledge that, nor would the men and other women. Very briefly she had my address and I hers, so we kept in touch."

"She had your little boy Amos," says Fred. His gaze was gluing her to this moment.

"I decided it was wrong to inquire about him, or about her, the fate of the village and the rest. It was best for us all, for the pain, mine, to harden and heal."

He released her from saying more, retreating from a subject he could sense might be a source of distress. Now scanning the intimacies of her room Fred says: "It's like a Moroccan bordello, all the colorful hanging sheets and clothes and your strings of beads. Not that I'd know what a bordello looks like, Moroccan or otherwise."

"Come," Roxie says. "Let me re-heat some sweet potato soup." She leads him by the hand back to the cluttered kitchen. "Sit. Forget all these pastels and drawings. Here, try my cashews, dear man, you must be..." She thrusts a bowl at him in lieu of completing that sentence.

"Yum," pronounces Fred.

He really is sweet at heart and wonderfully simple. "You know Chinese Five Spice powder? I bake the raw nuts with that and sea salt and lemon juice."

"Who needs hotdogs? Is there no end to your artistry, madam?"

"Don't put me on a pedestal. Remember I'm your witness not your master." She stirs the soup on the stove. "True for yourself, too, dear Fred. You don't master or conquer the yoga positions. We stimulate the whole body, never forcing it, one easy step to the next. It's meant to take a lifetime. Last a lifetime." He has that blasted worshipful look once again.

"Fred, lets try *self*-portraits next time."

"Oh, there's to be a next time?"

"I was just making a point before. Look inward. You know those incredible self-portraits that Rembrandt did forever, especially as an old man? It must be like writing an autobiography. One doesn't recognize oneself from the distance of storytelling. It's like Rembrandt was looking through himself into the plain bloody matter-of-fact flesh, the inky shadow of one eye but not the other, the crumpled purple lip edge juxtaposed to the highlighted pink sliver. All broken down into slabs of meat, really, but how miraculous taken as a whole. So arbitrary and neutral. The wounds healed or not. Truthful! That's how I at least can look at those paintings and see some part of myself. Or you, anyone. A revelation."

"I'm afraid you're burning the soup, Roxie."

"Damn!" She scoops up the top and ladles it into their bowls. "Oh well, I'd made extra so you'd have enough to take home. Now you have to stay lean and mean." She jostles his shoulder and sits.

"I forgot the bread," she says.

"Sit," says Fred.

At this she beams and bows to her soup. She's never famished like this.

They finish the soup. Their time is up. Yet neither makes a move.

"We've talked ourselves silly. At least I have," says Roxie. "Let's get on the floor, back on the mats in the bedroom. Ten minutes. No thinking best you can. Let your monkey mind hop about and leap away. Just float with your eyes lightly shut. You asked how I meditate. Let's give it a try."

And so they do. She knows Fred by now is up for anything that she suggests. Must be careful, it's about him not me. It does please her that she's been a sort of vessel to contain and direct the warpath he's on. And she is constantly struck by him as a vehicle for her to detach and lose her mind, forever a challenge.

"By way of transition," Roxie says when they're comfortably settled, "this is the Corpse pose. Not just lying on your back but imagining your entire body is getting very heavy...your flesh melting into the earth. Slowly leave your body and picture a beautiful pink and salmon sunset...the place where your soul is at home..."

She lowers her voice to a monotone chant. "There is just your breath...always there for you...your best friend...surrender never force." She leaves a long pause. "Lids lightly closed, breathe through the nose, gently warming the air before it reaches the lungs...not holding the inhale or the exhale, just allowing the natural flow, at one with all of the elements surrounding you, supporting you..."

The ten minutes pass. She wonders if he's asleep. She cranes her head. He is, but she knew that from his deep breathing.

"Hello, dear Fred," she says softly at which he opens his big gray eyes. "Wasn't that nice?" She wriggles herself onto her side.

"I fell asleep," he says.

"Now don't pass judgment. At least you weren't lost in thoughts. Mindfulness is much larger than thinking—kind of like peripheral vision getting included with whatever's obviously in focus. Visually, though, it could be an overload. That's why you made such a god-awful mess of my face with your drawings. But you're going in the right direction, sweetheart."

Later, alone, the state which has kept her company for—all these years, Roxie experiences a rare assault on her equilibrium. Inept, I am, at all this interaction. Lovely on the surface, but... Looking out the kitchen window, quietly seated, her eyes fog over. So glib, my recitations by rote of children in Tibet, children in Africa, my children, the way of strangers babbling on about their past, so much minutia filling in the blanks. What is truly relevant? She cannot erase the woman, the Tibetan refugee haunting her every night upon arrival in the camp, and still, a lifetime later. The woman whose little girl wandered aimlessly about as if this woman could not muster even the merest maternal attention. Roxie had done so in the woman's place, this woman whose family must not have fled from their homeland, or survived the trek to Nepal, or was haphazardly slaughtered by the Chinese. Months later Roxie learned quite graphically the circumstances of this woman's perpetual stupor. The motley assemblage of her fellow villagers was crossing a river only shin-deep but with the fiercest pull. She was clutching the hand of her little girl aged five when suddenly the baby girl she was carrying slipped out of the sling across her back and into the rapids, the child instantly swept yards from reach. The woman screamed, her young daughter screamed, the woman made a few futile leaps but was forced to her knees, the five-year-old grabbing her neck. By the time they struggled to their feet the baby was but a small ball of flesh gradually bobbing out of sight. All this was told to Roxie by a fevered witness grasping his own children, every single soul straining mightily to gain the river's opposite bank, the woman and her little girl among them, although the woman remained mute for the rest of their desperate journey and for the entirety of Roxie's time in Nepal.

The image of this horror replays itself often to Roxie, as now, staring blankly out her kitchen window piercing another day of pleasantries with Fred. And all these years later, somehow the recurring river scene tempers the leave-taking of her young son Amos in Africa. He was alive, he still may be, she should be filled with gratitude by contrast to the agonized mother of Tibet and the millions like her, before, after, and still to this day.

Chapter 11

FRED

HE IS PACING THE FLOOR OF HIS SUPPOSED-studio in the dingy ranch house. That this place is crummy does not matter. The squat little rooms, at best, contain him from the elements. But he is boxed within his kaleidoscope of thoughts from which he knows he must escape.

The art table stands idle, attempting to insult him with each blank sheet, every dry brush. At this he barely registers a blip of concern. If it should, he dismisses this with a shrug: I'm lying fallow, but "fallow" is your Pollyanna speaking. Louder is its hectoring rebuttal— —you know very well you've exhausted whatever crumbs of creative possibility you've always assumed for yourself. But even this falls flat on the floor of this dump, his interior dialogue consequential as a burp.

Fred comes to a halt in April's end of the room. It's achingly empty—no crib, toys, baby crap. Months ago Nell decided to work mostly from her apartment with April officially a toddler. Gradually he's become inured to this void, after the shock of realizing the extent to which Nell's dashing in and out and his long stretch of grandfatherhood had orchestrated his days, kept him from sinking into the sepulchral gloom he came to make of solitude.

He leans against the hollow sheetrock wall, his bulk near bending it. How he first savored the solitude, the shabby surround invisible after his coiffed suburban splendor. This faceless house indistinguishable from the dozens of slap-dash others: for him it was as exotic and thrilling as suddenly being deposited in a black African country whose name he didn't know or language he couldn't speak, leaving him blissfully removed from responsibility and routine. What harried housewife, what bedeviled wage earner let alone an artist of merit wouldn't sell their soul for such a reprieve?

Fix some of Roxie's herbal tea. Calming, she claims. Dare he admit to her it's she that's calming, the tea could be tap water. Still, he puts the pot on to boil. Soon he's collapsed at the funky, chipped Formica table astride the hot mug. Sipping it ever so slowly, trying to identify its exiguous flavor, in drawing this out for the better part of an hour: could this count as mind-numbing meditation?

However does Roxie do it—live so seemingly at peace with herself, okay, with a chipmunk or two and the birds?

She occupies her hands in the garden, busies them to make her living out of a patch in the woods. Maybe that allows her head to float in neutral. *Breathe,* she gently scolds him during their yoga. *Tell me what to do, Roxie, yes, please, keep up the patter, never as innocuous as it seems on the surface: what shade lies beneath the blood-black in this Jasper Johns...do you think the fennel overpowers the peppermint in the tea this time...is it time for our hike up the hill...*

Fred takes another sip, failing to taste this fucking stuff, yearning for a beer.

He closes his eyes. And yes, takes a deep breath. Life with his little family was so foundational he'd never took notice. Whoever is aware of the concrete so monumentally in place compared to what meets the eye? For countless years it was June's vapid new kitchen curtains and, worse, her elation over discovering placemats to match. Now he confronts all that as a massive crane from which he was agreeably suspended. Paint today, or draw? Re-do this watercolor or cut it up for birthday cards? Besotted he could be, forehead pressed against the big studio window of his precious estate, at the juxtaposition of those gorgeous magenta hollyhocks in full bloom with the rose-pink clematis spiraling their delicate tendrils up and around the elegant stalks. The hollyhocks were proud and erect, the he-dancer, supporting and twirling the clematis, his ballerina, like a baton.

This is how I lived half my life!

Meanwhile June changed the kitty litter even though it was purportedly the job for one of their spoiled brats.

Fred is again advancing the elusive tea onto his tongue as if it's a rare vintage Champagne; he's accomplishing that much.

Of course he loved that Freddie and Nell were enabled to mere pay lip-service to their parents. They were proxies for the counterpoint of his own stiff toy soldier, the role he never questioned until it was too late.

Now he worries about Freddie. Not that he dropped out of business school to make a go of it on his own;

that delights his dad. It's not even that he's in the city pushing paper and a computer keyboard — "Dad, it's a start. Nowhere to go but up." Of more toxic potential to Fred is the girlfriend. Work and money are easy for a man; personal life is more like aiming the telescope at a random star and locking down.

"Mom, Dad, this is Trudy."

In the foyer of their sprawling home, the entrance walls papered in pale ivory with a meandering vine design — Fred's selection, the other three of this group were erupting in smiles and extended arms while he stood there and pretended. He knew. Immediately. Even before June and Trudy became glued.

Blond Trudy was impeccable in her Laura Ashley skirt but not too prissy. She could blend in anywhere, would take pains to do so. Freddie beamed like a tomcat.

"I love your drapes," cooed Trudy. Again, in the public domain, fabrics his doing.

"You kids must be starving." June, face flushed in pink, complimented Trudy on the pebbly cotton of her blouse.

"Can't wait to see the rest of your lovely home." Trudy carried on with June, arm-in-arm towards the kitchen as the menfolk shuffled behind. Freddie punched Fred in his upper arm and winked.

My boy, all brass up to now, is following literally in his father's footsteps, thought Fred on the spot. He's going to marry his mother and be happy as a soft clam in a hard shell. Or, he'll spin wheels for half his life before he wakes up, Fred now ponders, his tea ice cold, the sink-side dishes crusted over, paint flaking off the wood of the curtainless windows. Which course is worse?

"Dad! So glad you're here!" A few days later Nell bursts upon Fred's present stupor, shattering the utter silence of his house, sealed and airless as a bomb shelter.

They hug forcefully. This is Nell, or him at least with her. Her long, usually lank brown hair is trussed up in multiple braids wound up and around in a bun. On top of this her get-up for today is a blouse of puffy sleeves and a kind of jumper shoving up and out her milk-laden breasts.

"You're looking evermore maternal," says Fred.

"Oh, this? Another dollar find at the recycle shop."

Fred laughs. "In that dirndl you belong to the Trapp family, not ours."

Nell squeezes his forearm and leads him to the kitchen. "Sit. I've got news." This is nothing new. Nell is always in overdrive. A parking ticket merits a phone call or tweet peppered with exclamation points.

"I'll fix some tea."

"Forget the tea. Dad. I'm getting back with Suleyman. He's working, fulltime, for this thriving catering business downtown. Bookkeeping, can you believe it? Totally clean, Dad. He still goes to meetings, but it's been a year. He's counselling at three inner-city schools!"

Fred inhales deeply, unnoticeably he hopes.

"Sweetie, I'm happy for you. And Suleyman." Pronouncing this name is like trying to chew peanut butter.

Nell thrusts both hands across the tabletop to clutch his. "He's April's daddy. It's only been sporadic visits. You know I haven't allowed otherwise."

She is reminding him that he does, somewhere deep down, have a pair of balls that his daughter has co-opted. Even when she was skewering them as a snarling teen, shoplifting, smoking dope — or hash? — in the school parking lot, there was a sliver of applause he had to stifle, him the brown nose until he was forty.

"It's going to double our income! Oh," she's sighing, still gripping his wrists, "all the good things I can get for April! There's a toddler *reading* group in the library, fabulous supervision, I can even get back to the Center three days a week. How I've missed my clients, the wretched, abused women, oh doesn't that sound frightful of me, but I have been so helpful at this work."

Finally, she sits back and releases her father. She already knows she has his blessing. How can I pass judgment on Suleyman, the ex-zombie, Fred thinks, as I circle this squalid chamber like a schizo in a ward?

Nell chatters on about her new arrangements pushing Fred all the further into his obsolescence as a parent. Hell, I let go even before it began, in her case, not Freddie's, he's ruminating, nodding at his girl. It was all in her eyes. She was so very present, meaning insistent: I am here. I will have my say. Fine with him, he recalls. His own self was enough of a warship navigating the high seas. Not that Freddie was a drag being all-adoring and adorable from the onset. It was such a tonic for June to have her perpetually-agreeable boy to counter Nell's push-and-shove. As their children grew, Freddie loved to have his mom select every outfit, Easter to the ballfields, whereas Nell shrieked in protest in the department store at her mother's choices, alarming the shoppers and salesgirls as she stormed into a dressing slot and slashed the curtain shut.

Fred sees the three of them—June and the kids, each in their way—composed the invisible armor that encased and held him together. Still. Even in their physical absence. How can you summarily draw a distinction between oneself and the world let alone your "flesh and blood?" I miss April! I want to hold her and have her clutch my fingers like her mother has just been grabbing me here and now. I need to smell her baby fragrance to offset my stale sweat and yet know we are one and the same. This is not weakness. This is not abdication of my solo flying mission. Nor is what can seem as clutching at Roxie. Roxie! My savior, yes, but comrade-in-arms, in art, in endlessly poking into god-knows-what odd, captivating, seductive angles lurking just beyond stasis for her, miasma for me.

Dear Roxie. Thank bejesus we now get together twice a week, both times at her cabin. One day we're making art and then yakking our heads off; the other day, hiking, strolling, yoga foremost, and, since we can't control ourselves, the second talkathon of the week. Stir-crazy keeping my own company the other five days but since Roxie it's worth it. Her sweet all the more so because of my sour.

"You know Mom is dating that guy, the co-director at her crafts place, Andrew somebody?"

This seizes Fred's attention.

"He's on a trial separation from his wife! Isn't this incredible? She's told him you're getting a divorce and all, but can you believe it? Mom? Getting all giggly and girlie, going to the movies of all things, at her age!"

Fred is fading again from her effervescence, so

completely of her own making, certainly not his. The business of June just another trumpet blast from Nell, but no: this one is going to crack open his carapace. Forget the jurisprudence. *Till death do us part.*

"So what's with this woman you're spending so much time with?" Her eyes glare like asteroids and defy him to look aside.

He parts his lips, smiles, hesitating because he simply does not know where to begin or how to condense this woman.

"Oh my God, Dad!" She pounces on his having paused. "You're having sex! Fantastic!" Nell squeals, jostling one of her neat braids to unravel. "Tell me! You know you and I can say anything. I will not breathe one iota to Mom."

Fred shakes his head. "Nell. She's become a truly wonderful friend. Really my first ever. I mean, all the guys in the bowling league, the cohorts at work…" His voice goes slack.

"And so you're sleeping with her, too. Part of it all. That's cool," Nell says flatly for once.

"She's just a friend."

"So what? If you're attracted."

"She's elderly."

"Elderly. What the heck does that mean? You are, too, the way you mope around. Besides, what does age have to do with it? And who the fuck cares?"

"She is in awesome shape."

"Ah-ha!"

"Now take it easy, Nell. I think you're getting motherly with me. With April you've got more than your share."

She presses her lips together, tilts her head with

exaggeration. "You're squirming, Dad. I know you. Good. Keep it to yourself. For now." She collects her limbs, interview ending. "Tell me her name. Tell me that much."

He does.

"Roxie! Love it. Aging Las Vegas showgirl on the make with my dad!"

"Don't be daft." He playfully shoves her towards the door. They hug and kiss even more aggressively than their greeting. He gives her an extra squeeze. "I know you and Suleyman are going to make this work. I want to take you out for supper, all three of you."

"April in a nice restaurant, you kidding, she's a squawker. Like me."

"The place doesn't have to be nice."

"Bring Roxie. We can have a four-way."

He kisses her again in lieu of more words.

"Go for it, Dad. I love you." She grins and scoots off.

Fred rides the tailwinds of Nell's jet stream until it peters out, as it must, thankfully resumed by and sucked into Roxie's vortex a few days hence.

This is their day for art. Fred has forgotten to bring wraps from the Green Grocer, a jug of cider at the least. But no matter, Roxie's domain is a cornucopia of goodies, edible and otherwise. She greets him barefoot in a simple white tunic and drawstring pants, unadorned by her usual dollops of gold or stone or fanciful trinkets at her ears. A whirlwind awaiting him she is not.

"Hello, dear Fred," she says and receives but doesn't reciprocate his loose hug. It is uncharacteristically neutral of her. Not understandable like the recent awkward embrace with June when he and she met over some ongoing financial items and exchanged courtesies. Fred, reading June's stilted body language, assumed the stance of a hazmat expert dismantling explosives. They are still adjusting to their lives as ex-spouses.

"You seem withdrawn, Roxie. If this is not a good time..."

"Oh it's perfectly fine. Let's sit on the porch before we begin. I'll grab my cardigan. You're okay in your hoodie?" It should be golden spring but, true to northern climes, it's misbehaving.

She steps off as he settles into her wicker rocker, a bit creaky but trusted and passed down generations like an heirloom cradle.

"I'm a little off key, yes Fred," says Roxie sitting in a matching wicker chair by his side. He hesitates to rock, to intrude upon the sudden perfect silence save for light wind in the trees, a bird call here and there. Her equilibrium, for him, is so infused in her every pore, the effulgence of her eyes never dimmed, that he cannot believe whatever she's about to share could unhinge her.

Still she doesn't speak, and so Fred reaches over and briefly strokes her forearm, her hand lightly draped over the end of the armrest but not gripping it.

"There's been some correspondence with Harold's estate. Totally out of the blue, and of little import. But for the first time in — oh, how many years? — it contains Abby's address and mine as well." She stops, her gaze like his held by the undulating outer limbs of the feathery hemlocks doing a hula dance.

"Are you thinking of getting in touch?" he asks, not facing her, not imposing, not sure this was the right thing to say.

"No. Not really. Just to have this information is, well, like a bulldozer roaring into my homestead. It was always Abby's, Abigail's insistence that we part ways, her deep desire to construct her life apart from mine, that she was at peace with my choices and this helped solidify her own. A clean break, as they say. And I respect that. Harold was her single parent. His family her family. Their lifestyle, values, the lot of it suited her precisely. You well know by now, Fred dear, although I could never fit the mold of mother that did not dampen my pleasure, my passion really, to devote myself to the welfare of struggling mothers and help-less children."

"Maybe you're unsettled by the vibes of Abigail's children, a role you could have for them. Complete their puzzles, their natural curiosity."

"I've thought of that. But I have to answer to myself without regard to any such demands. So much in my past simply isn't relevant. Knowing Abby's actual whereabouts just confirms this, a reminder to me that here..." and she gestures with a gentle wave of a hand, "with my solitude and my gratefulness and abundance and good deeds done over a long life and you, dear Fred, when we're together — I'm overflow-ing. It's all I can do to simplify it. Savor it piecemeal. I am so blessed compared to the misery of the world — I became all too familiar with it. It defined me. It forced me, if only a voice of one soul, to take a stand. Here I am. Here's what I believe. I mean, here's what I believe in. It's not about me."

"It's beautiful, what you're teaching me," Fred says.

"Thank you, sweetheart, but I'm not a teacher.

We're all just students of what we see and feel, what we make of it, ideally helping some others in the process."

This time Fred leaves his hand on her arm. "You're a utopia of one. Two, when I'm at your side."

Roxie taps both arms on her chair, as in this-meeting-is-adjourned. "Our self-portraits!"

"Do you have mirrors?" he asks.

"Hmm. Next time we can find some. How about another go at painting each other? Surely once is not enough. And there's more to us, let's hope, than meets the eye."

Orange, yes, there's even scarlet-orange, loud streaks, right there slicing her left cheek. Fred is using oil crayons, so bright and unforgiving and fun for a change—so emphatic. He and Roxie are sitting opposite each other at her all-purpose kitchen table, he regards it, her "play station," she corrects. Roxie has chosen a deep umber ink and several pens, sedate compared to his crayons but better for matching her mood, he gathers.

Green carving that eye socket. No, not forest-green, too cozy-woodsy-safe, but viridian, electric, alive. Next he's plastering under her chin with Prussian blue. Wait. This needs the opposite so it pulses. Throbs, even better. Again with the orange, the complementary color. This he tentatively dabs. More intense. Vermillion, layered with Cadmium yellow bright—on he goes in search of an even more fiery orange.

So today he is the thrust, she the parry. Is this what friends do…mix 'n match their demeanors? Friendship, loose, rather than relationship, tight. He shudders at the thought of tonight and tomorrow and the next day shackled to his doghouse of depression. I should spray-paint the walls with phosphorescent DayGlo like the mumbo-jumbo letters and gang insignia festooned over subways and highway embankments. How do those kids do it without getting arrested or run over? Three AM? I should get up in the middle of the night and paint like this when I don't know what I'm doing...sleep all day instead of playing nursemaid to my nosedives.

She is standing at his back and looking over his shoulder.

"How long have I been carrying on? Golly, Roxie."

"Eyes not lined up. Crooked nose. Missing ear. I love it."

"No more white hair, not this time, missus."

She leans down and lightly kisses the top of his head. "What a gift," she says. "To us. Such a joyous celebration. Whatever do you have in there, dear Fred, knocking so loud to be let out?"

He twists about to face her. "This is all you, Roxie. You're the most colorful character. Even when you're pensive. So what did you make of me today?"

He reaches over for her sketchpad, careful since he can tell the ink is still wet. "I look ancient. Haggard."

"And wise," she adds. She sits back down. He's never beheld her so withdrawn.

"I think these are self-portraits as well," Fred says. "The subject is mostly the starting gate. Today you're gray and monochromatic. I'm manic. Being with you. Then I go home and come down from the high. You. Always on your even keel."

Roxie doesn't reply. She does, however, sidle her attention to the table edge.

"It's Abigail, isn't it? Your Abby."

She faces him again and allows the merest smile.

Yes, he understands her to be saying: you're quite right. These things take time if they are to be addressed, digested, and not squashed into submission from which they can only lash out with even greater force and wreak havoc. Her lips slip back into repose having acknowledged him, his care and concern but signaling her retreat, nevertheless, on to her private perch, a Lotus position for her heart and soul. This, too, he comprehends about this incredible woman, their intercourse unspoken but plain as the white clothes she's wearing this day. He wonders how much more he has missed in these moments as he stands, stoops behind her, and returns a kiss to the top of her plush white hair. Yes, there is so much more she could say or imply, that he could hear or glean, but he is filled to the brim and resists being greedy.

"See you soon, dear Roxie," he says and takes his leave, letting her stay seated at the table, knowing for the first time that his presence has graced her without rending the nimbus, both impenetrable and sheer, so artfully spun, in which she resides.

Weeks go by. Fred is coasting, neither forward momentum nor treadmill of doldrums, no quagmire of doubt. It's not a visit this time but a phone call from Nell, more typically urgent.

"Dad, we're moving to California. Suley has been offered job at drug counselling that will be coupled with getting his high school equivalency, I know, at twenty-two, but he can then enroll at the junior college in their work-study deal, oh Dad, isn't this fantastic? I've been welcomed with open arms at the women's shelter..."

He is listening while also picturing in vivid detail their clasping over his kitchen table, wrists, hands, finally fingers sliding apart, them each sitting back, still connected by the warm air between them, the velocity of her words, the uplift to her voice.

How like she is to Roxie, he sighs. How true she is to her compass and with the passion that I lack.

Roxie. Roxie eclipses all else. He regards her an angel, himself an ox. How untenable his passing fancy, but for now, hold on tight.

Chapter 12

ROXIE

ASPARAGUS IS JUST TOO MUCH WORK, ROXIE is thinking on her hands and knees in the small patch that for years she has groomed like a formal rose garden. She's experimented with every conceivable mulch—a chopped newspaper slurry (what about ink residue?), shredded fall leaves (shrieking machine Hank had to rent), black plastic (ugh), but she's always relished the hand work, her "coolie labor" meant with respect. She shifts the pad to cushion her knees to tend the next section, groaning with the effort. She presses her gloved hands into the small of her back and arches her torso upright, craning backwards, to relieve the ache along her lower spine. Yoga is one thing, gently twisting and capitalizing on the strength of her core and legs to ground her. But too much of her day in the garden locked into the stance of a floor scrubber—it's long past time to reconsider this whole scenario.

"No, you can wait till I get back to the house," she tells Sammy, the "alpha" chipmunk, poised on his hind quarters. "Now you're begging." She tosses him a clump of witch grass. "True, I'd miss you bandits holding me hostage."

Roxie hoists herself up. Enough for this round. Supplying Hank and now Fred, there's still a surplus of these delectable spears. She brushes herself off, returns the cushion and hand tools to her lean-to, makeshift shed. The icy-crisp spring air, this she can inhale anywhere. With her pitchfork she turns under the topmost layer of compost in the pungent, steaming bin. She is daydreaming now with regularity about a cavernous but single room in an old building lovingly kept aloft by artists, most likely. It should be a room with gigantic, energy-deficient windows which flood the space, dawn to dusk, with ever-shifting, dancing splashes of light. No carpet! Aged planks. Elbow room for yoga, of course. She strolls back to her cabin taking deep breaths with barely opened eyes. The path like everything here, bathed four seasons in utter verdure thanks to the evergreens, has shaped her very being. Imagine in my heyday believing a plot in the woods could overwhelm one nonstop—parachuting birds out of the blue, the polyphony of buzzing insects day and night, oaks and maples chatting with each other in the breeze, the first slivery green beans demanding their harvest before tough with seeds in two days. But simplify I must.

In the kitchen, smoothing her hands and forearms with silky beeswax lotion, she sits and reviews the stacks of books patiently waiting to be read. Then there's the clutter of papers and art materials piling up after so many months of her sessions with Fred. Fred is wonderful company but he too is a distraction. Goodness, he's due again day after next.

She rises and prods the embers in her tidy,

Scandinavian tile woodstove. She buys the cordwood but Hank, bless his heart, splits it and stacks it for her under the porch, armloads always at the ready stove-side. She's too dependent upon him. The cabin is too much in the shade. Crazy having to deal with morning chill even in early summer.

She selects a slim volume of Thich Nhat Hanh and settles in the Boston rocker, amply padded now she has it. Here is simplification, pearls from a Zen master she knows by heart but prefers to read, sometimes aloud, another way to sidestep her rambling self and become centered.

Do not say that I'll depart tomorrow
Because even today I still arrive.

Eyes closed and who bustles in? Manny, you devil. And I don't believe in ghosts nor an afterlife but here you are again, damn it. Oh I know, it was my dream of dancing in a decrepit ex-warehouse, a make-believe ballroom. To think we never married that way, thank goodness; just in the flesh and the gut-rocking laughter and the Ethiopian restaurant with no English— you were trying to teach them Yiddish and of course got them all giggling trying to pronounce michegoss, tchotchkes, verklempt, and the tango contest leaving you writhing on the floor with a kneecap momentarily out of joint and you're bellowing with laughter along with the pain, and riding you and you riding me in every possible contortion and sometimes laughing ourselves silly and clambering up off the floor and flopping back onto the futon for proper coupling but in spite of all our years that was never to happen, truly, before the arteries seized up and said enough of this rodeo for one lifetime, you've had more than your fair share of foie gras and Champagne and scotch and especially this Shiksa whose life you've made and then some…

No, it was not enough, thinks Roxie, her eyes wide open now, her heart tapping like the gusts against her loose windowpanes. Better you're not still breathing life into me. The avalanche of memories is more than I can handle. At my age! She almost feels moist down under from a teardrop of lubrication, a reminder she's very much alive on her own. Of course Manny is never that far removed.

"That was a fantastic fuck, my pet. Who'd have thunk: a Boston matron."

"Manny, you're so vulgar. I love it. I have to admit I think 'fuck' is wonderfully descriptive."

He grinned ear-to-ear, pursing his fleshy purple lips and pinching his bulbous nose, as if clearing his mind for his rejoinder. "We have been known to make love, sweetheart, when you put on Mantovani."

She got serious again, her habit. "But why on earth is there all this negativity about the word that takes beautiful sex, our birthright, into its opposite? Fuck you, I'm fucked, fucking this and that, go fuck yourself. It's disgusting."

He stroked her bottom, that big hand with its hairy knuckles. However did he draw his exquisite architectural renderings with that mitt, she often wondered.

"This is too much work," he said of her discomfort with the F-word. "The undoing of a debutante. You should go back to Wellesley and see how they teach Chaucer these days, darling, if you're truly curious about the advent and complexities of Old English."

Roxie breaths again at her kitchen table, palms

upward in her lap, attempting to let Manny go. Okay, darling, you've had your say. Can I please get on with my...day? I can't say my life since you'll probably be here tomorrow. I can do yoga alone or with Fred or others in the someday-loft, she thinks, but dance like in her dream? That's seen my better days. With these thoughts, too, and the ones that follow, she lets them enter, greets them with a mental nod and lets them drift off.

Further relaxing, Roxie recalls a poem, no matter it's source, but its essence portraying people, ideas, theories as armloads of leaves one has gathered and is clutching and carrying, the leaves falling from one's grasp, to one side and the other, falling, scattering as one moves forward until, inevitably, the leaves are gone, the arms are free.

"Look. Fred." She punctuates these words. "All our heroes, these art books, it's very simple. To a man they were miserable, angst-ridden, wading through the muck."

They and the books are spread across her bed, such as it is, her lumpy padding on the floor, a mattress but primarily a log-jam of fat pillows piled every-which-way.

"Well, yeah, Munch here for sure," says Fred. "His solitude and sickness."

Despite her better nature she is feeling the teacher, impatient at the obvious. "Van Gogh, release of madness. Klee, grotesque distortion like Picasso. DeKooning, dementia. Don't tell me they were having fun."

"It's transformation, but brutal," Fred agrees on the spot.

Will this chap ever do otherwise than play it safe? Roxie thinks and continues. "Gaugin is escaping with the romance of far-flung primitives."

"Are you suggesting, Roxie, I have to lose my mind if I'm ever going to get anywhere?"

"I'm suggesting that our icons—irrational art to the rational audience we've all been—suffered from the demonic violence of their yearnings. However discombobulated I think they are striving toward inner order."

"This makes me feel so petty," says Fred splaying his big self across the mess, head supported by the triangle of his hand and anchored elbow.

"Well, feel petty if you must. I'm just sharing my take here if it's of any use. We've been at this for so many months, dear Fred. Much of contemporary art can seem berserk but in it we can see ourselves, as humans, flailing. It's not like they were seeking truth in general or even having a goal of making sense of themselves. They just plunged in." She's grounded in the Lotus position. She doesn't like almost towering over him, the reverse of their usual. But she can see he's enjoying this, her upper hand, if only he can get beyond that dopey look of idolizing her. One step at a time. But another year?

"What about these Leonardo's?" says Fred paging. "Mona Lisa?"

"Renaissance art, that's something else. But the struggles, the balancing act, it's there. Heaven and earth." She grabs the book, fans it open. "See how in addition to the pretty clouds and mountainscapes and the angel wings, right here in the foreground is low life—moles and snakes and dirt and dogs, children, bleeding bodies and the like. It's blending the godhead with the grime. Glory, dear Fred. Those darn college courses are at the tip of my tongue!"

"No, this is great," he says, sitting up again. "Mona Lisa mesmerizes because she's Mother Mary as well as Everywoman, right? Enough so we can identify, at least get included. Unlike these vacuous Gainsboroughs, Reynolds..."

"They were commissions. Study Constable's clouds. Or the unctuous sneer Velazquez manages — his how many portraits..." She quickly flips some pages. "...of King Philip? The court painter but he got in his licks. Michelangelo was paid by the pope but god knows he tells his side of the story."

She closes the books, one after another, and gathers them into stacks on the floor. "Well that was fun. My, can I bloviate! As if I know what I'm talking about."

"Of course you do," says Fred. "Me, I've only regurgitated what I've been told. I never studied art from multiple points of view."

"I'm not sure any of my comments hold up. I do sense, at least, for you Fred my dear — I'm past my prime, that there is some kind of descent into some sort of void and a battle of wills that can take place. Like a void is where conception happens."

"That's what you've claimed about meditation, Roxie. Allowing for the void."

"I like that," she says. "More void. Fewer volleys." She smirks recalling Manny's recent incursions; his sort of wisecrack, not hers.

"It's funny to lie on your bed," he says. "So low to the ground. So cushy. A playpen."

It's more than his tangle of limbs that suggest he's

uncomfortable, Roxie thinks. He raised the subject of her bed but had to make light of it. "Our yoga!" she declares. "Here is the only space in my cabin and, yes, it's getting more playful for you, dear. You're limbering up. Relaxing through some of it, this is good, what we're after." She hands him the mat and repositions the area rug for herself.

Fred pulls off his soiled hoodie and is left in a T-shirt, its inscription Roxie can't quite fathom on Fred, not that she's a prude. She blinks and re-reads it then laughs. "What on earth..." She stares at the motorcycle regalia, a black-leathered man riding his bike with a big-breasted woman at his rear grasping him tight. "Dix are for Chix," she recites.

Fred looks down at his chest, and his face flashes fire-engine red. "Cripes. One from Nell's pile of rejects from the recycle store...said at least they were clean and then I could chuck them." He feigns a laugh. "She was so grossed out by my mountain of undone laundry..."

What fun to see him flustered. He sheds his sneakers and socks and kneels down on his mat, preparing for down Dog, up Dog, three-legged Dog, her remonstrations to breathe. Roxie is ready to call upon her calming voice to lead them after the hurly-burly of art talk, the two of them so eagerly delving into that each week. I must watch it, she thinks, my tendency to pontificate which is taking me a lifetime to tame.

They proceed through the familiar poses until Roxie demonstrates Crescent Moon, a back-bending, split-legged lunge.

"No way," pleads Fred. "Sorry, Roxie, these jeans! Afraid my sweat pants, too, are buried alive in my laundry room."

"Take them off. You don't think I've see a pair of men's drawers in my life?"

Fred is far more embarrassed than he was by his homophobic T-shirt. "I—my laundry is so back-logged—I'm not..."

Roxie chuckles. "You don't think I've seen men's equipment in my day, every model on the road?"

"No way Roxie. Jesus."

She gets up from her mat, avoiding eye contact, although she can tell the blush of his cheeks reddens to the shade of his curly hair, his ursine torso slouched, heavy arms hanging low. "I have an idea." She rummages through her piles of things and pulls up a pair of stockings like a bird yanking out a worm. "Here, these should fit."

"You're joking. *Pantyhose?*"

"Elephantine. When I was much heavier one time. Go ahead. I won't look." She returns to her yoga mat.

"How about we go instead for a hike?"

"It's raining."

"This is going to distract me, mess up the whole point of our practice. How can I not think like I'm a girl?"

"Fred," she snaps from the floor, out of sight so he can't see her smiling. "This can enhance your time today. You can leap beyond your stilted fix of gender, one of the absolute stupidest strictures of our culture. Haven't I gone on and on about the men in Africa with their skirts, their purses and adornments of feathers and rings, face paintings and what not? Oh, please. Shape up, sweetheart."

He is groaning, he's shed the jeans, he is yanking

the T-shirt down as far as it can go, but he's complying. He's doing what he's told. One of his weaknesses, she knows, ordinarily, but for now it's all to the good.

"You ready to start over, Fred dear?"

"Sure."

So they do. And breathe. And climb and bend and stretch smoothly from one posture to the next. They are standing in the Tree, one leg elevated and partially facing each other. He's apparently moved beyond the craziness of his clothing. He is with her, lost in the lullaby, the sing-song of her yoga chant. "...connect with our Prana, our vital force...wind, energy, strength..." He seems fine but it's she who is jolted by glancing at this fellow, at her bedside no less, acknowledging his state of arousal, or mercy, the natural lay of his manhood, at which she is at first mortified, then somewhat excited, finally amused, employing all of her wits, in the spirit of Zen, to let each intrusion come and go. *Breathe.*

"There's still time for tea," she says later, hustling off to the kitchen so Fred can reclaim his modesty in peace.

After the visit, late afternoon, Roxie dons her quilted jacket to brave the bracing outdoors. It's stopped raining but it's raw. Must toss morsels to the chipmunks, fill the birdfeeder, pick up twigs for kindling. She knows she is using these as an excuse. To distance herself from her disheveling. The wildlife tended, the progress of snow peas noted, she folds arms against the chill and walks, soon, she realizes, in circles around the linkages of her various garden paths. She slows her pace to better steady her inspection of the raspberry staking needing replacement after winter, the glut of scrofulous brassica stems to uproot and collect as compost, all the toil she has vowed to eliminate with her hypothetical return to a sensible urban life. The years of self-sufficiency have come to folly, she muses. So, today would argue, has my friendship with Fred. He may need to become entangled like the remains of these pumpkin vines from last season—she taps them with the toe of her boot, but some of us are simply meant for the less-traveled road. Not contrarian, just staying attuned to our pacemaker calibrated to slow tempo, beginning to end. There is a reason for everything, for Fred and me to have crossed paths, each of us at a pivot-point. So many possible turns, like the free-fall of these winged maple seeds we are, casting about in the breeze, no idea where we will land, but land we must. Some take root, others not so lucky. Roxie thinks of herself at this moment, beholding the deepening indigo sky, as a person forever shifting gears, switching places and people and loved ones the better to isolate her and distill her purpose. Of course I'm still in pursuit of that. At my age? Whoever do I think I am?

She shrugs and heads back to her cabin. I have absolutely no idea who I am. And isn't that the point? she ponders approaching her cabin with its glowing little windows, an alien spaceship no longer of her world. I may indeed be nearing my final resting place surrounded by whatever happens to be there, warehouse or woods, enfolding me, dissolving me into the vast galactic vat. Sublime.

Sammy is perched on her porch rocker for his final offering of the day. "I know," she sighs, fetching the bag of peanuts. "You're not through with me yet."

A few days later the phone rings. She knows it could only be Hank or Fred. She is finishing the pinning up of a bedsheet on her clothesline, does that and then walks back to the porch, up the steps and into the kitchen. She can take her time. They know she's not a sprinter, agile as yoga has equipped her.

"Roxie?"

"Hello, my dear Fred." She's surprised to find herself annoyed. The sun streaming over the hemlocks, unfiltered as it reaches her aptly-placed clothesline, was warming to the bone.

"You know, Roxie, we've talked about Turner so much. And here is this retrospective of his watercolor studies at the museum. I could drive us to the city, we could stay at a nice bed and breakfast, separate rooms of course. Supper at something off the wall — Philippine fusion or borscht and noodles. Steak!"

"Yes, yes, that would be lovely. So much one can assimilate from books. From our talking, talking."

"And my hellhole, Roxie, it's stagnant. I know that's part of the process, forcing me into my — no rush, you can think about it. A change of pace for us. Lord knows what we'd make of such an outing, as if we've ever run out of words."

She switches the receiver to her other hand, resting it against the opposite ear. "Fred, dear Fred. I have thought about it. I don't think so. I've garden chores galore. I like to take my time with them. Every bud these days is a minor miracle, I hate to miss a thing." She cannot resist softening her answer, impressed she could do so without forethought — to let him down gently rather than simply saying no.

"Of course, Roxie." His voice has dropped a few

decibels.

"Maybe another time."

"Well. The exhibit's just begun," he says. "See you day after next. Full body portraits! Properly clothed, no more of your tights! You should be proud of me, Roxie. I've actually done my laundry."

"Me, too, as a matter fact. I was just…"

"So I'll see you Thursday. I'm bringing my biggest sketchpads. Maybe I'll prop one up on your counter like an easel. Maybe I'll change my mind and do it on my smallest pad. Devoid of cluttering detail. See what mood seizes the moment."

"I look forward to it, Fred. Thanks for calling." She replaces the receiver.

Lovely, she heaves a sigh and returns to her clothesline. Not a tad of guilt.

Chapter 13

FRED

FRED IS DIVERTING FROM HIS PERIODIC, perfunctory phone chats with his soon-to-be ex-wife by having lunch with her at The Green Grocer.

"You're looking terrific, June. Okay, Mrs. America, not quite the Miss of our college days but damn adorable." They're splitting a curried chicken salad wrap sans the side of seaweed. The place is bustling with people half his age, although that seems to be standard fare for Fred nearing fifty.

She smiles without her habit of blushing at compliments.

"You're looking a little peaked, Fred, to tell the truth. But I'm not worried about you. That's a shift."

He swallows this. "I'm not eating right but at least I've shed a few pounds. The food here, actually, is the best stuff I get."

She quickly nods but is ready to move the conversation on. She's touching up the graying roots of her rich mahogany hair, he can tell. Lost some pounds herself. "I'm sure it's a relief for you, Fred, our selling the house."

"We can settle the money for good," he says. "And it's right for you, June. A clean break."

She rests her nibbled sandwich and looks up. "I'm buying a condo out in Cedar Park. A five-minute drive to the crafts center. With Nell and the baby gone…"

"You're missing them, too?" he interrupts.

She pauses a second before responding, as if adjusting to the non-sequitur. "No, not really. Heaven knows, Fred, for most of her years Nell and I were at loggerheads. It's wonderful for her in California, such a fresh start after her endless troubled teens." She takes a sip of her iced tea. "Are you missing her?"

"Them, I guess. April sure filled my days. I was just getting into the grandpa thing."

"Your painting going well? It's certainly the fresh start that you've wanted." Nary a scintilla of resentment; she's simply stating a fact.

"It's going, June. It's work, it's been tough. Listen, I'm so pleased you're flourishing at the crafts center. And – Andrew, I mean, Nell told me." He shakes his head. "You've never not been a beauty, June. I know, Nell used to call me a 'looksist' but I'm delighted you and Andrew are an item. You deserve every bit of appreciation…"

"Fred," she interjects. "We're not moving in together but my condo is a half-block walk from Andrew's. We're taking it one step at a time."

Days later Fred is back at The Green Grocer for lunch, a reunion of sorts with Stratton. He's faithfully attended her Sunset Pilates class but they've skipped the Friday night suppers after their fling. Sometimes he's aware of the heat in his face along with the exercising whole of him, picturing her stripped of those tights. But they are "just friends" or more accurately coach and client in the business of Fred's struggle for fitness. Approaching fifty years old has been more of a motivator than his presenting a trim figure to a possible female playmate or partner. The lunch date popped into his head when Roxie had to cancel their next session so Hank could drive to a far-off medical facility for "her annual." He was crushed at the break in their routine, but was damned if he was going to slog through another few days in his dump and feel sorry for himself.

"So how's it going, pal?" asks Stratton once they're settled in a booth, she with her kefir shake and Fred with a veggie burger.

"I'm eating better, thanks to you. This has become my hang-out."

"Although you still choke on even marinated tofu." She's near bouncing in her seat, carbonated if ever a body could be. A loose sweater dwarfs her body suit, but Fred's imagination is fired all the more so. Eye candy, man, he reminds himself. Feast on it but you don't have to swallow. He teeter-totters on the brink of suggesting a replay so she's permanently deposited in his memory bank.

"Thanks for taking your break with me, a half-hour slot," Fred says. She's beaming genuine affection for him while he's beginning to squirm. "I'm happy your classes are booked solid, Stratton. Day and night."

"The Sunset session is my final for the day. Then I'm all play and no work. I don't wear it in class but Brad has given me a ring!"

Fred skips the next Pilates and gets a stationary bike. He spins in silence hoping to blank out his mind, maybe Roxie saying it could qualify as meditation. He cannot bear the drone of his tiny TV, so loud and piercing as if compensating for its size like a Jack Russell terrier bullying a black Lab. Stuck in the squat ranch house often reminds Fred of his mother Rose, commanded by her laundry, her shopping lists and church ladies guild, listening, yes, to his father, but fabricating a whole world of her meats and gravies, her special twist on cornbread or a pineapple upside-down cake, whatever it took to not so much shut Al up but seal herself off into whatever her present cast of fortification.

"What do you call them?" Fred once asked of his mother craned over the stove.

"Kartofel kloesse. I call them glace," she said. "Not ordinary dumplings. But since I'm making sauerbraten for your father's birthday I'm going full-hog. German dumplings this way really bring out the gingersnap gravy."

She seemed happy at the task, Fred thinks cycling, witlessly pumping away on the stationary bike. At the time and for years later he resented her being chained to that stove, that lousy kitchen, the bombast of her husband, her life. Forever clad in a threadbare but clean housedress and apron, never a token dash of makeup nor piece of jewelry, perhaps her neutral bearing was perfectly suited to keep her invisible, and intact.

"Here, Fred, why don't you chop up the parsley for the glace? A man can wield a knife, you know. Why not preparing food?"

This moment, that remark, he never forgot. Perhaps right now it holds a message for me, from my woebegone mother of all people, like a miraculous koan scrawled on a slip inside a bottle tossed to the seas and coming to light years later. Young Fred and Rose had their special bond but somehow he drew from it his singular role as her protector. How ironic, he is reflecting, if it were the reverse. It could have been she undermining his father as principal role model, paving the way for Fred to be alternately wired. Indeed, he was to be in the first generation of serious househusbands.

The pace of Fred's cycling has slowed but he is in no rush, in fact he's savoring the sweat. Logically enough he captures Al in a moment of tenderness that stands so apart from the shouts at his family, the slurs against everybody else. Fred was struggling to assemble a kite. The parts and paper and string had become for him at twelve a Chinese torture puzzle of complexity.

"Let's separate all this damn stuff for starters, kid," said Al getting down on his hands and knees.

No more was said. For once his father was silent, intently focused on a challenge with no relevance to the failures and stupidity of the human race, his wife and son included. Fred fought to follow his dad's agile fingers, the common sense instructions he was muttering to himself, not to his boy, which distanced Fred onto an island of momentary observation. He found himself sucked up into Al's warm breath, of all things. Fred remembers his dad accidentally brushing his shoulder, the man's large hand touching his own as he took a piece of balsa wood Fred had been holding, triggering a seismic tingle up and down his spine, his shuddering, his thinking for the first time his father actually loved him. But that was too womanly, too motherly, at least for Al ever to acknowledge outright. No, Fred above all was to be a real man in the making. He may or may not have been successful in that enterprise but here I am, Fred now thinks and lets the cycling bike come to rest. Missing a baby I've held in my arms, missing the chance to tell my children in their formative years that my love for them has never been on hold.

Interesting how peddling away on the bike has easily displaced his painting.

Fred has to fill another day before his next with Roxie. Being so alert to this is taking its toll. Craving her company. What better way to drive her off, shut her down, sabotage their wry and fascinating connection than by slipping a poisoned arrow of neediness into what's been fashioned as a sport. This he knows but cannot help dwelling upon the scores of nurturing women in his boyhood, the women in grammar school and Sunday school, the widows whose sidewalks he shoveled and lawns he mowed, the shut-in ladies to whom he was devoted and delivered the church bulletins, all of them older, wiser, whose very lips curling this way and that, speaking or not, told him Fred you're wonderful, Fred this is marvelous, Fred you're a sweetheart, Fred you are perfect, a superior being, God's gift to the world...and don't listen to yourself, he would think. They're women. Of course he couldn't believe them. It was their very nature, their sole purpose on earth to utter sweet nothings, to ensnare the men, to weaken them and disguise the possessors of true power.

Fred gets a beer, fuck it, he is drenched in sweat.

There was Marion, she was special among the matrons at the village art center he snuck off to when he was supposed to be at football practice. All of the women in the studio lapped him up but it was Marion who insisted he sit at her side. She didn't just explain the different paints and pencils and tools, but suggested other ideas for his work that day. Criticized it on occasion. She would lean over, take up his index finger, and guide him into smudging a charcoal line too blatant which was outshouting the others. He drank in her perfume. Her breasts would graze his shoulder. She was elegant, smart, so worldly, telling him of the origins of watercolor in Japan or name-dropping the masters. She was a tad irreverent, the two of them often in the rear of the circle, her confiding in his innate talent compared to this gaggle of bored lady patrons. Marion was beautiful. She was Venus, the others were housewives. She reminds him of Roxie.

Fred is driving home from another solo brunch at The Green Grocer. Without thinking he detours into the hinterland, closer to his old haunts in the swank suburbs, and stops by a meadow. No homes in this stretch, just a field and its border of lush trees, all of it former farmland but manicured like lands sweeping from the manor of an English lord. It is idyllic. I used to paint here, he declares as if he can't believe it. Ineffable watercolors of gray-green, gray-blue, celestial shades of pale violet and pink melting into each other as only watercolors can. Insipid, he now reacts. Not many years back but is this at least some scant evidence I'm moving beyond? To where who knows… He slams the car into drive and takes off. He cannot wait to discuss with Roxie a broader view of beauty than what has defined him, held him handcuffed for so long.

Fred stomps into his house and rapidly arranges his watercolors. He tapes down one of his biggest sheets, near two by three feet, to disallow any possible dainty, decorous microcosm. He dumps a cup or more water over the whole of it, thoroughly soaks it the better to slash away. Blues, black, he attacks his palette, impatient. No, a deeper dark with red and Winsor green, but any red will do, and any green, blended together are deadly and indelible ordinarily let alone at this level of indulgence. There is no turning back. And yet here I am thinking entirely of that meadow of tepid green, ringed by feathery, pellucid trees now becoming this impenetrable morass of stygian bleakness, bleeding away but impossible now to staunch the stains, to blot up and soften the story. Fred flails on, writing an alternative ending no matter how well it plays.

"Freddie, it's dad. How're doing?"

"The exec committee has asked me to make a presentation of the stats from our study of buying habits..."

Fred listens dutifully, prodding his son with queries here and there.

"If this isn't my first real break, Dad, I swear I'm on the verge. I've been told I speak well and, hell, I plan to get included in a sales pitch to Atlas Gas by the end of this year!"

The lad is in overdrive as he should be, as I was, Fred is thinking while listening and picturing himself in the ad agency as a graphic artist revamping soap labels. Fred lets the vivacity of Freddie's voice seep into his system, a much needed infusion.

"How about I get into the city and take you and Trudy out for dinner?" Fred asks when Freddie peters out. This has landed like a puncture wound given Freddie's lengthened pause. "Just sometime," adds Fred. "Be nice to catch up with you and get better acquainted with Trudy."

"Super, Dad," says Freddie with a speed suggesting more relief than appreciation.

"Good luck with your progress at work," Fred offers by way of concluding the call and releasing his son. "Keep me posted," although that has not been the case nor will it be likely.

"Don't berate yourself over your watercolor career," Roxie is saying as they organize themselves for full-body sketching, the theme they concocted for today. "Just because we've discussed how much your art could plow more into the opposite of peaceful landscapes, more troublesome but enlightening material, that doesn't mean that beautiful paintings aren't valid, even essential."

They are standing in the cramped cabin kitchen, their pads and pencils on the table, facing off but not sure how to begin.

Fred is near manic with relief at Roxie's amiable chatter. Serious conversation about art, this is how we began, he thinks. This is how we will continue. Here is where Roxie is open and available. For Christ's sake, enough with the invitation to a bed and breakfast. Whisking her out into the world, museums and beyond.

"Think of it this way, Fred dear. Thanks goodness we have beautiful paintings to keep the terror of the

199

world at bay, to hopefully lift us up and beyond it, aerating the soul. For all of us day by day, more often than not, is deadening routine. Rot and mayhem are barely below the surface. Making beauty is one of the best of things we can do—to assert the finest in ourselves. I've been to the caves in the Dordogne to see these fantastic drawings from tens of thousands of years ago, etchings of bison and horses and woolly mammoths and what not, to honor, they speculate, the elements they were dependent upon. The forces that could annihilate them in a flash."

"Remember, Roxie, you mentioned that article about art combining both the disease and the cure? I like that."

Upon arriving he'd told her of his being repelled the day before, stopping by the tranquil meadow, one of his innumerable watercolor sites, and realizing how besotted he'd always been by the sheer splendor of nature. His escape from reality. "So maybe I can look back and see the underbelly of what really prompted all those wispy watercolors. I shouldn't isolate the beauty bit as if that's all on its own."

Roxie is still poised with a fistful of charcoal sticks. "It's not just the artist, dear one. What you make isn't complete without others seeing it. Think of the years of pleasure you provided those hundreds of customers—you've often reduced them to suckers for your sentimental art. This is utter nonsense."

"Thank you, Roxie. You're my life preserver. We should sketch while we're still standing. I must shut up and not keep dipping into your storehouse of perspectives. I'm greedy, I admit."

"Please lean that way on one leg, Fred. Just for a

sec." She dashes off more lines. "Now you're less like a guard at Buckingham Palace. More equivocating."

He does what she asks and then begins in earnest sketching her sketching him. They work through multiple pages, quickly, energetically, happily for Fred. Roxie is both compact and lissome, each an amazement for a woman, anyone, in their high senior years. It's more than yoga, of course, he is thinking as he's feverishly drawing. It's her hold on life, her seeming not to miss a moment. She makes everything protean and respectful of attention, from articulating a slice of art history to brewing her herbal teas. Can I do this for myself...become inspired from a source only hinted at to date? Meanwhile it's good to focus on her frame, her figure instead of her face, that alone a universe of information.

The sun streaming through the kitchen window is near blinding them, bleaching their sketchpads. It's suddenly summer, nature having enticed them to trudge on through the endless mud season, the roiling drek of gray clouds.

"We should continue outdoors, don't you think, dear?" says Roxie as they pause. "One of us can pose and the other sit and draw on the tree stump. I won't even need my down vest."

Fred agrees, glancing at a few of her sketches. "Am I really stooped like that, Roxie?"

"It's the low ceiling," she mitigates.

"No, I'm bowing down to you in your inner sanctum."

She wrinkles up her nose as if to say, that stinks. "You are a big man, Fred. Taller than most everyone. I suspect your way has always been to bend over and fit in. Make others feel comfortable."

"Okay. I'll try harder to stand tall and claim my space."

"That's the spirit," she agrees as they gather things to go outside.

"It does mean I'll have to look down on people. Especially you." He hopes this will needle her.

"Yes," she says solemnly. "That would be an eminently sensible idea."

Fred sits on the stump and sketches while Roxie strikes various yoga positions, raised arms saluting the sky and then relaxing into rounded shoulders, inward thoughts. They trade places, the two of them often acting drunk on the sudden warmth, soon sweltering in the blaze.

"Enough!" cries Roxie collapsing onto the soft ground at Fred's feet. He's shed his flannel shirt as has Roxie her painter's smock. Each is in a T-shirt. Roxie removes her shoes. "Delectable," she says flexing toes in the bright new green grass. Fred unties his sneakers, yanks off his socks. Roxie supports herself with arms extended in back, her head and willowy white hair sunken into the concave dip between her uplifted shoulders. Fred follows suit and flops parallel to her side. He settles flat onto his back and cradles his head with both hands, eyes shut tight, aiming his nose pointblank at the show-stealing, coruscating sun.

Fred becomes engulfed by the orchestra of insects tuning itself before the performance, their buzzing like strings, their whistling as the winds, an occasional thud, the bassoon, probably a bird nose-diving her pond.

She interrupts his reverie. He can tell she is getting

up. Through squinting eyes — good god — she's removing her clothes.

"I'm plunging into the pond," she states as if what could be more logical as he looks aside. "It'll be like ice. I've come to terms with my Nordic blood living here in the tundra. Wishful thinking but it gets me in and out!"

She slips down to the pond edge. At first she tiptoes into the water and then hurls herself in. Submerges!

Fred bolts upright. Is she alright? She pops up with a positively girlish grin, slapping arms onto the surface, bouncing — it must not be over her head. The billowing white hair is suddenly black in this light and plastered to her scalp. She turns about and faces away, not beckoning him, not sending another signal, simply immersed in the explosion of summerlike spring, the unstoppable glory of the moment.

He rips off his things and rushes to the pond. Just at the second of his galloping to pond edge she spins around, him greeting her full-frontal. He reaches Roxie and whoops and shouts and leaps up and down. It is freezing but thrilling — a baptism, the mind-blasting spontaneity, the two of them naked and frolicking instead of dissecting Rothko on dry land.

A minute later — it seems an eternity — they are scooting up the bank and back to their clothes which they clutch more for toweling than coverage. They step lightly back to the cabin as if the spring grass, too, is as cold as the pond. Inside without rushing Roxie fetches them towels. Though she's petite, her breasts are remarkably plump and round, her body defying the facts of her face. Fred withdraws to a corner of the kitchen to complete his drying off and dressing, straining every fiber of his being to appear casual and not catatonic.

"Well, sweetheart," quips Roxie when fully reassembled. "This is how we met. At the figure-drawing workshop. Only it was the models who were nude. Now it's us. With art it's all the same."

Fred suddenly remembers Roxie's rendition of the male model on the occasion of their meeting: a whole page of an enormous penis!

Driving home Fred cannot reconcile Roxie's air of ease at this happenstance compared to, for him, its overpowering intimacy. I must take her at her word, unspoken but obvious — we are friends. We are artists whose paths are intersecting. For the time being. This is just another likely albeit impromptu angle to our linkage, stretching out now for well over a year. She's fond of saying how we often need to complete ourselves with important peoples' ideals but not make of them icons. Just keep feeding yourself this line, ole Fred, he silently commands and repeats and repeats. Just keep reminding yourself you're on your own at this stage — she sure as heck is. Don't think of her in the category of Stratton or June for that matter as eye candy just because from the rear her bottom, her shapely legs, the calm and grace with which she carries herself says female through and through. Not that her mettle hasn't been more than enough to hammer a stake into my heart.

Damn you, Roxie, for jumping into that pond.

Chapter 14

ROXIE AND FRED

ANY WEEKS LATER ROXIE'S GARDEN HAS done an about face from viscous mud to blinding green growth. Snowdrops, crocuses, violets sprung forth in rapid sequence, already gone by. Presently Fred is assigned to thin radishes and carrots while Roxie is fixing a lentil soup for lunch. The task of thinning seedlings is painstaking but at least Fred appreciates the tight focus manipulating his large fingers around and about the delicate sprouts. This is taking his mind off his latest oil, neurasthenic as a corpse. With its indecisive composition, it nevertheless stands bold as a battleship on the easel in his home studio, blanks on the canvas like pointed guns. It assaults him first thing in the morning and upon his return from Roxie's. It ceaselessly dictates his moves on the days when not retreating to Roxie's cabin or yard chores or yoga mats, the hikes, swims, their non-stop badinage and musings over art, from his own recent paintings to those by the masters. So blessedly simple to be here in her garden on hands and knees. He's in T-shirt, shorts and low work-boots, the footgear the better to anchor him this morning at the chopping block, splitting kindling to refresh Roxie's supply. One by one he's taken on several of the tasks requiring manual labor, relieving her ever-reliable Hank to concentrate on his day job, custodian at the local school. Although paying him handsomely with garden produce Roxie admits that Hank, father of four, is mostly doing her a favor by handling the homestead heavy-lifting. Fred now comes to the cabin more like three days a week instead of two.

He stands and stretches before hunkering down over the next vegetables in need. Without her asking he knows to thin the spinach and chard, all of this edible and apt for a salad along with the soup.

Roxie plucks some rosemary from her dried bundles strung up to the beam. It's for Fred, to add some kick. She herself is losing interest in fussing with food — with much of anything. She doesn't miss their twice or more weekly sessions of making art. This, too, is for Fred, she thinks, poking into her bread box. Slim pickings of her homemade. Maybe Fred won't tell the difference in the ten-seeded, twenty-sprouted or whatever brick she added to her shopping list for Hank. Dear Fred has no idea how dependent she has been on Hank for so much more than tilling the soil, hauling the trash she can't compost, on and on. Driving the jalopy to Fred's those times over the past year she became infuriated at her creeping along, let alone the drivers of cars queued up to her rear. It was she not the jalopy setting the pace. Am I willing to increasingly rely on Fred for a helping hand? She leaves the rosemary bunch on the counter rather than climbing back up her low stepladder. She's all too aware of elders prone to falling and breaking a hip. She glances out the kitchen window at Fred now spading a plot for a second planting of salad greens. Work is fine, she thinks, so long as others are doing it. Apart from practicing yoga my energy now is best spent keeping watch on the changing seasons, strolls with Fred through the meadows and up into the hills. Effort is for stilling the mind, grounding the spirits, navigating the next inevitable hurdle which always requires a leap.

Fred carries a bowl of greens to the cabin. He loves that Roxie has no lawn, just paths made by compacting the tall grass. The untrammeled grass, by contrast, gets to host Indian paintbrush, clumps of daisies, the odd stalk of wild lupine. The weeds, too, free range. He never saw Joe Pye weed or skunk cabbage in his tidy suburban cocoon. Never inhaled such foul, funky odors—raw, natural, believable assaults that make his former lily-of-the-valley patch seem synthetic as a lady's fine perfume.

"We can have a little salad, too," says Fred in the kitchen. "Don't need to rinse." Roxie is leaning against the butcher-block counter, hands loosely clasped. He suspects she prefers this shift in their routine. Less talk, more loose companionship. She no longer dons the dangly earrings and African skirts, almost flirting, she was, he's thought of their first months of reconnoitering. She's so relaxed. His presence finally is no big deal. The network of wrinkles in her face is definitely less defined.

"Why don't you fix dressing, Fred? I love the way you can just lift an arm and pluck a few herbs. Plus spicy mustard with the olive oil, like last time. And you brought me rice wine vinegar. Goodness, I've done nothing but olive oil and Balsamic since day one." He's so happy to be useful, to be told what to do, she thinks smiling and sitting down. And pleasing me, this positively inspires him. Let him be, no arguments here.

Fred heats up the soup, tosses the salad, plates some bread and sets the table. He pours them tall glasses from the jug of iced lemon balm tea he brewed the other day.

"I'll make an omelet for supper, Roxie," Fred says, delighting in the lunch. "A crime not to use the fresh dill. There's still some cheddar I got all those weeks ago at the farmer's market. I'll just scrape off the mold."

"Lovely," says Roxie. "So nice with the longer days we can eat on the porch on our laps. You're spoiling me, sweetheart."

"No, Roxie, it's the opposite. This is a slice of heaven after incarceration in my matchbox."

They continue to eat in silence, the comfort that comes to couples, Roxie thinks, when there's no urgency to sooth, explain, defend, incite. Just be.

"I've always wanted to make pickles," says Fred wiping his mouth. "I bet the young cukes will come about when there's still dillweed or the seeds for sure."

Roxie briefly shuts her eyes remembering the tedium of canning, drying on racks, fermenting, freezing, root-cellaring, the compulsory storage of every last Hubbard squash the size of a watermelon, enough for an army, half of it rotted by spring.

"I'm going to plant more dill so I'll be sure to have it mid-summer."

Roxie is amused at recalling Fred's tales of his ex-wife's obsession with placemats, floor polish.

"Oh Roxie, all my years of slaving away over flowers. They were beautiful. I painted them. Good god, the salmon poppies will only last another day...quick get the watercolor block! But here with you so much of the time, the gorgeous fruits and vegetables...and we get to share them."

"Maybe this is where you should live, Fred. After I'm gone."

"Roxie!"

"I meant, after I've moved to my fantasy ware-house. The one single room."

"Oh, that," he says rising, enormously relieved. "You want to simplify. I'm helping you simplify, my dear."

Roxie looks aside. She would have to sell the place to move. Would he buy it? Could he? Roxie decides to let the subject of this conversation rest. For the time being. For now, she tells herself, just luxuriate in Fred's animation, enough for the both of us.

He's got the dishes done, the napkins re-folded. "Now," he announces with Roxie still seated, his cap-tive audience. "I'm recharged and want to finish that spading. And pitch-forking both compost bins. They're begging for it."

Roxie reads on her bed the next hour. At some point she props herself up with pillows, eyes open and alert, holding a steady gaze to a strand of beads hanging opposite on a nail. The beads from some flea market likely having fired Manny on a whim, glistening a life-time ago, are now idle and opaque from wood smoke and pitch. She lets this slide past as if she were quietly sitting roadside and watching a hometown parade of yesteryear stride by. She sighs and settles back into the vacant, neutral place she appreciates best of all, devoid of walls, trappings, kindred souls, her own as well.

Meanwhile Fred heaves his bulk about as if the whole of him is a sledgehammer. The work is calling the shots. I'm just a medium. Like when painting is going well. My hands are minding the business of what hue goes where, which color comes next. This brush too dainty, this one too brash. The palette knife gets picked up erasing a fraught-over patch in one swipe but startling him with its wake of dazzling crenulations. Split-second decisions happening as if a robot is manning a control tower at JFK. I just watch, he thinks. I witness.

He's sweating freely. Plenty of time to attack the fence posts. His heart is pounding in protest. The stabbing at his temples forces him to drop his tools. He rushes to the cabin. Will she have a painkiller here in the woods?

Roxie climbs out of bed to greet him. She can see he's suffering, the brow tightened as in a vise, his bright reddish curls darkened and flat.

"I've got a splitting headache. June used to blame this on my weekend warrior syndrome, going at it like a gladiator after being on my ass all week."

"Sit down," she says softly.

"You have aspirin at least?"

"Better. Here," she says and pats the edge of the bed. "Close your eyes." She kneels behind Fred and rests hands over his forehead. "Slump, dear one. I'm in charge. Let go." And so she proceeds to press his temples, can in fact feel them throbbing. Slowly she rotates her middle fingers in small circles in the center of his forehead. After a moment she shifts them further apart, continuing with the same motions. Little circles of pressure. Very gradually she travels to the sides of his head, and next lower to astride his ears.

So strange and yet normal to be holding him in my hands, Roxie muses without missing a beat of her massage. He is big, she is not, they are light years apart in age and yet each has become an offspring of the other. She thinks of the shock of beholding a newborn tossed from the genetic roll of the dice but instantly unquestioning that both parties are as one.

After several minutes she is going higher, above his eyes, no longer circles, just gently pressing in a pulsing fashion. He is sighing, his breath ever slower. Having traced over the eyes she lightly runs her middle fingers along the lower bones of the eye sockets. She places her entire palms against his eyes and lingers there before sinking fingers into his hair and massaging his scalp.

"This is so wonderful," he whispers, absolved of pain, swooning from her touch, from her assurance as with everything she says or does.

"Shush," she replies, her hands rotating over his head and becoming more aggressive, her fingers working into the soft folds at the base of his skull, at some point tugging his earlobes, lightly pinching them up and around, a little tap-dance before stroking the fleshy lobes once again.

She rests hands on his shoulders. She is at peace which she assumes as well for Fred.

"You're a sorceress, Roxie," he says.

"Mama Milly was my education of a lifetime. I should have stayed in Africa and become a witch doctor."

"Amazing. My headache's gone."

She taps his shoulders. "Time for the pond. You men. Muscles over mind. Lucky you didn't strain your back like last fall."

Roxie gathers dry towels. They undress at the kitchen table, casually draping clothes over the chair backs, and stroll outdoors, Roxie leading, Fred rousing himself to mimic her spritely step. Rows of emerging vegetables wiggle in the light wind, soliciting their attention along with the woodpile to stack, the volunteer cosmos aching to be cut and celebrated as a proper bouquet indoors. They drop the towels and test the water with big toes. As if to steady himself, Fred grips Roxie's shoulder; by dint of flesh and bones he has lots more to coordinate prior to easing into the spring-fed pond. The day has turned steamy but the pond barely varies, majestic and poised as the mountain of evergreens looming overhead.

"Huhh!" he grimaces as his testicles touch down.

"You baby," laughs Roxie gracefully diving in.

He follows and they splash about. By now they've skinny-dipped a dozen times. We've been so serious for so long, Fred thinks dunking up and down, the headache a thing of the past. He needs to play. He hopes she does too rather than just another way he amuses her. Still it is hard for him to see himself beyond an accessory to the fulsome solitude of her homestead. I will not, must not, give a modicum of credence to the notion of living here, with or without her. Is meditation so intrinsic to her core that she could co-exist with me yet keep herself on track? Stop right there, buster. Play! He noisily swims circles around her, Roxie floating on her back, her modest breasts barely breaking the surface.

Whenever did I have such spontaneity as an adult let alone as a child, Roxie is thinking. A sliver with

Manny sandwiched into years and years of all the rest...

Fred comes to her side. They grip both hands and start circling in the waist-deep water, leaning back, their eyes seized by the joyful cerulean sky. We're like youngsters in recess before called back to class, Roxie thinks. She leads Fred out of the pond clutching one of his hands. They spread towels on the soft ground and lie down flat. The brilliant sun has set the agenda; they tried drying off standing once before but the air was way too cold. Their fingertips touch, like making snow angels, Fred thinks. Roxie's mind is a blank screen, as if the sun and breeze dappling her skin have devised a language all their own, happily excluding her.

Roxie releases Fred's hand and twists onto her side. "I'd like to play with your lovely penis. May I?"

Fred's head yanks to face her. He's speechless.

"It's been so long. But that's not why I want to touch you. Even before you, life is so physical here. Very much in balance. Now for us as well."

"Roxie..."

"You don't have to touch me. You don't have to become aroused, I know you men, although that's fine if that happens."

To say something Fred spits out the details of his affair with Stratton. "Truthfully, Roxie, I don't know where my body wants to go in terms of that direction."

"Well, listen to it. Pay it some attention. Those muscles of yours, they're capable of more than wielding paintbrushes and thinning seedlings." She giggles and puts a cool hand on his hot forehead, covering his eyes. "Oh darling Fred, just feel. Forget me. You are being embraced by all of nature — sun, wind, me, whatever."

Fred is beyond a point his rational self can cleave to. How can he possibly creep into and hide in a mental crevice and blot her out? There is sensation on his toes. He lifts his head. He's relieved his genitals are inert despite her heckling that men feel diminished unless posing fully-loaded.

"Please, Fred, keep your eyes closed."

He relaxes back as she traces lines on his feet with a single blade of grass, he caught that much.

"Really, now," she says, "is this any different than my sketching, but on you instead of on paper?" She runs the grass up and down his legs, the outsides not the overly-sensitive, erotic insides of his thighs. Up onto the chest, circling but not touching the nipples, down his flanks and belly but retreating from the slumbering man-parts. She rises and kneels over him to reach his arms, the sides of his neck and the top of his head but not his face—not to chance tickling. His broad penis is swelling from its nesting pinkness. The light reddish hairs above are transparent in the bright sun, making his shaft appear even more elongated. She taps the nipples with the grass, then the navel, the frizzy pubic bush, studiously avoiding the penis which has stretched with its pulsating bluish veins, flopping up and side-to-side like a big fish on the floor of a boat, fighting for its life. She grazes the blade of grass over the balls. They're churning. This thrills her, as if she's been allowed into the cage of an enormous gorgeous beast, each eyeing the other without an immediate notion of how to proceed. Manny is decades ago. What did she do? What didn't they do? Fred's genitals are roaring into a life all their own. She doesn't want to be cruel. She takes her hands and sets them on his chest.

His eyes bolt open, at first with the most quizzical look and then he belly-laughs.

Fred sits up and envelops her in his arms, respectful of her fragility. "Oh, Roxie. You are too wonderful." He stands and assists her to her feet. It is she whose face is now flung into astonishment. He lifts her into his powerful frame and carries her like a child-bride up to the cabin.

"We're going to lie on your plump bed. Side-by-side. No sex, now. It's my turn to play with you."

They crawl onto her futon, their unintelligible guffaws eventually replaced by sighs, deep breaths, ready for Fred to make a move. He does not know what to say or do, this turn of events like a sudden tornado ripping apart the unsuspecting plain. What a huge mistake. He feels like a kid on a wild ride at the amusement park who suddenly wishes he wasn't. She has lost touch with herself, her body, her wits, it's now all his doing. And it's devilishly good fun.

Fred sits up, bewildered. Just stop here. He surveys the cluttered little room. He's inside of a gypsy caravan laden with odd ornaments, yoga apparatus, fanciful clothes.

"Is that a *dildo?*"

She shifts up supported by her elbows. "It's called a vibrator."

His smile burst into a wicked grin.

"What?" she snaps. "You don't think if you're still alive you give up pleasure?"

"Roxie, lie back down."

"No penetration, for god's sake. I'm dry as a witch's tit, we used to day."

He flicks a switch and the big plastic thing pops out of his hand and onto the floor like the energizer bunny. He retrieves and turns it off.

"I take masses of lubrication. Not today. It was just a flight of fancy, darling Fred. You're like an Eagle Scout, but you're not getting your badge in doing old ladies."

"Close your eyes. My turn."

She settles back down, laughing or cursing she isn't sure, nor is he.

Fred steadies himself into the Lotus position at her side and glides the smooth, quiet wand over her arms...atop her lush hair...against the soles of her feet, hoping to surprise her, keep her off-kilter. It's her cabin, she's the commander-in-chief, but I'll settle for her steward, clerk-of-the-works.

"Not the nipples," she whispers. "No longer in service. Hurt, sometimes painful to the touch."

"Shhh," he says, continuing over her neck, wrists, calves. "Spread your legs some."

"Not there."

"Talking about the insides of the thighs."

"I'll stop talking," Roxie says, "if you will."

This triggers both of them to laugh. Fred sets the vibrator aside, crouches over and kisses Roxie on the lips, first time ever. Then he cradles her aged yet somehow supple torso in his arms and legs, encircling her, his erection wedged somewhere in the tangle of limbs.

"This is lovely, Fred," says Roxie. "So innocent." She is thinking of straddling Manny back in the day.

"Innocent? I suppose. After all, it's just our bodies, my dick, your tits, mostly skin. Less intimate in a way than sharing our stories, your being exposed to my ongoing wreckage of artwork." He rubs his nose to hers, the hard-on now less so. "Although I only know bits and pieces of what has taken place for you and what does now in that nimble noggin of yours."

"One thing at a time, darling Fred. Whatever words get recycled even though I may think they're fresh — we're each of us left to weave the threads dangling about. You make whatever of me as I must of you. We do this with and for each other. It makes me think of primitive art, each hand stretching out and holding one of the next person's on each side. Like children's paper cut-outs in a chain."

"A powerful image, Roxie," Fred says entwined with her more loosely. "But we're only two in that linkage."

"Yes. I know we're all of us meant to be connected. The others are still there. Before and after, for you. For me, you're the last in my line."

He leaves a pause. Something clicks. He flops onto his side, facing her, their legs still interlocking. "Wait a sec, Roxie. Long ago we had this conversation about history and our perception of it. We in the West you said insist on stringing it horizontally, one thing after another, as if there's no overlap. Remember? You're all before World War Two, saving tinsel from Christmas trees for the tanks. 'Before your time,' you lorded it over me from a totally different era, unscathed by such cataclysm. The Easterners you said consider it vertically, everything and everyone stacked so it all filters down and infuses cultures. You said one of my problems like for any artist is going it alone, expected to produce miracles every time rather than part of a process, a legacy to lean on as well as bounce off of."

She looks him in the eye. She unscrambles herself from their humid coil of arms and bellies and legs and perches on top of him.

"Alright," Roxie says. "I'm stacked on top of you. Here on your chest, not below, not yet. Forget the omelet. The snow peas can wait on the vine one more night. I'm channeling my Manny, I'm going back decades—the best of it, not the calamities. It's all coming back in a flash. Darling Fred, I may be an old crone but you really are a babe in the woods."

Chapter 15

FRED AND ROXIE

THEY ARE WALKING THROUGH THE UPPER meadow, taking their time on the home stretch. Even hiking up and down the hills, Fred following Roxie particularly through the narrow passages when brushing between prickly pines, they more amble than hike on this occasion. Traipsing through the meadows is always less arduous. There are no paths. At this point they are simply going for a stroll. They are holding hands.

Roxie releases from Fred's clasp which borders on a grip. She must take care he doesn't inadvertently crush her when they're supposedly at play. She makes her way to inspect a clump of chicory, so sky-blue, arriving early this summer. She always leans down to take a sniff even though she knows fragrance with wildflowers is a rarity. Maybe honeysuckle, she thinks, when it first blooms in early spring.

Fred's feet are planted wide, arms folded, happily waiting and savoring the pause. He and Roxie say very little on their walks, especially so today. His eyelids lower, limiting his peripheral vision and letting him better frame the riot of color in the foreground. The milky-gray whites of Queen Anne's lace and trembling yellows of buttercup practically shout when isolated against the green-black intensities of grass and stems, shadows and earth. Hey, I'm painting with my eyes, he thinks merrily. Who needs a studio, the rigmarole of brushes and oily tubes? What's the difference between what I concoct in my mind's eye and what transpires on canvas?

Roxie returns with a clump of feathery weeds, inserts her free hand into the nest of Fred's big mitt, and they resume their leisurely pace through the meadow.

Many weeks have passed since the escalation of their intimacy. Roxie is transported so far beyond the usual perception of herself. The self-stimulation and occasional release: that's been a given forever. Now another body combined with hers? It's one more layer of wellbeing, tending and harvesting her interior garden of goodies. There's her mindful meditation, her yoga exertions from opening Vinyasa and closing Savasana and all the asanas in between. Where in truth, she ponders, do body and mind not overlap, enliven and provoke one another? She knows Fred for his part is straining to behave, not rush to this now-regular activity in their routine. He's like a devoted dog used to sleeping on the floor and suddenly permitted onto the bed.

Reaching the garden, they release their intertwined hands and walk single-file.

Pods of greenbeans have gone unpicked, the beans swelling to marble size, the seams split apart. Dead-ripe cherry tomatoes have dropped to the ground, a banquet for the birds.

They've collected themselves amidst the bed pillows, naked before their romp, Fred of course at the ready but placing a corner of sheeting across his lap.

"Sex is such an inadequate term," says Roxie. Fred feels himself wilt but, for now, that's fine. "It's like shoving it to the corner of the dinner plate or like dessert, only one course at a time."

"Stratton said the same, but with us that was indeed the whole thing — sex and none of the rest. Great for her but ultimately not for me."

"We might not even touch right now," continues Roxie. "Just look into my eyes, Fred darling. What do you see? No, what do you see in me of yourself?"

"Well, I don't see any trace of apprehension in you that I'm feeling."

"Keep going."

"Bare skin, relaxed shoulders. I'm becoming at ease because you are."

"Deeper, dear."

"I sense a place of composure, on your surface and through and through, that is part of me, too. I never had this with June. Or rather, we could never make that wonderful — what should I call it? — retreat for ourselves. A desert island all our own."

Roxie smiles and nods. "Let's play Chinese. Japanese? Stretch one leg to me, I'll do the same, and we'll caress a foot. Take each toe and stroke it like you would a baby."

At this they proceed.

"It's like an offering to the other," says Fred. "It's not easy to receive at the same time, though."

"Close your eyes. I know what you mean but, ever so gradually," croons Roxie, "doesn't it feel like two synchronized parts of the same...hands of the clock... moving in tandem?"

Soon they switch their extended legs. Next she suggests they lie flat on their backs but lace fingers and linger like this for a while. Never has Fred not piloted sex, except the gymnastics with Stratton, all her doing, but that shouldn't count. Roxie reaches over to run fingertips up and down his arm, the backs of her nails prompting a reaction from Fred which hovers between shivers and sleepiness.

When she withdraws her hand he says: "I can't reciprocate. You're too tiny, too close. My elbow would club you in the face."

"Reciprocate? Silly. Sometimes pleasure is a one-way street. It's all good."

They fondle earlobes, then necks. Roxie takes a finger of Fred's in her mouth and sucks on it. He lets go of his squeamishness. He tries to let go of all but the sensation.

The morning carries on. They've abandoned any set time for lunch. Roxie breaks the silence of their interlude, she being tucked into a fetal position at his side, entwined in his long, strong arms. She is entranced with each part of him — pale skin so pink it's almost childlike, undersized nipples dotting the massive, rolling expanse of his upper chest. It's all so familiar and yet it's not, Roxie considers. He's the aroma of a peach left a day too long in the bowl. Not quite sweet, not quite stale. Manny, gefilte fish, forever with garlic breath. It's like wading into a different, eutrophying swamp with its own unique smell. Harold, prep school onward, the same blasted after-shave. Amos in Africa reeking of jungle flowers and whatever bird or animal dung clung to his boots. How did she, how does she still, distinguish between that man and the dirt and their pheromones at one with the shrieking insects and howling beasts with which they shared the night? But Fred, darling man, imagine something newly minted at the end of my life...

Fred has lost contact with his limbs let alone any thoughts, his flesh having melted deep into the pillows, the mismatched bed linens. He's vaguely aware of the outermost membrane of his body as Roxie's palm touches down here and there, the gesture barely acknowledged by him. In time it seems the whole of him is breathing up through the touch and directly pulsing into her palm.

Roxie breaks the silence. "Please get onto your hands and knees, dear one. That's good. And I'll slide underneath, like so," and her legs stretch under his shoulders and arms as she positions her head beneath his crotch. "I can reach you with my hands," she says and cups his penis and balls, equal handfuls at first. "Just feel, sweetheart, don't think. All you have to do. Don't even move. I know that's asking a lot of a big hunk of manhood. Goodness."

Fred is no stranger to his dick having a mind of its own. No problem doing as she says, as she toys with him, frequently releasing his enlarged penis to finger his ball sack and dance from there along the perineum to the opening of his arse. Fucking fabulous. He prays his knees hold up and don't buckle.

"Alright, sweetheart, now lower yourself best you can so I can at least get to the tip with my lips. Glory, I'm so inflexible...you'd think with all my yoga..."

Lowering to more of a pushup, tough as a damn

plank in the gym, but this he does. And he lowers beyond her lips, lets himself sink as much into her mouth as she can manage. Good god, plus her grasping his shaft in one hand and cradling balls in the other... no way to hold back...

Roxie pulls away, smoothly but decisively. "Just for starters, darling, we're in no rush although I should be, my age." She erupts in a throaty laugh. They right themselves on the bed. "Now wasn't that nice?"

Fred knows with his slackened jaw, gaping mouth, he must resemble a baboon.

"Shall we sip a little tea before we go on?" says Roxie. "My turn next. I'm saving you for that."

An hour later, after tea, after more laughs, they are back on her bed.

"Oh, Fred, I was joking before. You don't have to get another erection. Ever. This is for fun. There's my vibrator, if it comes to that. I'll certainly be using that on you."

Fred is neither relieved nor disappointed. She's driving the pickup and he's in its bed, bouncing along.

"Besides," she adds, arranging Fred on his back and straddling him, taking her time. She can no longer move quickly; her transitions from one yoga pose to the next are in slow motion. Fred's sex once again is stiff as a smokestack. "I'd have to be an Amazon to get all that business inside." She can't believe she is talking like this. It's either all too new to be recognizable or it all comes naturally, wired at birth.

Roxie gingerly fondles Fred. With her assumption of command, he has abdicated any shred of guilt at being so passive. Maybe after all these months, he thinks, with Roxie at whatever the activity or conversation, in some way I evaporate. He merges into a delirium as now, some whirling, nebulous outpost from which he cannot see the ground let alone safely land.

Roxie taps his rigid self against her softness. She has smeared herself with gobs of lubricant from the bedside jar. She gradually rocks against him, holding his erection with both hands and hoping the rubbing is as nice for him as for her. Every time she looks at her hands she notices yet another cascade of brown spots or a formerly violet vein now purple and even more pronounced. Thank god these palms wielding him are still satin-smooth.

I must not come! Fred barks to himself, although he knows for her, with her, that would be just another ripe cherry to pluck from their tree. Have I entered a narcosis and slipped into sleep? He wants to keep going this way, Roxie groaning slightly, more a hum, as she tentatively places his swollen tip on her sweet spot. An uninvited memory crashes the party. He'd be on the verge of carpel tunnel syndrome massaging June's clit, determined to hear her howl for once.

She guides him in barely an inch. No more! Her lovely vibrator has suited her for how many years? It's hardly a precursor of Fred. Wonder if I can find that feather-tip as an attachment? She pushes aside this thought and relaxes into a rhythm, soon prompting the recollection of that Tennessee walking horse when she was a teen, when she was exploding with hormonal fireworks and found arousal at this was perfectly safe. A debutante in riding school! Golly she had them all hoodwinked.

Fred cries aloud, gushes semen into her fists. She laughs and leans over to kiss his mouth, misses, her lips smashing his left nostril.

"Oh but you were going great guns, Roxie," he moans.

"Yes. And no stopping me now." Gracefully she slides off Fred's belly onto her back and spreads the handful of his guck over her labia, inside the folds, her guttural giggles at first compromising her sighs.

Fred tucks a hand high up on her thigh, not massaging but hoping to aide her momentum. He cannot see her fingertips yet he knows, he knows a woman knows herself better than any man no matter how well she's schooled him. Let her mastermind the finish but let him do his part from the start.

Long moments later, it would seem after her third attempt or third achievement—how would I know, he thinks, a lifetime of June set about my pleasure and never her own—Roxie and Fred have collapsed into the tossed salad of rumpled pillows and soggy sheets.

"Well," says Roxie. "What a lovely way to spend the day. Skipping lunch. We can go right to supper."

Fred's upper arm serves as a hard cushion for her head. He's at a loss for words. He cannot even speculate where this tryst could possibly lead. A one-time layover in their meandering journey of acquaintance, or the first of countless possibilities, according to her. Fred hasn't the foggiest.

Roxie rises and slips into a kimono, black silk embroidered with giant red and pink hibiscus. "I haven't gotten this gussied-up in many a moon. I wonder what's a-foot?" She tickles his big toe, Fred still splayed on the bed as if he's the paying customer, she's the madam whisking off to the next. In fact it's a total reversal, he posits. Somehow it's she who has taken her pleasure and he who has serviced his queen.

I should know better than to entertain such folly, Fred thinks and heaves himself up. Roxie so firmly believes there are no rules in this business or any other, for that matter. For the time being he's happy to give her the benefit of the doubt.

"Try a bite of the eel," says Roxie. "I haven't had anything this exotic since — Nepal — Rhodesia. I must say Zimbabwe. Such ancient history, before your time."

They are regaling themselves at a remote Asian seafood eatery in the city after their day at the museum. Cartoon-colored paper lanterns festoon the low ceilings like festive flags on a cruise ship, formerly bright but now tattered. Strung from exposed plumbing are lines of twinkling Christmas lights, the greens more poison-yellow, the reds, pale orange. It's perfect, thinks Roxie. "Trashy but authentic," says Fred.

Fred samples the eel and lifts his eyebrows. "Squid, sea urchin, raw clams. All kind of rubbery." He dives back into his lobster salad. "Garden greens it seems we live on, my dear Roxie, but all this succulent meat for a change! Love it."

Roxie nibbles a little of this and that from the huge platter of fish like miniature dim sum. Mostly she is experiencing herself a gazillion years ago, the young miss on her first date.

"Roxie, you are simply stunning in that ivory dress. Showing off your wonderful necklace and rings."

"All from Mama Milly. Not the dress. Can you believe I saved this frock from the days with Harold, don't ask me why. And it fits!" He's so observant. Yes, she skipped earrings to let the elaborate African beads and stones be the stars.

Fred is on his second glass of wine, a Chardonnay. The first he insisted be Champagne. Roxie pretends to sip; she wants to stay absolutely alert to the evening's end at the little inn. It simply cannot sink in that they've been so sexual. This dinner is like they have just met on a blind date. They're going backwards.

Fred in his best button-down shirt reaches across the wooden table, carved into a patina rivaling Roxie's butcher-block. He's polished off his first course as well as hers. He strokes her two hands flat and crossed on the tabletop. "Remember when I suggested we get here for the Turner show, stay at a B and B? You recoiled like a turtle being poked."

"I try to honor each day, dear Fred. I don't think ahead or look much back."

"I'm glad you declined the idea at the time. I think this Chagall exhibit is a much better match for where we are now. So—visceral. So bursting with humanity."

"I hope the vivid colors inspire you, dear. Your painting can still be shy that way. I mean, according to you. I think your subtle tones are heavenly."

"I used to think of Chagall as sentimental. Cozy village shtetl life, everything connected, the donkeys and virgins and angels and rabbis and the rest. Thank you for pointing out the eye of God, an almost pagan innocence, the images transcending the horror of Jewish pogroms, the daily toil. So much in any one work!" He pauses; yet there's more. "The promise the divine holds for renewal. Light shining through night."

Roxie taps a finger at Fred. "Thank you, sweetheart,

for seizing upon the brides, lovers, breasts. We know your present fixation. But with your next oil—what about dream fragments? Semi-human forms. You've done so much portraiture and figure drawing." She grasps her multiple strands of bright beads and beams. "Oh, Fred. Little did I ever expect to spend a day at a museum instead of—one more year as the nun I've made of myself, the cabin, the gardens, a bloody convent."

They squeeze hands and release them to make way for the huge platters of steaming bluefish, replete with bulging eyes as if there's no such thing in the world, along with Chagall, that isn't bursting with life.

It's another month well along in summer, green leaves in the mountain trying on a touch of ochre, the beefsteak tomatoes teasing with fringes of bright red. Fred and Roxie have tackled the garden, agreeably harvesting heads of broccoli, snatching up a young zucchini before it bloats into a submarine overnight.

They frolic in the pond knowing time there is short. On the odd occasion of a chilly evening Fred has fired up the woodstove. Fred is now installed in the cabin with periodic forays to paint at his place. He flails away at one oil after another but no one work is actually finished. "All part of a process," Roxie reassures. He knows his painting, in truth, is on the back burner. Time with Roxie is foremost. Taking cues from her, he is not thinking of what lies ahead. She herself has set aside her talk of selling the homestead and moving into much simpler quarters. Both of them speak their minds but each of them seems to him-or-herself to be skirting topics of the future, a no-fly-zone of sorts. Life is to be celebrated for the here-and-now, the essence of her slant on Zen which for Fred is contagious.

As such, Fred is presently selecting a tunic for Roxie approaching their pre-dinner soiree as she showers. Roxie re-enters the bedroom, her big towel a sarong.

"I call them my glad rags," she remarks of the shimmering tunic. "I really did love once upon a time to dress up."

"This one's enormous," he says of a brilliant blue wrap marbled with tiny gemstones plus bits of mirror or glass.

"One of Mama Milly's own she sent me years after. A man could wear that."

"No way."

"Which gender, my dear, dons the vibrant colors in the wild? Humm? The he-cock or the she-cock?"

"He who struts. I get it."

"So why have we, measly mankind at least in this day and age, thwarted nature?"

"I know, I know," Fred says, a tad exasperated. "We men turn you women into Barbie dolls, ornaments for our amusement, so the concubines have to force-feed their feet into binders, pluck hair, paint faces every-which-way..."

"Put it on," says Roxie squirreled upright on the bed. "Take off your things. C'mon."

Fred scowls. "I was just making a point, my dear. I may be so 'before your time' as you say but I was raised with feminists. Cornell was not a boys' club."

"Maybe so. But you're not man enough to switch roles? And what's wrong with a man acting feminine and vice-versa? Remember Leonardo's 'John the Baptist' and 'Bacchus' with their wily, androgynous smiles? Anima, animus, we're all drawn, Fred dear, from the collective unconscious."

Fred while agreeing with her intellectually doesn't do a damn thing for his getting into this rig.

She gets up and fumbles among her plastic jewelry. "These, too." She thrusts at him a necklace and pendant of brass big as a breastplate. "It wasn't just Nefertiti who was bejeweled."

"That was in the pharaoh's tomb. After he was dead. To get buried with his gold."

"Why are you sweating, sweetheart? Because you know I'm serious. If you want more nookie in a few minutes..."

With that he can't argue. He strips down, to humor her, heaving the exhale of a snorting bull. She helps slide the sparkling cobalt chemise over his raised arms and he wiggles on in. He spread-eagles his arms like Christ on the cross. "Satisfied?"

"Not yet. Sit on the edge of the bed." She places over his head the brass necklace, dazzling in the late afternoon light. She picks out rings, sized for her thumb but just making it onto his pinkies.

"Now what?"

She scrounges through another floor pile of bright fabrics. More like a towel, she stretches the yellow-and-black, faux tiger-skin scarf good and wide, folds it once and again as he follows her, spellbound, slumped, no longer taking part in this zaniness, just bearing witness. She wraps the material around his face, nudges it upwards so he can see, finally twists and tucks it like a huge spiral of soft ice cream.

"No Turk without his turban!" Roxie cries. "Stand up, onto the porch."

"The chipmunks will be scared halfway into the woods."

"Wait!" She fetches something from her feminine toolbox.

"*Lipstick!*" he shouts.

"You've come this far, darling. What's a little icing on the cake?"

"C'mon, Roxie. What if Hank shows up?"

"We'll tell him you're rehearsing for Halloween."

She leads him by the hand and out into a rocker. Roxie skips into the kitchen and returns with jelly jars of jug wine, it normally being Fred's job to serve them both when they hunker down for their Happy Hour, to take stock of each other and another fine day.

"What about the nookie?" he groans.

"Let's just say this one's my turn, but who's keeping track?" Roxie says, her grin to him a mile wide.

Chapter 16

ROXIE AND FRED

ROXIE ASSUMES IT IS NOW AUTUMN. THE browning of leaves and vines in the garden tell her so. It's been years since she's followed a calendar, although this particular day is of note. Before Fred returns from his errands and painting in his home studio, Roxie is putting finishing touches on her dessert to celebrate the occasion of his birthday, so he reluctantly informed her. In a large bowl she has cut up chunks of dense chocolate cake layered with whipped cream and the richest possible chocolate ice cream and crushed chocolate wafers, coarsely chopped, bits of a Belgian bittersweet chocolate and gobs of sour cream here and there to cut some of the sweetness. She now ladles a chocolate fudge sauce she's warmed up and folds this in as well. She told him she wouldn't fuss. She lied. After all, he's turning fifty today.

Roxie covers and slides the bowl into the fridge. She sits for a spell at the table, more tired from the effort than she would expect. Is he tiring me? she wonders idly fingering a teaspoon. So much merriment or simply togetherness have invaded her system like the most welcome of guests, but still a stretch. She has lived for so long on her own, requiring a minimum of propulsive energy. Just to lay silent with Fred can seem taxing, draining a psychic tank held in reserve for contingencies but now drawn upon every day.

Use it or lose it, isn't that the byword? Fred's age is advancing but not my own? She's never dwelt upon aging until now, saddled atop Fred's thoroughbred.

Fred bustles in, arms loaded with gear and supplies. Roxie does not rise. All the better to kiss the side of her elegant neck, Fred thinks, taking aim. "Thank goodness I rarely check email," he says, unloading foodstuffs onto the butcher-block counter. "But special ones today from the kids, of course, and June. Plus congratulations in my voicemail. The mailbox was crammed with cards. A reminder of how incomplete has been my escape into the woods!"

A computer, Roxie thinks. Emails. Instant access. Anathema. She does have a phone and always should, for emergencies she supposes, but it's really for Fred who keeps contact with his children.

"Did you call Nell and Freddie?" Roxie asks.

"Oh yes. Nell is in orbit with her job and still in groove with her mate. Same for Freddie. It's so freeing for me." He is readying things for his birthday dinner, no different from their usual routine. "What's in that bowl?"

"Don't look, dear. You deserve at least one surprise."

Fred assists Roxie to her feet and enthuses over her selection of an exceptionally festive, long floral dress for the occasion. He leads her to their bed and helps her lift out of the colorful frock. He, too, disrobes and they settle into the mass of pillows, Fred near swallowing

Roxie in his embrace. Her powder-white hair, forever fragrant, nestles under his nose.

They lie still, slowing their breaths. This they can do, have done, for hours, often sleeping entwined like this. Strange it can be, Roxie often thinks, so cuddled with Fred she can retreat into the waters of her calmest cove, Fred's vastness billowing beyond her capacity to visualize it.

Before long, as is his way, Fred kisses the top of Roxie's head and allows his fingers and hips to initiate their journey in slow motion. Ever so gradually he tightens his grip, as if rocking the two of them in a lullaby, neither one the mother or the dozing child. Fred can see them so disposed in retrospect, never in the moment, as now. Still, he senses something odd, as if a third party has intervened.

Fred's large hand feels leaden to Roxie. "I'm fine, sweetheart," she whispers, preventing his hand from lowering below her navel. She proceeds to lead him to arousal and groaning, marshalling her delicate touch the best she can in spite of her singular, sudden loss of stamina. "Flow, dear one, go right ahead and receive my gift. You're the engine for the both of us today."

There have been several killing frosts. The outer leaves of cabbage have curled and blackened, the carrots and beets left in the ground. Fred has spent long days at his easel, painting in his studio upon Roxie's announcement soon after his birthday a few weeks prior.

"It's high time for me to sell this place, Fred," Roxie said lingering over spearmint tea, their mid-afternoon hour of mindless chatter, ordinarily dealing with the weather or the wood supply. "I cannot face another round of root cellaring and weather-stripping the leaking windows, even though you, darling, are doing all the work! Look at me. I'm old…"

"I do look at you, Roxie," he interrupted, "and get near blinded by your glow."

"Yes you are blind," she replied.

"The wheels in you spin so fast it's no wonder you have to meditate. Or try to, with me clunking around."

"Enough with false flattery. You know perfectly well, dear, what I'm trying to say. If it hadn't been for Hank I would have left here ages ago. And then with you, well over a year now, I've simply prolonged the fantasy life of my homestead."

"Relax, Roxie," Fred said, attempting to placate. "I can do it all. I love taking care of us. Of you, I admit, much of the time."

Roxie smiled but shook her head. "How I need your help is to find the warehouse, my next, my final fantasy. I already know of a few possibilities, one an old place converted to studios. One room. One big room, one single space. You can share it with me. Or you can get a unit that's adjacent." Yes my wheels are spinning, Roxie thought, and I'm serious and it is taking every ounce of my fortitude to state all this and watch sweet Fred's face crumple with apprehension.

He brightened. "Yes. And while we're at it I can dispose of that dump of a ranch-house. I am absolutely ready to simplify as well."

Roxie and Fred are going about the business of dealing with a real estate agent. Presently they're in the cabin bedroom as Roxie selects clothes to keep, laying them across the bed, while Fred carries armloads of her rejects, neatly folds them on the kitchen table, and packs them into cardboard boxes. They've agreed all but the most glittery things will be much appreciated donations to the local charity center.

Roxie has one hand wedged into her lower side and bends back. "Goodness, I'm exhausted. Everything takes so much effort. Totally sensible to be making this move!"

"Lie down, Roxie," Fred states quietly.

"Yes, you too," she says and pats the mountain of tasseled and fringed and wildly-patterned pillows, all of which she cannot take to a new abode. "I need to be still and you always help me with that. Darling Fred, my personal tranquilizer."

Fred knows this is not the moment for intimacy. In fact, it's been many weeks since any rollicking love-making. Their yoga is at a standstill, Roxie having avoided the strenuous standing postures in favor of Cobbler's pose and Lion pose, well-grounded on the floor.

They are on their backs, eyes closed, holding hands. To her Fred's hand is enormous, on the verge of hurting her own. To him Roxie's hand is unusually cold.

"For the time being, sweetheart..." she begins.

Already his heartbeat escalates: another pronouncement.

" — I'd like to suggest you practice solo sex. I know, you don't have to tell me once again how much our coupling has opened a multitude of pathways... for you to give and receive...or simply approach an abyss, a vexing or provocative dead-end. For me, too. But you — it's like you're exploring a cave, trapped

in there—forgive me, but it's as if you're discovering
cracks of light. Burst into the open, darling. And don't
rush to orgasm. Or don't orgasm. Play with your toes,
neck, all over. Bring that back to us and we'll see what
delights will follow. Or not." She rolls onto her side
and crawls into the familiar musk of his armpit, folds
into his various limbs as fingers into the perfect, soft
leather glove.

Fred has downshifted from his racing motor of
nerves and blood. Eventually he is deeply breathing as
is this miraculous, fragile woman in his midst, beautiful but fleeting as a hummingbird. To where next? I can
be with her, he thinks, but she will always be hovering
just beyond my reach. It's not her, not Roxie, but what
she embodies. How can something so transformative
at this crossroads of my life be flat-out tortuous as well?

Fred begins a new oil. Two by three feet, not large,
not small, it's the last blank, stretched canvas in his
studio before their move into the Art Factory, the reno-
vated albatross of a shoe manufacturer long since put
out of business by overseas sources.

He's not had a single prospect to buy the ranch-
house but Roxie's cabin and woodland spread sold
the week after it was put on the market to a wide-eyed
young couple with no kids, of course. "Love at first
sight," the girl said of the asparagus bed alone. Roxie
insisted on a price reducing the agent's fee to near negligible, but she didn't want to linger in limbo. The money
was of no concern. The Art Factory was perfection,
Roxie exclaimed, Fred reviewing the sequence of recent
events. Even if the ranch-house doesn't sell, he thinks
today will surely be his final effort in the drab studio.

I'm enjoying this, he tells himself scraping a slap of pure amethyst purple over another, equally brilliant smear of chartreuse. Why has color, real color, eluded me for so long? I'm a control freak, he answers. I'm afraid of commitment. Yes, but with oil nothing's indelible. You can keep changing your mind and your palette, so what's the big deal? This could end up as muted and limp-wristed as your watercolors...

He makes a wide stroke of acid yellow, not listening to himself. Or rambling is essential to keep his mind distracted from monitoring the brushwork with DNA all its own.

No more isolation in this dreadful place. Maybe making it a true studio burdened me with the crap of expectation. Output. He is flailing away, as if it's the first time ever to taste abandonment...to crush to the floor the accelerator of a car with no brakes...

A few hours later it's time to return to Roxie. She's so wiped out from packing, sorting, just thinking and dealing with details as opposed to rocking on the porch. On the other hand, she was planning a long nap to take advantage of his absence. Better not get back too soon, Fred thinks, soaking and cleaning brushes in the "powder room" sink stained a mouse brown as adjunct to his studio.

Sweet Roxie, such upheaval.

The painting is a wrestling match of contradictory colors in search of a theme. But golly it was fun. Maybe it's actually good? Most folks beholding Pollock and the like quip their third-grader makes better art. Think of it as breaking the stranglehold of — what? — whatever's been held in place, making room for the next round of possibilities. Disjointed colors that manage to cohere as a composition...or barely discernible hues that express an emotion while lacking one single line...

Roxie is asleep which Fred half-suspected, and so he tiptoes about the cabin.

She is keeping her eyes closed even though she was aware of him peering into the bedroom. Another few minutes to reflect on the new space she's moving to. How can this be any simpler? A delusion. Fred in tow. The balm of nature no longer beckoning overhead, alive with breeze and birds and happy, fickle clouds, now to be witnessed through a window, a world away. Neighbors. Nattering artists, no less. What is wrong with me? She feels listless as a woman with too many children and no means of support, as if the endless years have borne far too many projects, outpourings, dependents, but, most demanding of all, her onslaught of opinions and ideas. I never could pull the plug, she is thinking. But now I am. Can feel it in my bones, my aching back. This frightens her instead of consoling her, being on the verge of the peace for which she has longed the last few decades of her life. The factory loft is the logical conclusion to the homestead but taunts her as if this place, too, will be transitory instead of her last.

"Roxie, I've fixed some supper. Maybe it will inspire you, the final butternut squash. No more weeding! We get to buy it all from the farmer's market."

"Darling Fred." This is all she says instead of a comment or two by way of response. She slides her knees over the edge of bed, fumbles for her slippers. For a second she is shocked at the thought of her lower frame no longer the trustworthy foundation for her yoga practice let alone for spirited walking, for hiking up the hills. This is a momentary setback, understandable given the weight, psychological and real, required of her to undergo such a massive move.

Fred sets down the salad and soup. "You know, Roxie. I think this meal, one of our last in the cabin, may be the first I've cooked entirely on my own."

"I'm afraid for your sake, Fred, even with yoga I'm sliding down to Corpse pose. Becoming a rag doll."

"So we're mostly cuddling of late. I'm so happy we're together. Starting from scratch, really, in the Art Factory. Damned exciting, Roxie."

"I appreciate your feeling that for us both right now. I'm just so weary."

"And you're not hungry, you poor thing," notes Fred. "Not to worry. If you get truly sluggish I'll fish some of my leftover birthday chocolate bombe out of the freezer. Have to finish it anyway before we move."

As if given permission, Roxie rests the fork on her plate, the spoon in her barely-touched bowl of soup. "It's all delicious," she says feeling a rueful smile force itself for Fred, the least she can do.

Fred too pauses, his hands on the tabletop. It seems he lifts her eyes to his from the force of his gaze.

"Roxie, I love you."

"Oh, Fred, darling. I'm not sure I understand what we say is 'love.' It's sort of like when we've talked ourselves silly about sex. It's all so amorphous." How can I be this cruel? she thinks. Is this bluntness best for his own sake? "I know I've become a part of you, dearest Fred, and you're a part of me. There's such a range of possible connections...I do cherish ours. I do cherish you."

Fred rises, touches his lips to the top of her hair, presses down to the scalp and starts clearing the table. His instinct is to leave stand, unfettered, not only her remarks to honor them, underscore them, leave them unalloyed, but also to accept them as truths for him as well.

Finally Roxie stands and shuffles to Fred's backside at the sink, encircles his waist and squeezes to the extent of her strength.

Anything Fred can do to make the various proceedings less stressful for Roxie he entertains. Winter by the calendar or otherwise has arrived for real. It is one of their final nights in the cabin, made especially cozy with the woodstove at full blast and the extra-thick down-filled comforter hauled into service.

"I've been reading about Tantra," Fred says. "I'm sure you know all about it, Roxie, but I thought it might come into play, at least for me."

"Tantra," says Roxie picturing a referee in their bed, but so what?

"It's much more than sex. It's not far removed from our inhaling each other's breath," Fred says. "And not necessarily orgasm if we're sexual. It's intercourse as soul-gazing. Perhaps it will help me experience sensation head to toe," Fred adds as he gets up from the bed, from their warm, comfortable spooning, and lights four candles he resurrected from the trash. "Please bear with me. I bought some scented ones, too, and this aromatic oil." He returns to her side.

Roxie is amused, hardly annoyed. Fred is Fred, this will not change. He's adorable and she adores him. But this part of her shares the stage with her antagonist that is not negative but neutral. These halves hold each other at bay, no one mood predominant. She floats above all. She wishes this was true for the nausea, not from his meal which she'd hardly touched.

"Our next climax or just yours or just mine, that doesn't matter, could be electric. Roxie I feel every day we've become more merged. Like we are right now. My sharing these thoughts and you taking them in. And then letting them out. It's like my last painting. Being on some layer with no bearing of what is above or beneath. You have paved the way for this, my sweet one. And I know you don't consider yourself enlightened but learning still, still open, which enthralls me all the more." He is running a finger he's dipped in the jasmine-scented oil lightly over her forehead.

Roxie wobbles on the fine line of sleep aided by Fred's soporific voice. She inhales the brew of candles, oil, wax with each breath and always the honeyed-rank odor of Fred, unique to just this man. It is easy, it is dark, as the curtains of her eyelids are drawn for another day. The whites of her eyes are slightly discolored which she can dismiss in the solace of release into his broad, firm arms.

Chapter 17

FRED AND ROXIE

"WE WERE LUCKY TO GET THE LAST PLACE with a wall of windows facing the brook," says Fred gripping knees to his chest, butt planted on the yoga mat.

Roxie nods in the affirmative. She can sit in the Lotus for ages. In fact she doesn't want to move from this centering on her old square area rug. They've finished another hour-plus practice although she cannot call it that, rarely moving from flat on her back, maybe a few seconds lifting her hips in the Bridge. It is Fred now who leads them through the poses, the seated mindful breathing on to vigorous Warriors and Triangles which Fred can maintain for ten breaths, she barely one. They end with motionless postures like a long Child's pose of complete relaxation. That she can handle.

"You doing okay, sweetie?" says Fred. "Holed up like this? No more roaming in the woods from the cabin and now here with two inches of snow."

"The windows are all I need," Roxie says. "And I just close my eyes and poke about anywhere. The rhubarb patch, the woodshed, the meadows…the mountains of Nepal, the Rhodesian veld for that matter." Carefully she rolls back onto her spine, swings her folded knees side to side. No one position relieves the pain for very long.

"I've got to set up my paints," says Fred. "This place is big as a banquet hall."

"I love the empty space," she replies. "Makes me just a speck."

"For me it's oddly expansive. Elbow room to day-dream." He hoists himself up from the floor and goes to the makeshift kitchen, starts the kettle on the hot-plate. They do have a little cook-stove with its oven no bigger than a breadbox, the microwave, the huge tank of bottled water on its stand. They're not slumming it despite the ramshackle former factory with its tall ceiling a crosshatch of rusted ducts, oversized drafty windows, the floorboards croaking loud as the old pond bullfrog with every step.

Roxie is still splayed on her rug. "As a young lady in Boston I had the obligatory ballet lessons in a room like this. And at the girl's academy the boys from the allied prep school would arrive weekly for rehearsing the foxtrot, the waltzes — two feet apart in those days!"

Fred serves them store-bought lemon-ginger tea. He flops on the bed as Roxie resumes the Lotus on her old square of Tibetan carpet. "We didn't skimp on furnishing this place," Fred says, "but, boy, our dressers, the cushy sofa, kitchen table, my easel, it's all so dwarfed. We'll have to share it with a hundred others for emergency shelter if ever there's an earthquake."

"It would be a hurricane, darling."

"What if I painted the ceiling and the riot of pipes and wires, the lot of it, sky blue! You know, like the ceilings of porches on Victorian summer houses?"

"I like it decrepit, dear. I don't stand out."

"Screw you," snaps Fred beaming.

"I wish. Those days, I'm afraid, for us a thing of the past."

"We're practicing Tantra, just without — ecstatic release."

Roxie snickers. "We did have our moments of flash-flooding, at least for you, sweet man."

They sip from their mugs of tea. They fall into silence by mutual consent. Fred regards this habit of theirs as clearing the air, allowing a pause so the weight of the prior subject can filter through without the interference of more words. Prior to Roxie the whole arena of sex for him was pelted with anxiety, unanswerable questions and provocations that nagged and became embedded like canker sores in the brain. Here and now the thought that sex may be relegated to their history is just one more piece in their shared collection of beautiful art, priceless only to them.

Roxie's breath is approaching that calm of a few hours after midnight when all of the earth — plants, animals, air — call a truce in their ongoing scramble of pursuits, herself included. She takes the slightest of sips. Maybe if I don't move a muscle and don't speak, we can prolong this quiet interlude so the pain can be temporarily outwitted.

This is so different from silences with June, Fred is thinking. There, forever a pressure would build, June waiting for me to unload my thoughts as if whatever they contained was of greater import than ideas of her own. She was poised to applaud, support, acquiesce. If I took this as a victory, it was hollow; if as an inadequacy of mine, a reminder of our imbalance from the beginning and I should have known better.

"It's good you've made the appointment. Day after tomorrow?" Roxie inserts into their reverie. "I do lose track of time here in these woods, too."

Fred is relieved that Roxie has apparently blanked out the desultory spread of sagging homes and idle buildings surrounding the factory. To him even the woods across the brook are bone-bleak. Half the trees are decaying on the ground. Any upright evergreens are missing whole sections of limbs and needles like Roxie once described scantily-feathered chickens madly plucking sere, scorched earth in Nepal for a pin-prick of sustenance.

Fred finally addresses Roxie, motionless and ashen as a petite sculpture of Buddha. "The light massage is helping, you say, but the dark urine, the fluid in your middle despite your losing weight...we've waited long enough, dear Roxie." The whites of her eyes are unremittingly yellow. He would be reduced to abject trepidation were if not for Roxie's nonchalance.

"It's the next road to travel," says Roxie. "I find it curious but not of great concern. Physical travails— childbirth, dysentery, literal heartache, whatever I've slogged through, it's all the same. The body does what it must. But the mind? The miseries of the carcass are no match."

Rambunctious Roxie, a mere few months ago! So abrupt it's blocked Fred from taking her inertia for real. He joins her on the floor and assists her onto her back, his belly a cushion for her head. He strokes the glorious sheens of white hair; that will never quit.

"I hope you're thinking about starting another canvas, Fred."

"I'm lying fallow."

"You're fixated on me. As always. Now it's my illness."

"Excuse me? We're in this together."

"Yes and no. Anyway, have you considered that taking up your paints at the other end of our huge hall would please me no end?"

"You win. You always do."

"I should. I'm well versed at getting my way. Others could take it or leave it. The takers, of course, like you, dearest, find the reverse of deferring to me...rather an open door to their own agenda. It's worked for us, has it not? Note the amazing trajectory of your art!"

He bends over and kisses the bridge of her nose. He lifts her into his arms and carries her to their bed. "Time for your nap. I'm going to deal with food. It'll give me a breather from the sage...so I can think about my next painting."

Roxie elevates her still dark, dramatic eyebrows. "But gestate. Don't think. When it happens you'll let it flow."

"Yes, madam. I'm at your beck and call. That's what pleases me."

There is one piece of art on their vast walls, not one of Fred's but the only oil painting Roxie ever did, her agreeing with Fred it could accompany them to the loft. The huge white hand, the tiny black head, the strange beige torso — they remain so troubling to Fred and unresolved.

Returning from the oncologist a few days later, they first stopped at the pharmacy for the various pills he prescribed. Fred lines them up on the small counter. "You can begin this one now but the others at bedtime.

Don't worry about it, sweetheart. I'll keep track." He is acting like a nurse to anesthetize himself, he can see.

"Thank you, Fred dear. But I will do with them as I please. Not quite ready for this infusion."

Fred pauses to restrain his pounce. "The bile duct is blocked, maybe from a blood clot. Maybe a cyst. It's serious, Roxie. We both know that now. No reason not to alleviate the pain."

"For now I'm fine."

He sighs. "It's why the fluid stays in your abdomen. And the swelling in your left leg."

"You sound like a lecture in anatomy class." She gives a little shrug. "That's how I think of all this, too. It's so mechanical. Things I'm observing in a separate being. What's it got to do with me?"

Fred turns his back, must shift gears. "How about we read?" They've taken to picking up one of the precious books she saved from her stacks, Fred reciting aloud to spare Roxie from sitting upright. They settle on the lovely old sofa facing the big window, Roxie engulfed in the squishy pillows and Fred soldier-straight.

"Here's one I've wanted to dig into—several pages with your yellow highlighter." He reads: "Artists extend much further down into the warmth of All Becoming; in them other juices ripen into fruit."

"Freud! Forget it. Yes, it's an old favorite but I've hacked it to death."

He tries again at random from the pile.

"This one's on religion and art, I love it. And look at your pages of notes here!"

"Do with me what you will." She rests her head against his shoulder. "Your voice is so soothing, whatever the words."

He scans the faded sheets. "Now this applies to me. You write and I quote: 'There are no longer the collective formats of ritual and religion, bankrupting artists in a way and forcing them to achieve what's not been done before. If not submitting to an authority, one has to create on one's own.' A familiar theme," Fred says. "At least I quit the church as a boy, got that one right." He pages on. He can't tell if Roxie has fallen asleep; her eyes are closed.

"Primitive art is abstract belief in the soul, not in the concrete gods of higher religions that objectify a god who then becomes the rationale for art. You with me?" She murmurs. Fred continues although he senses, faster than he recites, that the ideas are treading very closely to their present crisis.

"Practicing art like practicing religion is a bid for immortality. Both strategies attempt to ameliorate fear of death."

Roxie lifts her head. "I couldn't agree more. That's why I'm not afraid."

"I know you don't believe in an afterlife, Roxie. Nor do I," says Fred plowing ahead if this is where she wants to go. "But doesn't that exacerbate the issue? Here and now is all there is, and who wants to give it up?"

"I'm not thinking about it, Fred," this said matter-of-factly, Roxie sounding neither friendly nor hostile. "I am enjoying my feet against your thighs and that pool of sunlight warming my legs."

He takes this in, a variation of what Roxie has so often expressed. "Alright," he states, his head and shoulders erect. "So this is it, our brief fling on Earth.

Well, that's a reason I want to be more than earth-worm food. I'm not thinking immortality. What I leave behind. Who cares?"

Now Roxie shifts herself up from slumping on his shoulder. "That's excellent, Fred dear. We do need to do good work. Freud said all that. But despite Darwin — we can't set ourselves apart from all living things, we most certainly do have a special gift. There's a tricky point of balance here. But it's not fear of death or striving for immortality in your case of pursuing art. It's what your bloody good at. Now if you'll please get your rump off this sofa, fix a lovely salad which I'll nibble and you'll devour, so you can get over to that easel this very afternoon. Get about your business, sweetheart. That's what I'm doing."

The snows have arrived in earnest. Even Fred is housebound, having lost interest in occasional treks across the frozen brook. His attempts at tromping through the vacant, dystopian woodlots surrounding the factory featured the crunch of discarded cans and broken bottles underfoot. At least peering through their wall of windows he can slow his heart rate and reduce his worries, prompted by open skies then distracted by the unpredictable, passing clouds. He has started and stopped and started again a new oil painting, but this like the window-gazing is constantly in lockstep with Roxie's distress. Periodically she swallows the litany of pills but increasingly suffers from chills, fever, and generalized pain.

A few weeks later they are again facing the oncologist after Roxie has complied with Fred's pleas to undergo various tests. These she has endured, he knows, for his sake not hers: the computerized tomography or CAT-scans plus a biopsy guiding the needle with ultrasound, hours in a hospital gown as Fred sat stupefied in a nearby lounge.

"The blood test reports a very high level of bilirubin," says the doctor, an eager young man, to Fred delighting in his mastery of this science, who goes on to articulate the first of several findings, paving a path to the dire, logical conclusion, not just in her individual situation but the rock-bottom, fucking order of the universe to which every living soul is inextricably bound.

"You have metastatic pancreatic cancer, Roxie. It has spread to your liver as well. Ordinarily there are options to alleviate pain, but because of your age we have to rule out surgery and resort to chemotherapy as palliative. The tumors are too advanced and disparate at this point. But I assure you both that your discomfort can be mollified if not eliminated."

They drive home in silence which Fred well knows is Roxie's source of comfort first and foremost.

He fixes them tea. Roxie sits tall in the sofa and Fred slouches into a heap.

"I learned as much weeks ago on the Internet," Fred says in a monotone. "Delving into this seemed more pressing for me than you."

"You should have told me. Better you than him."

"I'm sorry, Roxie. I—I was probably trying to…"

She puts her hand atop his. "That's fine, darling. We do what we need to do for ourselves. Then we can better help others."

"You make it sound so normal!" he near shouts.

"It is. I've known for months likely something

insidious was at hand."

Fred explodes. "It's rotten! I hate it. This is us not just you." His voice catches but he goes on. "I'm not ready to lose you, Roxie."

"You'll be fine when the time comes. But I am ready, dear one. Have been for years and years."

"I know. You're way ahead of me on all fronts," Fred says bitterly. "It's been your mission. You're ready. Well I'm fucking not."

Roxie slackens her shoulders but remains upright.

Fred realizes he is crushing her hand and relinquishes it, no need to apologize. "Of course I'm enraged."

"It will pass. Goodness, I was angry for most of my life. But now, not over this."

Fred drops his head into his hands. He cannot dam the tears. "I know," he utters, "you'll say this is all good, all part of the process."

"Please listen, my dear, I'm not going to move on until you, too, are ready. I wouldn't leave until you can let go."

Fred swivels his head about and glares at her. "What the hell is that supposed to mean?"

"It means, very simply, that there is no way I will undergo chemotherapy, morphine, tubes, hospital beds, beleaguered or insensate nurses and do-gooder staff. None of it. Darling Fred, do you really believe I'm capable of leave-taking other than when I and you have arrived at that time?"

"Not even painkillers?"

"It's not so bad now that I know officially. I can live with it. It won't be for long."

"Roxie...oh Roxie. Why should you be tending

me? This is insane, I'm such a dunce."

She takes up his big hand in both of hers. "Whatever unfolds for you, dear Fred, we're holding hands, going forward together. When my hands no longer work, well, we have our hearts."

Again Fred's head drops, chin to chest. He wipes his eyes. "I can't imagine my life lasting long enough to absorb let alone be guided by all you've taught me. I feel so undeserving, to bear witness right now. It's excruciating and yet a privilege."

"It has indeed been a union. And every smidgeon of what you take from me you must understand is returned to me in equal armloads. Now. However you operate that high-tech gimmick that makes music, put some on, sweetheart. Take me back to my debutante ball, in the grip of one dashing and handsome lad after another, no chance to open his mouth and ruin the illusion."

This he can do. Fred grapples with his iPad and soon the dreary factory walls, browns darkened with black as if incinerated at one time, are reverberating with — yes — Strauss!

He swoops her up. "Just step on my feet, Roxie, you're such a wisp. Clasp your fingers around my neck, don't worry if you can't, I'm holding you almost in the air." He's cinching her waist, he's doing it all.

Fred dips her and whirls her in dizzying circles. Her eyes are clenched shut but he can read the violent pulsing at her temples, her grinning like a hyena, her head thrown back on her lithe swan of a neck. The melodic, sugary waltz blasts on and on as if there's no end, just the two of them welded as one in the pillar of Fred's upright ox of a body, Roxie no more than a mere appendage.

"Oh look at us, Roxie. Pressed together, groin and guts, not two feet apart! What would your chaperones say to that?"

Soon enough they are collapsed side-by-side on the sofa, loosely holding hands. It's another of their silences, not pregnant with much unsaid that needs airing but rather a settling-down, like sprinters tripping in circles right after the race, dazed, whether having won or lost, it's over and done with.

"It's not death to be afraid of," says Roxie to begin again their wading into the swamp. "It's dying. In death one doesn't exist. Dying, that's something else. That's what's dreadful."

"Oh my dear Roxie," Fred responds, lifting and kissing the back of her hand. "You make it sound so—everyday."

"Well, darling, I'm not dying yet and I'm not going to. I'll be damned if I'll put up with any of that nonsense. Is all this sinking in…what happens next, legal or otherwise, with you at my side?"

"Yes," Fred says listlessly and senses that a smattering of her words, with or without his compliance, have wormed their way into his viscera with the stealth of a cancer cell, singular, lethal, and unseen.

Chapter 18

ROXIE AND FRED

As Fred goes through the motions of painting, many weeks now on the same canvas, he assumes Roxie is waiting, waiting for the right time. He has procured the recommended dose of Nembutal from Mexico; it was quite matter-of-fact; she is not the first. He knows her well enough to be convinced that what is calming her right now is not the resolution of conflict within her but his commitment to this painting, his largest ever, six feet square.

Roxie is propped up in their bed and facing the big window, her thoughts, such as they are, directed by the sky and its kaleidoscope of color, its indeterminate moods. It's as if I am painting along with Fred, she thinks, although it needn't ever be finished. It also occurs that she is using the configuration of clouds as a mandala, an anchor. Often she closes her eyes. The world then is utterly still while so expanded, diminishing her significance. The highlight of her day is Fred ending his at his easel and rolling it over the squeaking floorboards to her bedside. She has tried to take a mental snapshot of the painting after the prior session to compare it to what is presented twenty-four hours later. Usually she is startled by a total change of direction but sometimes she has no reaction, at which Fred declares, for example, the elimination of the former meddlesome edge of dark in the lower left and how thoroughly relieved he is. She smiles, she hopes not wanly, to second the motion but says nothing.

She can tell that Fred is not completely absorbed by his painting. Too often he will refresh her tea and too soon after replenishing her ice-water he will sit quietly by her side, claiming he needs a break from his aching wrist, which she takes as a loving fib.

For hours she lies still and savors the fact that Fred for the most part understands he needn't make idle banter to amuse or distract her, while at the same time he so reinforces her deep satisfaction at his very presence. No, most souls do not want to take the last steps entirely on their own; the final step, yes of course, but the watchful eyes of loved ones surely pave the way. Rose petals thrown upon the retreating bride, families madly waving and blowing kisses as soldiers board the planes. She has kept herself ample company for the second half of her life. What a marvelous surprise to be relieved of that, far more for the opportunity to care for this dear man than any need of her own to be the revered.

As Fred strokes and dabs away on his canvas he thinks increasingly of his children. What will I do when she's gone? the question plagues him, and often Nell and Freddie fill the void. The painting-in-progress commands him each morning to plot a near-military campaign. Yes there is a kind of general residing within and hurling orders, but Fred primarily identifies as a grunt in the trench. He likes to be told what to do. The present composition is way too centered and lacking that critical off-balance to keep the eyes in motion. This ratty gray may be boring but that slice of icy copper overwhelms the enticing subtlety — the lime-gray ebbing to interesting ivory — that does work. No! barks the leering general. You've fallen in love with that billowing mass of variegated grays. Time for the whole business to go.

Roxie's forearms have yellowed as much as the whites of her eyes. Fred will remark of this now and then without thinking or in a moment of weakness. She hasn't looked in the mirror in ages, even brushing her hair. Yes I can see the yellow but I cannot feel much pain. She decided to take the painkillers. She wants her leave-taking to be a gradual unfolding of the inevitable, not a bumpy road of petty crises. She cannot proceed without Fred. He paints and I fill my soul with one abundance after another to near bursting. A tender response from the Tibetan child whose neglectful mother was deadened by the drowning of her baby girl. A squeeze from the black single mother of five in Boston, her embrace near suffocating Roxie at news of the woman's acceptance as a legal secretary. Mama Milly adopting this lunatic white girl as one of her own. On her father's knee, him finishing the story and making the driver wait an extra minute before his being rushed to operate on his fourth cardiac patient of the day, or night. She often thinks of herself as the globe, a composite of so many tongues but completely whole. Over this she roams, one vision to the next, when the sky and clouds, her habitual media of release, are periodically at rest.

Fred nibbles now and then. They no longer share

meals. To him he is fully occupied. Between his canvas and care of Roxie he is devoid of decisions. Somehow the eerie and unspeakable have become quotidian, like a blind person focused on the remaining senses, forgetting the absence of sight, the pernicious condition its cause.

The window-wall is presently dimming but daily stretching illumination as winter hints at loosening its hammerlock. Roxie stirs from her memories and readies herself for Fred, to review his day's work, honor his accomplishments if that's what they are for him, or empathize with his disgruntlement, more often the case.

"Let me see, darling," she says without craning her neck; that would invite a stab of pain.

Fred stands aside his easel, blank expression like a presenter at an auction house, neutered so as not to obtrude upon the art.

Roxie can read him nevertheless. He's standing boyishly tall without a trace of slouching, the posture that usually claims him so he doesn't overpower people with his towering height.

"There's a blush of rose, I don't remember that, dear." She's usually silent and nods up or down in sync with his signals, but not today. He's determined to elicit her reactions. "It's beautiful, every conceivable shade of gray but it cannot keep a lid on—what?—a teasing effervescence. The pearly tones. Delicious."

Fred beams. "I've stopped fighting the beauty. At least with this round. Up to now it's been all bruises."

"Mine," says Roxie.

Fred doesn't disagree. "Mine, too. But a dozen shades of gray…can it hold together? So often I wind up with a milky blend and forego — a punch, a purpose!"

"Don't undervalue non-assertiveness, Fred. God knows we've got overdoses of the opposite. If your art is a reflection of you, it's real."

"Oh Roxie, you just love me. Whoops. Adore me."

"I can see you're pleased with this painting. For the moment. Now roll the easel away. It's time for me to indulge in watching you sipping some wine."

Fred returns to her, scowling. Wine for him, more tea for her.

"Don't fret, darling, I've had my fill...Champagne to rot-gut. Whoever knows those gallons of African moonshine I downed with Amos. I should know since it got me pregnant. But the fresh ginger tea you're making for me. Bliss."

Fred climbs onto the bed, the two of them basking in the amber twilight filling the loft. He pulls back the coverlet and runs fingers lightly over her horribly swollen ankles. They appear all the more grotesque relative to her attenuated frame from weight loss. Her cheekbones are more pronounced than ever, exaggerating the aristocracy of her roots.

Roxie chooses not to dwell on her advancing abnormalities. She cannot relish Fred's touch just now with the numbing around her ankles in particular. Instead she fills her heart with his sweet attention. Have all his loved ones been this fortunate? she wonders. Have I been singled out? She thinks not. She suspects his family and other relationships have had outpourings of kindness from his man but, unlike with her, they had to compete with the usual onslaught of emotions, obligations, Fred or any breadwinner for that matter manning a life raft and hauling onto the rocking little rubber boat one burden after another.

"Sit back now, dear, and relax," says Roxie.

"You've seemed fine today," Fred says.

She almost utters "considering" but checks herself. Of course everything he communicates, spoken or otherwise, is an honest, open acknowledgment of her life now. She inhales deeply.

"Today I let myself wax and wane with the birds in that ever-turbulent sky," she says. "I'm just along for the ride. That's always been the case. I'd think I was masterminding this or that or him or her, but not really. I was a passenger like everyone else. I have no option thinking otherwise at this juncture. But still. Very freeing."

Fred nods, releases her hands, cups his mug of wine. This sure is not true for me, he reacts, but is for her and that's what counts.

"Death," continues Roxie, "is such a physical thing. I've always been more physical than mental, so oddly this helps. It's the idea of death, the compulsion to imagine it, that infuses it with horror, outrage at the least. Since no one of us living has experienced death in the flesh, why should we enthrone it on a pedestal that looms over all? Honestly, truly, my dearest Fred, I don't think it's worth the worry. Death is overrated, a monster with no fangs."

"You're so incredibly alive, Roxie. It's unbelievable if I weren't here to watch and listen."

"Ah, the advantage of being old! I'm no longer in the business of wanting. Wanting life too much just enhances the terror of letting go."

"You've been talking like this since I've known you."

"Now it's for real, not hypothetical."

They let this conversation fade. It will resurface another time, another day, and for Fred at least it's essential. It's for me she says these things, he reminds himself, but no longer labels this as a flaw. In spite of the passing of his parents, he's a novice at confronting loss of life.

Roxie pinches together all the muscles of her face in consternation. "You know, I've thought I could be missing out on a semi-spiritual, numinous..." She tosses hands in the air. "...vision, some fantastic revelation if I were to carry on with ever-heavier drugs. Some midpoint between dream state and reality. But I've done nothing but lose my mind for years in the woods, staring at a tree until there's no difference between the tip of the leaf and the crust of the bark. How much more do I need to learn or experience? But bottom-line, darling, a 'peaceful death' to me, as you would say, is bullshit. Saturated with chemicals? More like being sterilized in a lab."

Her breathing slows once again after what she acknowledges has been a gale-force of expenditure with all that talk. The pain is negligible when every part of her is still, the plane on automatic pilot, a gull gliding over the sea. She lowers her eyelids and rests a hand on Fred's forearm.

The ringing phone causes them both to jerk, spilling liquid into their laps.

Fred leaps up. It could only be Freddie or Nell, possibly June on a rare occasion. He answers and soon hands the receiver to Roxie, she startled by his face drained of color, his mouth an open void.

"It's your daughter," he says. "It's Abigail."

Without missing a beat, Roxie exclaims: "Hello Abby, my dear. It's a shock but not a surprise. I suppose I knew in my bones that someday..."

"Outside of Cleveland—yes, lovely rolling land—that, too, is no srurprise. Horse country!"

Roxie listens, smiling, nodding. I should leave, Fred thinks, but where would I go? She could be faking it...she could pass out from such a blow! Her daughter, out of the blue, after a lifetime?

"Oh, yes, those papers from your father's estate I had to sign, goodness, after all this time..."

"My whereabouts—yes, the computer I'm told does it all..." She pauses at length.

"No, I'm fine, please tell me about you, dearest Abby, I'm sorry, Abigail."

Several minutes transpire, Roxie pressing the phone to an ear, listening intently.

"Oh I've not really noticed, Abigail, I can't keep track of the years let alone the days of the month."

She inserts fragments into what is apparently a monologue from her daughter. "Yes I still manage on my own. Well. I do have a wonderful companion, Fred. He's my savior...no longer that address in the sticks, I'm back in the city, almost near your spawning grounds...no, not there, goodness, those mansions of the past..."

Despite these bits of animated conversation on Roxie's part she begins coughing, soon near choking, and hands the receiver to Fred.

"She'll be right with you, Abigail. I'm getting her a sip of water." He does so.

Roxie has fallen back into pillows but remains mostly propped up. She clears her throat and picks up the phone. At this point Fred retreats to the stool of his easel, the least he can do as a bid for privacy.

"Actually I'm quite well, Abigail, although I'm dealing with an illness." Bit by bit she elaborates, obvious to Fred she is being grilled.

"Oh, that's not necessary..."

"Your children are — where, after college?"

"No, please..." Roxie is now flat on her back.

"Of course. Of course, Abby, if you insist..."

"Oh it's been a lovely day...we celebrate each one, Fred and me..."

"He can give you the details, you have the phone number, he'll get yours, our address will surprise you I'm afraid, not the proper part of town..."

"Of course it doesn't matter — thank you, thank you again, my dear, for..." and Roxie lets her voice creep to barely audible as she rides out the conversation, receives the barrage from the other end, the voice not recognizable but the steeliness, the assertiveness, those have not changed. Abby is from that other family of which Roxie was never a part.

"It would be cruel not to let her visit," Roxie manages later when Fred serves her fresh green tea.

He remains silent, the best he can do to support her pass through this fury.

"I always knew Abby would seek me out when it suited her. That's the hand I dealt her. You're-on-your-own. But she became my iron-fisted mother-in-law by age twelve, she did grab hold of that proxy. She needs something, to forgive me I suppose, to feel a tad better about herself. Abby declined my many bids to stay in touch. I wanted closure, she wanted to keep that noose around my neck." The tea is soothing, yes, purportedly an anti-oxidant or anti-carcinogen or some such according to dear Fred, he can't help himself. But she's preoccupied with her daughter and not the pain.

"She's in Cleveland?"

"Adelaide Hills. The most exclusive enclave there, I know them all from my prep school days. No question Abby's a society woman just like Harold's mother who presided and my own mother who pretended. I was out-numbered as a role model, even when I tried. In fact my dropping all that mock-motherhood hardly infuriated Abby. I always figured it propelled her to my opposite which suited her to a tee. Oh, you know this sad story, my dear. Why repeat it?"

"Because we're going to be hosting Abigail, I gather. Oh Roxie, she needs to say goodbye. You told her it was pancreatic cancer. Everyone knows that's incurable. If you say she's all protocol, this visit has to happen. And you don't know. Maybe she's got a warm heart. She does in fact share your DNA." Fred says this but his wits are splintering with confusion, even anger at this assault into their lives. "Roxie. This is not what you've wanted. It's like you and I are on a ship. It's already sailed." Shut up, Fred, he tells himself.

"It's not what I've wanted. But that is changing. It's what Abby wants. Her needs are greater than mine, darling. I have everything in the world with you. What difference, ultimately, is this going to make for me? She will come and go. Perhaps it's a gift of grace for me. I can look in her eyes and I can say goodbye to her. To a woman I don't really know but she does own a slice of me. She is that, I can't deny. Who's to say her wiliness as a child didn't work to solidify me at the time?

This could make amends for the wreckage I caused, the loved ones upended, Harold above all, the poor sot? At least Abby was a little tigress in the making. She let me off the hook in her way. I didn't mind her hatred. I knew that would soften, someday. I just never suspected it would take this long."

Fred gently lays hands on her distended ankles. He knows they are numb but he's the supplicant at her disposal. His sole desire is to empower her in this, likely her final challenge in life, to let it not be turmoil and rudely counterproductive. I do belong if not as blood relation, he reassures himself. Roxie said it herself explaining him upfront on the phone. They are every bit a couple in her eyes; for him it's never been in question.

Fred leaves her on the bed to fix some food for himself, re-heat a half-cup of miso soup for Roxie. The loft has been swallowed in shadows, the window glass gone blank and obsidian. He tidies things up, about to strip down to his boxers for some time on the yoga mat. This will allow Roxie to continue collecting herself, correcting her course over the formerly still pond abruptly whipped into a whirlpool.

"It was sweet of her," Roxie whispers. "She wants to take care of me, even if briefly. Seek approval as any child does, and should, and move on. She can tell me of her career as a remarkable mother, likely a wonderful wife and formidable member of her community. It's her only opportunity to have me proud of her. She may even need to apologize for abandoning me as I did her. I'm beyond apologizing to her and she knows that. But maybe she feels remiss to have lorded over me her superiority for so long."

Fred has come back to sitting by her side. "It's complicated," he says.

"Always. That's why I've tried not to cling to any one mode for explanation. At best I'm a filter letting it through. It took me forever, darling, to accept this as freeing instead of gratified for being right or punished for being wrong. All of it, at the end of the day, is trifling. And I am at the end."

By not replying Fred agrees. And then something erupts which he cannot suppress.

"But Roxie, why now? How come Abigail suddenly came out of hiding? She could know nothing of your illness."

Roxie smiles and tilts her mop of white hair, strands glistening with silver highlights in the rising quarter moon. "Serves me right," says Roxie, "heedless of a calendar. Today would be something out of the ordinary for most folks, but not for us, at least for me with you."

"It's—it's your birthday," says Fred. "Abigail would know that."

Roxie nods yes.

"But why this one and after all these decades?"

"I'm turning ninety. Today."

Fred jackknifes up from the bed, clumsily steps back, near tripping on the yoga mat. "No way. You can't be." His tongue refuses to make sounds. He tries again. "I figured late seventies, alright, maybe early eighties. This is the truth?"

Now it's Roxie's silence that answers in the affirmative.

"We are forty years apart?"

"Why should you be surprised? Our coupling has

been anything but conventional. We've gone back in time like cavemen, darling, where drawings gave voice to the world, where first mutterings and grunts couldn't even come close. Has art as the deepest source of expression ever gone out of fashion?"

He smiles with effort to bypass some inadvertently smarmy, oleaginous comment that would cloak his state of shock.

"We met over drawings," Roxie continues. "And then we devised a language all our own." She pauses, observing the fog of doubt glazing Fred's dewy eyes. "A little time with Abby will be fine, dear one. Nothing to do with us."

Chapter 19

ROXIE

S HE DOESN'T UNDERSTAND WHY HER STRENGTH IS not waning but holding steady after these many weeks. Fred says it's due to my lifelong habit of exercise, Roxie recalls, my light "Mediterranean" diet and all those sensible things. He also claims that her pure WASP genes go back to the first Pilgrims of Massachusetts. Although their own stock wound up as the aristocracy they fled, he says, those early Puritans had gumption and fortitude to risk their lives and start from scratch. Maybe she's just holding out for Abigail. Roxie can tell Fred is squeamish about Abby and this turn of events, however he's straining not to say a word. Well I can't tend his feelings, she decides, observing him at his easel with a heightened intensity. I can't let anyone, even Fred, distract me from progressing on my path. No second chances at that.

Roxie has noted that Fred straightened up the loft in anticipation of Abby's visit. A bench of sorts he's using for various cans and brushes has been angled with the sofa to make a sitting area. He has re-organized her medications in the tiny bathroom instead of their being broadcast bedside. He helped her select one of her few remaining festive shifts. She's still mobile enough to tend herself in the bathroom, to shower, to groom her hair and nails, to stand tall if she must on occasion, and this certainly will be one. I may be dying, Roxie thinks, but I am not on my deathbed. Yes Abby is coming to say goodbye, but no reason not to entertain this series of visits, hopefully short-lived, as a way for her to welcome me into her life. Mustn't that be what she wants? How can I take stock of my own life if not for its addressing others? I was consumed by attempting to relieve abuse or ignorance or starvation I could only imagine with those scores of frightful women. Otherwise I've been on my own—selfish, self-protecting, self-empowering, what difference does it make? Manny and I were the ultimate playmates, bless that sweet man. But the love that Fred enshrines in a chalice I've not shared with one other soul. That can make me an outcast, in my mind. However I must have clung to some notion or other of love that did include me, because I was alive and alert and breathing the same air as my men. Of course there was Mama Milly...

Roxie faces the window-wall as usual, but the flow of her thoughts on this occasion glosses over the play of wind whipping branches into vibration, inviting her attention to no avail.

My dear Fred, Roxie is mulling, him with the comportment of a giant even in their vast loft. Abby could keep me from dwelling upon Fred. I need him more than ever but worry about him on his own apart from our nest. Will he soar? Will he sour? For Roxie there is no more agenda. Her mind was made up the minute of her diagnosis. I will not prolong this for another "three to six months" with the host of attendant miseries, the endless tests and tedious consultations. She is ready when everyone else is. There are the doctors; it's not only Fred and now her daughter. And then the few neighbors at the Factory here who've been incredibly kind — mostly feeding Fred — but it's still a nuisance. I came here to simplify. The truth is, Roxie admits to herself, I miss the woods. The woods before Fred. How are the birds and Sammie and the chipmunks surviving the long winter? Appalling that I made them so dependent! Or, Roxie reflects, was it more likely the reverse?

Fred is out shopping. He insists on small sandwiches and snacks when Abby comes "for tea." He can't help wanting to make the meeting casual when it's obviously momentous, almost more so for Fred, Roxie thinks. She insisted he get bottles of Scotch, gin, and vodka to augment his half-gallon of bourbon, which he's been nicking at increasingly. He if not Abby may need to loosen up if the visit extends to Happy Hour, heaven forbid. An Ohio matron, Roxie judges, could be terribly Republican, especially Abigail raised by those capitalists without shame.

She snickers to herself, her mood lightened by her long-dormant rascally streak. Or maybe it's because of the threadbare trees across the brook tinged with tiny chartreuse buds. She wishes she could yank open the windows and at least hear the gushing brook unplugged of its stranglehold of ice.

She continues to file her fingernails and shape the moons. Her toes she must submit to Fred. This infuriates her. She rests the file and wooden cuticle pusher in her lap; Fred likes her sitting on the sofa rather than slouched in bed. It's uncomfortable but another way to please him, another of the host of minutia she employs to disengage, the owl perched and peering down, never one to fly in a flock.

This is no different than my entire life of putting myself at the disposal of others, she thinks. But this I realized even then was my survival strategy to covertly take command. For decades, she was heaped with encomiums of appreciation, praise to the hilt. "Oh Roxie, you are a saint for commuting through the horrible city winter sludge to the ghetto and those god-forsaken women!" Little did the society ladies know her career took shape so she could escape from them! I was no saint. Not for near-dying in Nepal, not in my desperation after that, fleeing to Africa. Not for leaving there my two-year-old baby son. Not for walking out on my daughter on the cusp of her traumatic teen years to salvage my own sanity.

Why doesn't anyone believe my side of the story? Manny wouldn't hear of it. Fred is too infatuated, still, sculpting me like a statue of Diana in response to his own peripatetic course.

Abby is another thing. How should I know? If it's not anger up her sleeve — understandable, what is?

A few mornings later their buzzer rings exactly at ten-thirty, the appointed time. Fred descends the stairs to greet her as Roxie rises from the sofa and leans against its backside. Invalids can still be erect. She's wearing a rather dashing violet dress, Fred forbidding her to be in her bathrobe. The long dress conceals her terribly swollen ankles. She has compromised with her slippers; perhaps on his she outfoxed him. Roxie is calm as ever but considers this odd given the circumstance.

I've become that numb?

"Rosa — I should say Mother!" The woman bursts in ahead of Fred and rushes to Roxie. She doesn't attempt to hug, thank goodness, but grips Roxie's shoulders and lets go, sensing their fragility. Her thick, ash-blond hair is stylishly layered, not just shoulder length but somehow feathered into an intricate helmet Roxie once could only picture on a movie star but is now likely pedestrian.

"Abby," says Roxie softly. "Abigail. Forgive me." Abby is broadly beaming. Roxie regards her with the pluck of a double-breasted Salvation Army bell-ringer assaulting holiday shoppers.

"You were always beautiful, Ros..."

"Call me Roxie."

Abby sighs. "No. I'm calling you Mother. For now. Of course you were Rosamund to the family. Daddy didn't mind my referring to you as Mother for years but never in his parents' presence. You were this woman, off on your own. Not a source of disgrace! Never for them!" She screws her pretty face into a cartoon exaggeration of hauteur. "You were more like a third party. Fine with me by the time I was fifteen or so. God I couldn't tolerate them — Daddy's sisters — Aunt Isobel, Aunt Caroline, Grandmother and Papa and all their rules? Ugh."

"Come sit," says Fred indicating the sofa. Without Abby's likely noticing he steadies Roxie to take her place at Abby's side. He settles himself on the bench, determined to be onlooker.

Abby twists to fully face Roxie and takes up her hands. "I've agonized over this forever. Your hands are so delicate. Such lovely nails." Her eyes are watering.

"I'm fine, Abigail. Been healthy as a horse for ninety years! So my time has come like it does for us all."

"I wanted to honor your wishes when I was a child," manages Abby. "Such a decision for a young mother to make. Oh, your subsequent invitations to check in — I just thought you were being polite."

"Politeness was the law of your land, Abigail. I didn't mind your ignoring me. In fact I thought it was a smart stance on your part, to forge head without falling back on a source of support you had every reason not to trust."

Abby swallows hard. She brightens, clearly her habit. "I have your hair! I'm very sturdy, too."

"I can tell. You're stunning, Abigail. And you're sixty-something."

"Sixty-three. Tennis whenever I can. But mostly I work. Kids are gone. Neil is gone with his trophy wife so I'm on my own, Mother. That scenario sound familiar?"

"Tell me about your children."

"Two girls and a boy. A tax lawyer in Florida, a screenwriter in New York, and head of a Planned Parenthood chapter in northern California. Four grandkids, two more on the way."

"I'm impressed!"

"I miss them and I don't. We talk and text constantly on our smart phones, but, to tell you the truth, after Neil I really am thriving in my way. I'm a realtor and do quite well." She catches her breath.

"You deal with those mansions in Adelaide Hills?" asks Roxie.

"God, no. All the old estates, the golf courses and meadows and woods, one solid block of condos. I live in one. I thank our lucky stars we put the kids through college before Neil blew the last of Daddy's trust funds. We did live high on the hog, Mother, for years, me being clueless about each of Neil's failed schemes, one after the other."

Roxie has no grasp of the wealth of Harold's family and never did. For her it was solely a launch-pad for service to others. Abby, meanwhile, is sitting here in an elegant mauve outfit, polished leather pumps, nary a hint of her reduced station.

"Neil was all talk and no show," Abby rambles on. "He charmed Daddy no end but then again, as you know, Daddy was pathetic as a businessman and mostly hung out at the club, so he and Daddy got on like a house-a-fire. Of course my grandparents were likely grateful Daddy never got his hand on the till. I was so spoiled it never occurred to me to think beyond getting through college and making a good match. I was never a feminist. But it's not too late, yes Mother?"

Abby kicks off her burgundy high heels and tucks legs under her rump.

"Don't you think it's ironic—although you were absent, you eventually became my role model? They despised you, Daddy's lot. Neil, too, in a way. And so I filed you away in some slot—wrongful mother—and then you simply faded from my life. My girls tried to wise me up, that's another whole story, because of course they suspected Neil of philandering. Just like Daddy who never remarried, you know. Why quit the game? Oh and Neil, come to think of it, was also like Harold. A knucklehead with money. Boy, did our kids bolt from Ohio!"

Roxie is fascinated by the saturated red, like glistening blood, painted on her daughter's lips. She wonders if Fred someday would indulge in acrylics instead of his traditional oils if only to achieve a color so brilliant. Synthetic but dazzling. She is also apprehending Abby's diatribe as a virtue. Such a Chatty Cathy diametrically opposed to how Roxie views herself. And so she's individuated from her parents, her mother for sure, and fashioned herself anew.

Fred gets up and offers them tea and nuggets of cheese and simple crackers. This interrupts Abby only momentarily from her runaway narration.

"You know this place could make somebody millions. Look at the bones of this old building." She cranes her neck about, licking her upper lip into an even higher gloss, mascara-lined lashes aflutter. "I admit, the neighborhood's a little dicey but, hey, it's happening everywhere. Poor people shoved further out of the cities so the up-and-comers can doll it up. This place in the suburbs of Cleveland would be solid shops — gourmet dog biscuits, salons, wine bars." She's stretched an arm across the sofa back in Roxie's direction.

"Maybe that will be your next venture as a realtor, dear. You obviously have lived in the fast lane."

She addresses Roxie, as if for the first time. "You're feeling pretty well now, Mother, but the time will come...have you thought about hospice...plus your friend Fred, here, do you already have folks from the visiting nurse association?"

Roxie is peeved at Abby's having seized upon "Mother" as moniker rather than Rosamund, but she lets this go. "Fred is all the help I need, aren't you dear?" she says as they simultaneously sip from their mugs of tea.

"You have a place nearby, Fred?"

"I'm—in the Factory, too." It's Roxie's not his license to elaborate.

"Oh, that's wonderful. I see the easel and all those paintings. So—you're working here instead of your own studio and helping Rosa—Mother?"

"Fred shares the loft with me, Abigail. We live together. We have for almost two years."

Abby looks confused, her dark, unbleached eyebrows pinching together. "I see. Well. You're in good hands." She retracts her arm from the top of the sofa. "So when you need more help, Fred, when Mother needs..."

"Abigail. Fred is all the assistance I could possibly hope for."

"Do you have a family, Fred? I gather you're on your own." Abby looks regal, the realtor wheeling and dealing, perhaps in the manner of her ex-husband but in her case a success.

"I do have a family," says Fred. "And they're on their own but I am not." He hesitates.

Abby tilts her chin upwards, aiming it at Fred.

"I'm with Roxie," he says. "I'm with your mother."

Abby is staying at The Sheffield, an old neighborhood hotel, a genteel dowager long since drained of her former glory. "It's like your Art Factory," says Abby upon leaving their initial visit. "This whole area of the city is so ripe for renewal. The hotel suits my budget just fine, and I'm within walking distance."

Walking distance! This comment indicating she is digging in is akin to Abby's landing from outer space in Roxie's lap. Ever the gentleman, Fred invites her to return the following day but for supper. "It's the least we can do," he says later, "if she's after some kind of closure. She's come all this way for more than these few hours. We should get on with it."

Roxie slips out of the dress and into her bedclothes. Fred plumps and arranges the pillows thinking the two women have just performed in a play for Abby's benefit, hopefully for Roxie's as well.

"I expected a gal from the upper-crust with lockjaw if she was anything like Harold's parents," quips Roxie. "She's turned out a regular girl. Betrayed. Divorced. Maybe a tad belligerent. But fair enough, to survive."

"I think she's an airhead," says Fred.

"You're being unkind. She's had to make her way in the world. Like we all do."

"She's going to foul up the precious last days of your life!" Fred exhorts.

"Darling, they're no more precious than all the rest."

"Yes, but…" Fred stammers.

"She can have her way with me, it's only words, and she can leave fulfilling some driving need. And airhead? I resent that, Fred! Part of me is in her head. She's got moxie, more than I ever did floundering from project to project, man to man."

Fred purses his lips. "And I'm your latest man."

"Well, yes, what's wrong with that, my dear? I'm not entitled, at ninety no less, to have had a history?"

Fred turns to the sink, yanks on the tap, rinses out the mugs.

"You know I've mostly been alone," says Roxie. "Like Abby is now."

"Roxie, if you want to keep to your plan, we will make that happen. If you change your mind in any way, you know that's fine, too. It's whatever you want that matters." He takes a towel and dries the dishes, still addressing the sink.

Abby, in a smart tweed suit for the first visit, dresses down for their next. She greets them in late afternoon in a simple blouse and dark slacks but one wrist armored with a bevy of silver bracelets.

"Cocktails," she chirps, her lips a less threatening light ruby versus the blood-red of before. "Never miss that! Vodka rocks," she adds upon Fred's recitation of his limited selection.

Roxie is planted squarely in bed, facing Fred and Abby on the sofa. She's in her bathrobe and clutching a mug of ginger tea. The small talk lasts about fifteen minutes. Roxie is taking stock of Abby's more relaxed manner on the surface which she assumes is the result of a firm resolve underneath. Once again Fred seems to be moderating the divergent personalities, this time setting a bowl of nuts on the bench and then swirling his pots on the stove, peeking in the oven, refreshing his and Abby's drinks. He's like a chemist in a lab, overly watchful of potentially execrable reactions. Roxie is bemused by this but also unsettled.

"Look, I'll get to the point," says Abby hoisting her glass of liquor mid-air. "We have two hospices in the area — the one in North Carthage farther afield but much, much nicer. God it was so easy to zip around the city in my mini rental car, the directions came back to me in a flash." She takes another healthy slug. "And thanks for mentioning your doctor and his clinic. I found him incredibly thoughtful and courteous. I like that man. He confirmed the prognosis and so we still have leeway, thank God." She drinks again. "I can stay here, of course—and work with my clients by phone and email—they'd be gobbled up otherwise in no time—but at least I can make sure everything here is all set up, the visiting nurses, too. When you need them." She nods to Fred. "I perfectly understand, Mother, why you wouldn't want to endure the bedlam of a hospital, inner-city no less..."

"Abigail," says Roxie. "I'm not electing to undergo chemotherapy. I'm pleased Dr. Rollins explained that to you, along with the bare facts of my cancer being inoperable."

"Yes," says Abby, her voice lowered.

"So a hospital is out of the picture," Roxie continues. "And Fred, as you can see, is wonderfully capable. You can leave knowing all is well."

"I'm not leaving just yet, Mother. And no, I do not think all is well." She sets down her drink. "You are not taking the full complement of drugs Dr. Rollins has recommended. This loft may be chic but the bathroom's inadequate, the place drafty as hell, I don't care if spring is near. You need a nurse, for God's sake, not a nursemaid. Proper nutrition, beef broth, this kitchen's no better than one in a broken-down RV. I'm sorry, Fred, I'm sure you're an excellent companion, but Rosamund is my mother, after all."

Her irritable husband was only half the picture, Roxie thinks before responding with words that will ring hollow, but best to let her daughter assume she is having her way. "Thank you, my dear. I do appreciate you are so concerned."

They manage through Fred's supper of chicken and rice and spinach; what hubris of Abby's to put him down. Little is eaten and less is said. The only thing to end their evening is for Roxie to yield to Abby's requests to visit again the following day but in private, face-to-face, to clear the air.

It's agreed by Roxie and Fred after Abby leaves that she is a storm to weather, and this they will.

They settle into the night, their usual rituals, Fred helping hold the water while Roxie swallows her pills although for this task she does not need assistance. It's more for the touch, Fred's one hand cradling the back of her slender neck. The warmth of his body is ordinarily effusive but not tonight, not given her chill.

"What do you mean, you've signed papers?" Fred explodes after Roxie's and Abby's private meeting. "Roxie!"

"It's fine, dear. You and I have nothing in writing. If it satisfies Abigail, she can go her way. One must have papers, 'the power of attorney,' 'advance directives,' the living will and so much nonsense — even for the hospice. She's determined to commandeer all of this. Oh, darling, let her. It's all she's got of me. This taking hold is her last chance to — to cancel the lack of her forgiveness all our lives, to give me something essential. She said she's always thought my having to leave my boy in Africa left me in a state of pain which I've had to deny in order to carry on. She said that's why I didn't have the wherewithal to nurture her let alone get re-folded into her family. She went on and on, rattled on about her years in therapy, her own guilt at a failed marriage for being preoccupied with a huge chunk of herself that was incomplete. She feels an utter failure. Her children gone not only from her but from each other to the opposite ends of the country. They think of themselves flourishing now without their dysfunctional parents. And so on. Oh Fred, my dear. It's the least I could do to temper the woman. She's a cauldron, poor thing. I'm not really a part of her life and never have been. That we're intersecting like this, at the eleventh hour so to speak, I'm simply a bystander. It's fine. Darling. Look at me. If anything, this is nudging me farther along on my path, of course with your loving support."

Fred is as solemn as she's ever beheld him. As at their most poignant, most crystalline moments, he is silent, letting her speak for them both.

"There's one more thing," says Roxie. "Really it will not affect me any more than Abigail's insinuation into our lives."

She pauses, needs this to sink in for her as well as for Fred.

"Abby's come into possession of volumes of paperwork, boxes of it from Harold's family's final affairs. It's why I had to sign forms from some lawyer in Ohio a year or so back, him representing Abby, which is how she tracked me down. There were files and records of mine from Rhodesia — my being black-listed, details of the baby and his murdered father. Financial statements of arrangements which Harold, bless his heart, continued to have his office oversee on my behalf. Above all there's correspondence with Mama Milly about Amos' welfare, snapshots, oh darling, I dumped it all when I left Harold and Abigail for real. Anyhow, since Abby made contact a few weeks ago with me she did likewise with Amos Sakuto in Harare, Zimbabwe. My son was given Milly's surname as his foster mother or adoptive mother or however it was arranged. And with the Internet and so forth, Abby found him. She told him I've not much longer to live. A father of five, a schoolteacher earning next to nothing, he's fifty-two, believes in the Lord and thinks this is the biggest blessing of his life. 'He is, after all, my step-brother,' Abby said. Oh darling Fred, what's it got to do with me? Twenty or thirty years ago, perhaps. But now?" She rolls into his arms.

Chapter 20

FRED

HE CAN'T IMAGINE PAINTING. HE CAN'T imagine having been painting for the last several months. All that Fred wants is to give his full attention to Roxie even if that means leaving her alone, reading by himself splayed across the sofa... pretending to be absorbed by reading, or painting, or dashing out on errands—pharmacy, grocery, bank—fabrications so as to not intrude.

Presently Fred lowers the book to his lap. He notes Roxie, alert as ever, observing him with a wry smile on her handsome face. Don't all of us look our best, he thinks, when happiness erupts from within, unedited? Yet this is Roxie's habitual mien.

"She'll be here again soon," says Fred. It's been three days, three consecutive visits. Abby has made arrangements with the North Carthage hospice which apparently satisfies the women but not him. He had taken for granted that hospice care could begin at home, their home, here. He trusts Roxie will forestall actually moving to the hospice by keeping to her plan, with Fred's help, well before she becomes so ill.

"It might not be so bad," says Roxie peering at the

windows. "You'll be right there, darling. I can swallow the pills, no one will know. I'm ninety, with terminal cancer. My passing on won't raise any concern."

Fred bolts up. "You make it sound so scripted, Roxie. I'll do whatever you say. But I do not want to be arrested. Nor do you want that. We should stay right here in our loft."

Roxie pauses, as she does to let him reap the full benefit of whatever his opinions, and then says: "Abby reports although they're lovely people, the nurses and all, they're understaffed. They are extremely pleased that you'll be there much of the time. You can even sleep on a cot at my side. Oh, dear one, it won't be for long. Just until Abby achieves her mission and leaves."

Fred attempts a smile. He doesn't want to refute her. Here she sits, upright from the waist as if she's holding the Lotus, collected as a cat. Here I am, bordering on a basket case.

"You seem to be enjoying Abigail's exertions," he says. Fred knows Roxie's being so pleasant is for Abby's benefit, but he also understands she isn't faking it like he is.

"She's like a swarm of birds suddenly swooping in next to me by the pond," Roxie says. "And then she'll take flight. Meanwhile I'll have been quietly sitting by."

A shudder stabs the length of Fred's spine. Soon she'll be taking flight and it will be me staring into space. He has promised himself not to turn maudlin, not to taint any one of their remaining days, hours, seconds with grief before he's entitled. But then he will have to dive into that pool of misery if he is ever to emerge from it and move on.

"Would you like me to read aloud from Thich Nhat

Hanh for a bit?" Fred asks, his eyes opened wide to dry them, to defy a thin wet veil to descend all the way.

"I think not, my dear. Maybe later. Abigail will be enough entertainment for the time being."

Fred does not take her at her word regarding Abby. Roxie has not dismissed this woman outright nor held her aloft. As for him, he's hovering behind a huge wall. Is she shoving me aside? No, he thinks, rising to smooth the blanket over Roxie's lap. Abby is not the issue. It's the space far apart from Roxie about to become the ground on which I have to stand.

"How are you today, Mother?" says Abby poised on the edge of the bed, tightly controlled as a gymnast before she bounds into action.

"I'm just fine, dear. You're a better dose of energy than beef broth."

Abby addresses them both, detailing plans with the hospice. "They agree, it's entirely up to you, and Fred, as to the timing. Meanwhile, a lovely girl named Marybeth will visit and check in on your meds and supplies, answer questions."

Fred looks about the loft, the thick twists of paint on his palette already hardened. Abby and Roxie natter on. It's out of my hands, Fred considers. I've begun the counter-clockwise turn of the vise to let Roxie go, along with my role. Partner reduced to caretaker. Knowing full well his is the cavil of an adolescent only makes it worse.

Abby has been handling her business in Ohio by phone. But she barges in and out at random as if checking in on Roxie is the centrifugal force of her life.

"Amos is arriving next week!" Abby squeals, rushing in unannounced. This reaches Fred's ears like a crack of lightning. Roxie is beaming. Fred can only hope for Roxie's sake that this will be enlivening, all joy, a greeting and goodbye wrapped up and beribboned like the most beautiful possible gift.

Several days later Roxie stands for Amos' arrival with Abby. Roxie's donned earrings and necklaces, found her lipstick and perfume, taken special care with her hair. Abby is babbling non-stop so Roxie can simply smile and allow herself to be engulfed by this man of light-mocha skin. His bald head makes his brilliant white teeth the focal point of his face. Of average build, he is stressing the limits of his ill-fitting, threadbare tight suit. He shakes Fred's hand, clasping it with both of his own, bowing, tears running down his shiny beige cheeks. This is all so bizarre. Roxie seems nonplussed. Fred thinks of diplomats at a foreign consulate in an excess of politeness, this thought a feeble attempt to distance himself. But this is not about him. He goes about fixing tea.

"Yes. I'm a schoolteacher! So is my wife Yeshi! Always we have been," says Amos as they hunker down into their seats. "We have many children besides our own five." He spreads wide his pale palms, totally white to Fred. "I believe you call it home schooling in America. No, no more schools in our district!" Is he genuinely enthusiastic or in overdrive for this occasion?

Roxie slips in a query when Abby, constantly doing the same, catches her breath. Amos is happy to oblige.

"There are no funds from the government. We don't know how the Mugabe regime can become any more corrupt. They just let us wither on the vine. It gets worse and worse! By the time Yeshi and I left our school in Harare there was no paper or pencils or pens. The children wrote lessons in the dust on the floor!"

He wipes his freely sweating forehead. "Oh but Miss Roxie! Christ has given me this visit as the most precious gift! Meeting you will fill me with abundance back home. Proof that God's son on earth truly does offer us salvation!" He is swaying in small circles from the hips. He is panting.

Fred wants to loosen the man's necktie. Amos rushes on, as if this is the first opportunity in his life to reach sympathetic ears.

"The English have all but given up on Zimbabwe for aid…it just goes to the fat cats and Mugabe's mob in Borrowdale Brook—that's the suburb of manicured lawns and big cars and golfing clubs and of course shops fully stocked with beautiful fruits and vegetables…" He heaves a huge sigh.

"You seem a wonderfully happy man," Roxie slips into the recital.

"I am! Our children, all of them in our village, are fed from our own garden! Yeshi and I alternate between teaching in our little school and managing the farm—carrots and pumpkins we market, the parents working in the fields."

"Glory," says Roxie slapping hands together. "That's what we did when you were born in the veld!"

"Mama Milly told me everything about you. Miss Rux she called you. She was my mother, God rest her soul, but you were a spirit-woman in our hamlet. I was special because my revolutionary father Amos was a hero and you, a white goddess from America, we thought of you like we Christians do Christ. How did you do that? I always wondered. A blessed union with my father. Like the Holy Mother the Virgin Mary!" He bellows with laughter and wipes his sweating neck.

"I was no virgin. Your father and Mama Milly knew that."

Abby is holding her tongue, enchanted as Roxie obviously is as well. Amos tells more of his country and his life. Fred puzzles over whether Roxie is enjoying this as mere storytelling or relating to it as a slice of her past. If the latter, isn't it so far gone as to be a fable?

Amos has hands on his knees, rocking back and forth. "I've been so blessed! Mama Milly taught me the finest English which allowed me the higher schooling denied to most. My fellow students, men and women, had to sell their bodies for sex on the side to keep in college but most dropped out. You know Rhodesia used to have the highest standard of education, the highest literacy rate, in all of the Sub-Sahara thanks to the English imperialists, but now? We're the most impoverished. A million children no longer schooled! I'm one of the lucky few, for which I thank God every morning and night. Our bellies are full, our minds are fed, we are Black Africans! We are reclaiming the whole continent one village at a time!"

Now it is Roxie streaming tears. She gets out of bed, her throne of pillows, and walks unsteadily to Amos on the sofa. She taps hands on his shoulders and then leans over to kiss the crown of his glistening head. Fred sees she has put her biggest ring on a thumb, a ring that could no longer fit on the shrinking flesh of her fingers.

There are two more days of Amos before a meeting Abby arranged for him in New York with a foundation providing grants for schooling African orphans. Then he must return home, being indispensable there. He and Abby had affably wrestled to take turns in regaling Roxie with the highlights and heartaches of their lives. A time or two Fred slipped out so they could wander farther afield in the web which connects them. He didn't mind. In fact he appreciated the break. He got lost in a forest of his own making. For a few fleeting hours he had no responsibility for a solid grasp of his bearings, as if Roxie did not exist.

"Thank God for the computer," announces Abby upon Amos' departure. "And my i-phone, of course. I'm dealing with a half-dozen clients, working with a colleague to show a few new listings, so I've got another week." She's already relieved Fred as chef with armloads of take-out. She's done the dishes, scrubbed the bathroom, and wielded laundry to and from the Factory basement facility.

Roxie is looking exhausted and paler than ever after this cumulative onslaught. "Being with Amos was more like a dream," Roxie confided when alone and they climbed into bed the prior night. "At this point I can't fathom that faraway land. I can barely look back and recall my wild African chapter. Amos my lover came and went. Baby Amos was just one more of the miserable children. Mama Milly, she's still vivid. But this grown man? Who is he? How would I know since I'm losing myself? Oh, but that's all for the good, darling," she added to reassure Fred, grazing his arm.

Perhaps she's accepted Abby's leave-of-absence here for whatever Abby's reasons, and can more or less relax, Fred thinks, now, the next day, fussing with sketchbooks, contemplating his unfinished canvases to leave the two women to their chatter at the other end of the loft. Abby calls him for the soup she is serving and then re-ties the bow of Roxie's bathrobe.

The soup temporarily replaces table-talk. Roxie has insisted upon sitting at the table with the two of them. She breaks the silence.

"Fred, dear, I've agreed with Abigail that I should take up residence at the hospice. Next week. I described the visit with Marybeth, the nice young lady, yesterday when you were out. She, too, thinks it's best. You know I haven't needed the nappies but, well, I have had several accidents. Fred, darling, you've taken that in stride. I have as well. But the timing is perfect. I'll be settled in the home before Abigail has to go."

Fred freezes. This turn of events is another of so many he has kept aloft like a juggler without letting any one of them fall. This is the least I can do for my sweet Roxie, he thinks. If this is what she wants.

"We'll use my car," Fred says in the aftermath of acknowledgments to Roxie's declaration. "More comfortable than your rental mini, Abby. You can follow. We'll both be loaded up with Roxie's nightgowns and slippers and what not."

"Just bring the books, darling. We'll need to fill in the gap after Abigail."

"Excuse me, it's Nell on the phone from California," says Fred after their dinner, Roxie again in bed, Abby retired to her hotel. He retreats to his studio end of the loft.

"Oh, no…poor thing…walking cast but still. Of course I'll check in…yes, her Andrew a thing of the past…oh, Nell, I would love it, April, it's been almost a year…no, I know June is fine on her own but she'll love you and April here for that week you can make it…"

He returns to the bedside. "June has broken her ankle. She's doing okay but she can't work for now, and ankles take forever to heal. Mostly, I feel so sorry that her relationship didn't work out."

"Darling, we live in our past, like it or not. June is the mother of your children. June was the first love of your life. You must cheer her up. So you're off for a few hours. I don't think my poor body can absorb much more of your kindness!"

Fred is driving to June's condo but he cannot stop picturing the latest photos of April Nell keeps posting on Facebook. Nell spoon-fed him directions for joining the social media so he is positioned upfront with every drool, every giggle, every mug shot of his flourishing granddaughter. Roxie is right, as always: his firm hold on his past with baby April is helping him survive her absence in the flesh. He misses Nell, both of his children. Even though he and Freddie now text it's not the same as feeding his kid, chewing him out on rare occasion, mostly praising him every year of school until he was out the door. He does not miss June or rather as the two of them were for years before their separation and divorce. Roxie has loomed so large for so long he does not belittle his intimacy with June, other flings before and after, so much as put them in little frames of remembrance, like dusty family photos though outdated still occupying slots on the mantel if not on the nightstand.

"Oh, Fred!" cries June upon his arrival. "You're so sweet, all these casseroles. They'll last me two weeks."

"They're from the store." He sets them on the counter. She's hobbling enough to take it from there. Ex-husbands probably shouldn't open the fridge.

"Sit on the stool for a bit," says June. "Lots easier for me than in a chair with all this boxy—Styrofoam?"

Despite her encumbrance she shuffles with grace. The loose cardigan does not hide the fact that her figure is better than ever. Probably eats like a bird with no husband and kids. No roots showing, she could be ready for another round after her Andrew.

"We're both older, June, but you'll be pretty to your grave."

"No excuse with so much time on my hands."

"You still at the crafts center?"

"Nope. It ended fine with Andrew, very civil, we've gone to the movies, the odd dinner, but, I decided to join a coop studio so I'm learning welding and making silver things. You know, rings, bracelets."

"Is that one?" Fred asks.

June nods and reaches her wrist to Fred.

He holds her wrist and then traces the nubbins and intricate curlicues. "Very Celtic. It's beautiful."

"I've sold two. Actually they're more elaborate. This was my first of this width." She's content, Fred thinks. Ordinarily she'd be blushing at a compliment. But what do I know now is ordinary?

They chat about their boy, about Nell, about her impending visit with April. June suggests a few meals at her place, Nell can cook if she, June, is still disabled. Fred offers to take them all out, April in a highchair, don't all restaurants have those? Maybe Freddie and his girl can join them too, he adds. June asks about the health of his older lady friend he's watching over, and he fills her in some but avoids the big picture, the floundering that lead him to the day he met Roxie. He avoids the trauma he's on the verge of. No, he won't go there.

They exchange a chaste kiss on the lips; it would be rude to do otherwise. June thanks him for the food, for the visit, but not profusely which at first he takes as appropriate, given their relationship, but registers as a slight. What is June, he thinks driving off, other than a geyser of female concern from which I had to flee?

She is no longer that overflowing vessel, he tells himself. And he no longer needs to flee. They are family, after all. My only family, such as it is.

The neighborhood hasn't changed. Suddenly Fred is a world apart from Roxie. He's in no rush to resume the blended family with Abby. Without intention he is driving by the Pilates studio and, a block later, The Green Grocer deli. He jams on the break, executes a U-turn, and swings into the Pilates parking lot.

"Fred!" cries Stratton in her skintight bodysuit, sun-glare yellow but not distracting from her long brown mane, her electrified eyes. "However are you? I've missed you in class!" Her breasts are wider than her slim hips, all of it accentuated by showgirl long legs. Of course she hasn't had babies.

He tells her about his yoga practice but stops there. She tells him about the expansion of the studio next door, knocking down the wall, her instructing others to teach Pilates. He takes in the outlines of her nipples which the miracle of stretch fabric can't possibly conceal.

"Oh it's so good to see you, Fred!" Stratton says and grabs his forearm. "You've lost weight, whew! But you look hardened. Yoga's been a good turn, yes?"

"Want to grab a bite at The Green Grocer if you're free?" he says without forethought.

She checks her watch. "Sure." He senses a restraint in her reply. "Why not?" Old time's sake."

They walk briskly to the deli and order wraps of mostly roughage. Stratton unleashes her ponytail, voluptuous even constrained. Once their orders arrive, Fred begins telling Stratton about Roxie, the whole of their connection, art class to cabin to her cancer. He tells her of his being hopelessly in love, some salacious details of their incredible lovemaking, their living together, the unbelievable fact of Roxie's age.

Fred has only eaten a morsel or two. Stratton is enjoying her lunch, nodding at each turn of Fred's story, signaling neither approval nor shock.

Fred's throat has become desert-dry despite occasional tugs on the straw of his iced verbena tea.

"What about for old time's sake?" he blurts out.

"Huh?" says Stratton, crinkling her delectable nose.

"You know, tumble in the sack sometime. Roxie has taught me a thing or two."

"What's Roxie got to do with it?"

"Well. She's stuffed it into my brain that sex can be for fun. Can sometimes, with some folks, be only for fun. She had that with her main squeeze, Manny. I may be the same for her. Frankly, Stratton, it's hard for me to tell. She's mostly dealing with the end of her beautiful life…"

"Fred. Stop. You're adorable as ever. Maybe even more so, off your rocker. Thanks, but no. You're here with too many strings. True my guy and I split, I know I told you when we ran into each other here. And I'm trying on a few others. But. Hire a whore. No shame in that. Our fling, I really thought you were hot. Even a possibility. But now? No way, cutie." She whips her hair back into the ponytail, picks up his hand, smacks his knuckles with a kiss. "I still think there's a place in your playpen for Pilates." She winks, stands up from the booth, places a ten-dollar bill on the table, and bustles off.

Within a week Roxie is installed in the hospice. Fred had not realized the large supply of diapers Abby had squirreled into the loft. He was grateful for Abby overseeing Roxie's settling in as he simultaneously secured things at the Factory, packaged her medications, bundled more of her clothes than she would now need.

"Please, darling. Straight to Goodwill with the lot of it," Roxie said to his deaf ears. He stuffed a shoebox with every piece of her jewelry but kept it in the trunk of his car. This, along with her fanciest dresses and portfolio of drawings he refused to leave at the cabin and also stashed in the car trunk. One of them had to be sentimental if Roxie seemed incapable of such. Every time Fred thought Roxie was being heroic he had to deny this, heroism implying her death was a sacrifice when he must take her at her word — this being a logical conclusion, in fact a peaceful not a tragic ending.

"For life to be lived, I suppose the dregs of tragedy must be given their due," Roxie had quipped at one point. "But they needn't dominate the play. I didn't make that one up but never forgot it."

At this he tried, unsuccessfully, to chuckle as she did, him relentlessly mired in the blunt fact of losing her while for the moment she was so very much alive.

She is not in serious pain, Fred drummed it into

his head. She is tired but she talks as if this day is not particularly different from any other. She is absolutely convincing in the unimpeachable sense of what she is about. Damn her for being so amazing! But why still? For the convenience of Abigail, this woman of marginal connection, her entitlement as capricious as a tornado?

"I would so like to be here with you, Mother," implored Abby at Roxie's hospice bedside. "Be here for you. And Fred," she added, dabbing wet eyes with the back of her hand.

Roxie reached for Abby's free hand and feebly shook it. "Thank you, Abigail. Thank you for Amos. My life is so full, more than any soul deserves. It is time for others to claim their share. Now go, darling. Please understand I keep you in my heart."

It's the first time Fred has heard Roxie utter "darling" to anyone but himself. I know she means me above all with this endearment, he reacted at the time. Believing this, however, dissolved inevitably as the setting sun.

Abby departed, Fred glances now, the second day, about the little hospice room. The off-white walls, the flimsy curtains devoid of pattern, a bare-bones dresser and cot for him which he's vainly padded with a few of Roxie's flamboyant pillows he couldn't bear to discard.

"You wanted to simplify, dear Roxie," says Fred. "You're getting your wish."

Roxie grins impishly. "I've still got you."

Chapter 21

ROXIE

A S SHE PREDICTED, THEY WOULD HAVE THE
lovely little room to themselves. Gail and
Theresa, the nurses currently on duty, are
occupied with the poor people in their last stages. Just
because I'm incontinent, plus ghastly swollen parts,
the ashen skin, that's mechanical, Roxie thinks as Fred
squirms to get comfortable sitting on the edge of the
small bed. With a lugubrious countenance he stares at
the big jug of water he's arranged for when the time
comes. It's been a few days, Fred sleeping on the cot.
All of this—the bed, the cot, the window in need of
cleaning, the room itself—are on the scale of a doll's
house, it strikes Roxie, compared to their castle of a
loft they just left. Fred's behemoth of a body eclipses
all else in her field of vision, as it should. He is more
than a man, her man and soul-mate. He's become a
bridge, not to the unknown but to my original home,
she goes on as Fred adjusts the pillows so she can sit
up straighter. Yes! It's a homecoming. A wedding, too,
of sorts. She sees herself commingling with the gal-
axy of other souls, animals, every living thing. She is
grounded, solid as the core of the earth. The carcass

has fulfilled its purpose. That's gone. How grand it leaves the spirit intact to join the swell of the oceans, the pull of the tides, the pulsating gills of every single fish, minnows to sea monsters and that's just a slice of it. What a joyride it's been, and it's beginning again! How would any of us know what is next…except to be a grain or two of sand on that beach at the very least.

She's startled by the cascading flush of the toilet. Fred has relieved himself in the miniature bathroom and joined her once more on the bed.

"I don't mean to harp, darling, but do take to wearing loose drawstring pants once in a while. All of us but mostly men cinch waists with belts tight as potato sacks. Like women in the olden days with our girdles. Remember to breathe!"

"This is what's on your mind?" he says allowing a laugh. "How can I forget anything you've lectured me on?" He is resting a hand on one of hers cutting off the circulation. No matter.

"Just before, Noguchi popped up," Roxie says. "You know those marvelous slabs of stone, all rough-edged and raw except for a mere portion he's cut off and polished?"

Fred nods. "We saw one in the city."

"That's how I'm envisioning myself. The polished part is all I've ever been aware of. My own brilliance, at first, then transferred to others—Father, teachers, loved ones. Mama Milly. Manny. I do think it came to the point where I was mortified by my fixation to the slick surface, how that couldn't be all there was in this business of living. Thank the stars I got to be an antique. It's only been a few years since I've identified that big old ugly boulder that's been my life's support all along! Truly Noguchi was a genius, but, you see? There I go again…"

"We go again," Fred says.

" — to infuse, what, a handful of folks to carry our load. The rabbis, the real priests, the imans and the shamans and swamis, the mystics and witches and prophets, they don't take themselves seriously. Rumi! Just something in the marrow of their bones that sneaks to the surface unawares. A manmade source of light. But we box them in and miss the message."

Fred lays a hand now on her swollen belly. "You're speaking about me. I've tried like hell to let you down from that pedestal, Roxie."

"But we're human," Roxie laughs. "I suppose if we were perfect we'd have no purpose. I do believe the groveling is central to the process. The fuck-ups as you call them — oh Fred, look how you've loosened the tongue of this old lady! — the botching up of it all, god knows that describes most of my life. How else can we hope that each step one takes can lead to the peace and love we all crave? It's not a given. We're not even conscious of our breath. You will do your asanas, won't you darling?"

"You're lecturing, my dear."

Instead of chortling she disintegrates into a cough and then turns serious. She wants to be quiet but can't help herself.

"It's so very odd, Fred. It's like I'm standing still yet moving forward. I feel like a child learning to stand upright instead of crawl, knowing there's a better way but yet to experience it. I'm being absurd. This is the end of my life."

Fred's rapt gaze holds her captive to the point she

must look aside.

"I'm sorry my children—they think of themselves as my children but I really don't—I'm sorry Abigail and Amos intruded upon us. Of course all that business was meant to happen. Part of my homecoming, I guess. We were going along so smoothly. I do hope each of them found some sort of grace note in me. If he'd be here longer I would venture to tell Amos he belongs to Africa, not to me or his Lord. He and I are no more united than any of us. I think we put way too much stock in blood relations. They serve their purpose but cause far more havoc than they should. Oh, not to say, darling, that you cut off your little family. Ever! And not June. Your love however you're linked now is nurturing. But this ridiculous boundary line. Relatives. Others. England. France. One's tribe. Despicable others. You agree it's insane?"

"Oh, yes. Wars equal the human race."

"But I was delighted Amos is getting it right. He cares not just for his own five offspring but the whole village. He is fighting in his way for the entire continent, he said. Fantastic."

She permits sufficient pause to let Fred respond. "Isn't Abby also reaching out? Shoved out of her advantage or whatever and back into the fray? She said her three adult children have abandoned her, off of their own."

"I tried to ignore her on the surface these several days while appreciating her stamina, so yes," Roxie says. "Maybe in some way I helped to light her fuse. But this is too specific, darling. I should no longer isolate and inspect myself. I was so bloody self-centered to survive but I always knew there was a bigger picture.

Oh, listen to me."

"I am, sweetheart. And I have! But I hope I can come to think of you as another of the many voices in my thick head. My jury, my judges battling away with all points of view. I will not, I promise, permit you to become Chief Justice with the winning vote!"

"In that I'll be dead should help. Just a figment of your imagination." She giggles, pressing a finger into his open palm.

"You'll be my Scylla and Charybdis. Impossibly alluring so I'll have to struggle all the more to keep a steady course."

"Lovely. I like that," Roxie says. She inhales deeply, stifling another cough. "I'm procrastinating. Can you believe I'm going on like a runaway train, dear Fred? Like I have to sum it all up? I pictured being in a trance."

"Oh, Roxie. You're just totally present. You're not really incapacitated. Besides, with Abby and Amos, you couldn't get a word in edgewise," Fred says, a touching try for levity.

"Serves me right. They probably got my loquacious gene which I repressed...until you came along to shake me up." She looks aside. "Thank goodness their visits were relatively brief, but I did quite enjoy them."

"I know you did." Fred picks up her skeletal hand and kisses it.

"You have all the pills?" asks Roxie.

"Whenever you're ready," he says, bravely to Roxie, clearly putting on the best possible face. She knows it's going to be harder for him than for her.

"My heart breaks for the people here truly dying," Roxie says. "And their suffering. In agony even with morphine."

"Every time I peer into the other little rooms," Fred says, "...gray ghosts flat as floorboards." He strokes her hair, addressing it. "Still...like shimmying rolling waves of white surf. You're so beautiful."

Her smile drops. "I can feel so cowardly, not courageous, avoiding what we all must." She sits up despite sharp distress in her bowels.

"Dear Roxie, soon you'd be suffering like these people. It's all the same."

"I feel so damned privileged," Roxie says frankly. "I think of all the wretched souls who don't begin to have the wherewithal, who aren't well enough, whose minds have gone, or the families are making the decisions, or the irrepressible doctors. The laws are changing, though, aren't they?"

"You're still a pioneer, Roxie. They passed an assisted suicide law in Vermont but very few have taken advantage."

"It's complicated. Like everything."

"But it's not complicated for you, sweetheart. I do know that. I hope I haven't thwarted you, moping around, dolorous as doomsday."

"I can't reach your hand, darling. Give it to me. Let me kiss both of them." And she does then falls back into the pillows. "They would never do an autopsy on a nonagenarian. It's another way I'm so lucky."

"You couldn't help the elevated station into which you were born...the heaps of good fortune."

"Enough of this. Enough of me. Dear Fred, I know you are going to blossom beyond art. Oh, very much with your art—sketches or murals, whatever—but you've showered me with so much love. I've just been a passing catalyst to unleash that. The next woman, and there will be one, will be incredibly blessed. As I've been and am to my last breath."

Gradually their chatter subsides, wordless for quite a spell, an agreeable habit of theirs to allow the weight of their thoughts to break down into assimilable pieces and become embedded, the most worthy lasting and retrievable. Fred runs a fingertip lightly over Roxie's arm. She follows her breath as it slows to a near standstill, as if with all her talk she'd raced a marathon which ended but took a while to come to rest.

Suddenly Roxie is gripped with fear as if her monologue was contrived to smother it. Seconds of pure terror are shattering a composure, an ego loss years in the making she has taken for granted. It's all been her doing, her insistence on aiming beyond the improvident denial of death forever founded upon the almighty individual, her specialness stretching for the stratosphere of enlightened ones who abandon selfhood for the greater good. Yes, I am afraid, she admits to herself. Must not to Fred! Why leave life now? The underbelly of fear assaults her once again. I am not a god. Unknowing is to be human. She struggles to let the fear come and go, not fight it. Open-mouthed, her breathing is audible. It's alright if I juggle what cannot be answered to the very end. I must make a place for terror, too, in the vestibule of my departure. Let it be. Let it all be.

"You okay, Roxie?" His forehead is clenched like a fist.

She inhales deeply and closes her eyes. Several minutes pass. Many, many more minutes than they would allow ordinarily.

"I can see a painting," Roxie says. "It's a new one of yours. I'm watching the brushstrokes up close. I can see the beautiful colors, the hesitation of your hand, pausing above the canvas, and then its stabbing and darting with a vigor, your vigor." She opens her eyes. "Actually, it was me painting. I was the artist and you were inside me. We were one." She smiles and lets her lips relax. "I'm ready, darling. I'm ready."

Fred sits up, mouth agape.

"You have the pad, the computer...I forgot I wanted you to play Mozart's flute concerto...and, yes, remember that lovely solo harp, can't recall her name."

"Of course I can play these." He rises, stumbling, and fumbles among his things.

"No, just the harp, darling. Mozart probably too peppy. Yes the single strings of the harp. Nice and easy so my breathing can flow in sync."

The music starts. "Too low...better." Roxie wants to fall back, sink into the pillows, but she must sit up to sip and swallow. "The lovely sounds, they're enlarging the space which has to consume me...into which I must disappear."

Fred has uncapped the pills in a pocket of clean cloth which he now spreads on the bed. He places a capsule between Roxie's lips and follows that with a drink from a large glass of water. "You could do this yourself," he says, his hand shaking.

"I know. I prefer it this way, my dearest."

"It won't take very long," Fred says. "You weigh but a feather."

"No, I'm just of a certain age."

She keeps swallowing, he continues for his part, his eyes gushing like waterfalls.

"I was planning to ask for big swing bands," Roxie says between gulps. "Tommy Dorsey. Glenn Miller. Guy Lombardo. All before your time."

"It should have been the Strauss waltz. That time we made our loft a ballroom I will never forget."

"Music. In case we were lost for words." At this they both grin. With a few more pills left, Roxie says: "This is indeed like a dance, the two of us. But then isn't all of life if you let it?"

Roxie is groggy when she comes to the last pill. She reaches for Fred's hand that is gripping her hip, his other tucked into her neck. Her eyes close but under her lids there blooms a punishing glare, like looking directly at the sun, and then it becomes a gorgeous dark umbra at the center.

"It's like I've been all day at an amusement park," Roxie says softly, "after the fireworks, the band playing its final tunes. The rides are closing down but I'm basking in the lambent afterglow. The light is gradually ebbing. It's so very quiet, the people drifting off to the exits, but I'm still standing in a state of wonder. I'm smiling and recalling all the thrills, the sweet treats, the exhilarating scary bits, bushwhacked with tiredness. My loves have left, they've faded into the shadows. It's time for me, too, to go. No regrets, no recriminations..."

She's slurring.

"All this gathers...in the softening light...everything in harmony. It's calm...it's good...all good things come to an end..."

Her hand falls away from Fred's.

"Darling," she whispers and is gone.

Chapter 22

FRED

T WO MONTHS LATER SPRING IS SNAPPING OPEN the buds, impatient at the long delay. By contrast Fred, with a leaden heart and lethargic of step, has settled the closure of their loft at the Art Factory. Fortunately this was easy, having been so modestly outfitted. He is once again entrenched in his squat suburban ranch and somehow marshaled the energy to completely repaint the walls. This project consumed him, leaving no room to detail the avalanche of conversational snippets—Roxie's ever-ready reappraisal of any one of his thoughts or her own. Rather, for now, let her loom as a canyon so vast it's beyond the dimensions of one single view. Cherry-red is now the kitchen, butter yellow the bath. A mellow toffee in the hallways but a burgundy bordering on royal purple in his bedroom. The large former living room, also his former studio, is a vague off-white to keep it noncommittal. The cramped second bedroom is where he has installed his easel which currently is securing a blank canvas six-by-eight feet. It dwarfs the room and overwhelms Fred with the breadth of the Milky Way. Its cover of pristine gesso rivets him with whiteness. This room he didn't repaint. Perhaps soon it will be splattered every-which-way. That will be enough.

For several days Fred has puttered about, ducking in and out of the little studio, eyeing the intimidating canvas, deepening his gloom. *Oh darling, just have fun. Isn't that what we were all about? Remember you being so serious, your eyebrows locked in fury, trying to draw me just so. And there I'm happily sketching you as a plate of scrambled eggs!* Okay, okay.

Roxie presides over Fred's every waking second, although true to his promise not to let her passing become an impassable roadblock, he's straining to reduce her to her wicked, sexy, borderline meretricious grin. Only halfway through a beer does he weaken and submit to insatiable grief. Only when he's suddenly idle is he caught off-guard. Someday, supposedly, he will let himself get sucked into that rushing river and over the rapids. Bellowing, tears exploding, whatever it takes. Not yet.

He picks up a favorite brush and jabs it into jet black. With this he makes his first mark. Next he introduces pale violet, smudging most of the bleak straight lines of black. They never stood a chance to go un-smeared, so much pure bold. Bold is best as a blend, an impenetrable dark mix of reds and greens or blues and browns or...

She is in me, no longer by my side. I'm left loving a heart that has stopped beating, so my tubes and blood and nerves are taking over. She will become my female, I predict, Fred is thinking as he takes a palette knife and runs it down the right-hand edge. The darks and lights are already duking it out. Female creates, male destroys. No wonder its she as the usual focus of art—song, poetry, dance. Well, I'm a painter. I have to do both. What's created must be destroyed; what's demolished gets reborn.

Very good, dear. Think if you must, just keep the paints flying.

Six by eight feet should keep it loose. No one edge predominant. But don't make it a bull's eye. Rectangles off-center are compelling. So much space here to explore! Oh do shut up.

I will listen to myself say this: do not repeat a passage let alone whole blocks "that work." This he has taught himself. Roxie all else, it often seems, but not this. And he scrapes off the entire top third that is becoming pretty. Pretty is fine. Not with this. Death is necessary but it's not nice. Fine for the dying, damn her, but here in these shoes…paint-splotched Birkenstocks…

Wasn't it wonderful when I made that god-awful mess of watercolors then dumped the whole tub of dirty rinse-water over? I wish you could have seen the look on your face!

Fred drops his equipment and dashes outdoors, grabs a handful of sandy dirt and piles it on his palette. He scoops some of it up with a broad knife and draws it across the canvas. More. Again. Much of the grainy, mucilaginous trail slithers to the base of the easel, but much also sticks. Talk about impasto.

Bravo, darling.

Two or three hours later Fred stands back. It's a loopy carnival of dizzying elements. He jabs away, more dots and dashes, the more details the better. It will all be submerged in a few weeks under multiple mudslides of layers, the odd refulgent streak allowed to peak through here and there. If that celadon line is lucky. What is painting, Fred thinks, but a process of

...mination? Like life. Distilling, boiling down, until you're left with the residue, the pure granules of a loved one, the best of your friends.

Way too much baleful grayish-blue. But way too soon to inoculate with some savage, untamed orange. He pauses, hoping she will intervene. She does not. So enough for today. Tomorrow he will confront the canvas and gag. "Morning-after remorse," he calls it, like when the girl says "I love you" and you feel more alone than ever. But Roxie will sustain him. In some ways it's as if she hasn't even left, yet. Probably why unmitigated grief is willing to wait off-stage for the time being.

Fred rinses out his brushes plump with water-soluble oils, making of the sink a madhouse of competing colors. *Maybe I should take a photo of this someday,* he ponders, *and leave it at that. A black and blue Pollock.*

He takes one more notice of the canvas at the end of its maiden voyage. An addlepated, fucking mess.

Remember it's about acceptance of imperfection, it echoes in his weary head. *You like it, you don't — you don't matter. It's a crazy-quilt you somehow stitch together. Otherwise it isn't art.*

He closes the door and ambles to the fridge for his beer. He feels like a snake that has shed its skin, so much has changed. But he's still himself, for good or ill.

No, Roxie corrects. *Good and ill.*

He chugs the brew and corrals his various limbs into the confines of the undersized, garage-sale-sterling kitchen chair. *Yes I did all the talking, our final chance. But you're right. It was your death, too. I called the shots while you were on remote control. I knew you were begging to ease me with your own words from connection to its loss.* No, it was all good, my dearest, Fred says to himself.

I was meant to bear the extinguishing of your voice for real, so how marvelous you shared it nonstop. If it had happened in utter silence that would have handed me more weight than I could bear. But onward to your most precious gift. *The greater the distance from dazzling ways, the rants of the world, darling...and the more I'm dumped into a seeming pit of unremitting emptiness, the more I come to love the world!* And you cut that noose I clutched to my neck, wondering at fifty years old what my "character" is...what have I got to show for my life. *Rather, dear one – what is there which needs no definition?* Yet still he asks: What is it, Roxie, you breathed into my life?

He's finished with his beer but will never be with her.

Such was Fred's weekend. It's now back to work. It is mid-afternoon Monday. It will only be for two hours – later for some mothers to pick up after work. And by Friday night, after all five sessions, Fred will be ready to slug back a few shots of bourbon, primed once again to paint.

He has purchased old desks from a school sale but most of the kids choose to be hunkered onto the floor. He has to limit the class – the class! the pandemonium – to twenty. Space enough in the living room although several children cling together, fighting over crayons or actually collaborating on a finger-painting when he pulls off a twosome at a nice big sheet.

It was an instant success simply from the few posters tacked up about town. Five bucks. For only those who can afford it. Most women do so because he told them it pays for the peanut butter and jelly. The supplies have been donated by the two local art stores which get to boast about their largesse. The women are single mothers to a one. Nell suggested that Fred include a poster at the city women's center where she had worked, and that alone near-filled his squad of shriekers. Fortunately not each kid comes every day, so he has room for extras from the immediate neighborhood, more often houses with broken windows, rusting cars. These women could care less about the art. The look of relief in their faces, the smiles showing missing or dislocated teeth, the glimpses of joy almost supersedes the kids rushing to the women when they come to collect the cute brats, kids sometimes ripping their drawings, waving them like the star-spangled banner on the Fourth of July.

"Ellie, that's fantastic," Fred says on his hands and knees mid-session this Monday afternoon. "You filled up the whole page. Every darn corner and edge. Good for you! You're a terrific artist, Ellie. Such exuberance."

"What's exbur...?"

"It means you use yellows and blues and reds — the primary colors — plus the greens and browns and all the rest."

"What's prime Mary?"

"Let's look at Tyree's. Tyree, I like these tiny lines. Beautiful little black lines, all in this cluster. Just the one corner. So delicate."

"It's a spider. It can kill you."

"Scary. Keep it in a corner, right?"

Tyree shakes his head of jet-black coils, his skin a black closer to brown.

Fred works his way around the room, the circus of flailing arms, faces with giggles, faces locked in stern concentration. These are like the cave drawings, he thinks. But here as then they're not honoring the beasts per se. Yes the artists of millennia ago were expressing raw hunger, dependence on the animal-godheads, Roxie explained. But more, as with these tykes, it's clawing away at some inexplicable force. Can I do it... tag along with a five-year-old? Fred pesters himself. Maybe I should ditch the oils and get a lump of clay.

"Thank you so much, Fred," says Marie arriving for Nathan an hour after the others have gone. Marie is the one bombshell, blond and twice-divorced. It's hard to believe any man would let her go even if she is a chain smoker, grammar-school dropout, saloon waitress and all the rest. She's eye candy and sweet to the bone and genuinely grateful. He is loathe to accept her twenty-dollar bill for the week — one day gratis she apologizes for, but he refuses to diminish her any more than the toss of the dice has already doled out.

Finally it is Friday night. Fred cleans up the big room in a fashion. This involves filling a trash can and wiping up the congealing islets of peanut butter and jelly.

Maybe I could catch the new James Bond, he thinks idly, pressing hands into the small of his back to ease the ache. Maybe I'll see if June is free. Maybe I'll guffaw into Nell's voicemail so April can reconnect with the sound of my voice. Say hi to Freddie. No, save that for Sunday when I can be serious like my son. For now Fred's too beat even to pop open a beer.

He finds himself in his bedroom and crashes down on the bed. Hands behind head, he arches upwards, scrunches up a pillow for better support. This is the way he likes best of all to end his day, after hollering urchins…after being sealed off in his studio, silent as a tomb. Here is my place of worship, purple walls and all, he muses. Resting on a nail is the clothes-hanger displaying the shocking blue, baggy but bejeweled dress she had him not only wear but parade about the cabin, his face probably as bright red as the dress is a blinding cobalt. It was chief among momentos of her Mama Milly. Now there was true love, even Roxie would admit. The shoebox of her wild adornments is front-and-center on his dresser-top. He's draped a few strings of colorful beads so they spill over the edge. I must have Nell sort through it and take what she wants. Save a few for April someday? Offer June the nicest ring? Fred's gaze is ensnared, as always, by the other two of his wall hangings. One is Roxie's drawing before their time together about which he had raved and she had to agree with its panache. *Goodness only knows how it happened. You're the artist, darling.* It's the rendering of a leafless tree upside down, a whirligig of interlocking limbs and twigs, gathered and anchored by the thick trunk rooted skyward, in reverse. The second sketch is unforgettably the one done at the moment of their meeting, the two of them still strangers in the life-drawing class, the male model all of them gamely attempting to take in as a whole but for one white-haired feisty lady, blithely tacking up her artwork at session's close on the big bulletin board, her depiction solely of the enormous, swaggering penis, her inspiration of the day.

"Oh Roxie, Roxie," Fred sighs aloud. "You sure made my day and then some, my dear."

ACKNOWLEDGEMENTS

I thank these friends as avid readers for their ongoing criticisms and support: Janet Ballantyne, Sara Alther Bostwick, Read Brown, Eileen Fitzpatrick, Lindley Karstens, Bill Kennedy, Mary Kennedy, Dick Lipez, Dianne Mooney, Alice Murdoch, Jim Selsor, Barbara Wagner, and Phil Wagner.

I remain indebted to these departed friends who also as mentors shaped my life and art with their bravura, risk-taking, and passion to the end: Lyman P. Wood, as an entrepreneur; Lawrence C. Goldsmith, as a painter; and Doris Lessing, as a novelist.

Most importantly, my career as a writer has been inspired by my former wife, Lisa Alther, and emboldened by my husband, Ray Repp.